THE UNKNOWN

by

TAYLOR EVANS

TELEMACHUS PRESS

This book is a work of fiction. Names, characters, places and incidents are either the product of the author's imagination or are used fictitiously. Any resemblance to actual persons, living or dead, or to actual events or locales is entirely coincidental.

THE UNKNOWN

The publisher does not have any control over and does not assume any responsibility for author or third-party websites or their content.

Cover designed by Telemachus Press, LLC

Cover art:
Copyright © 99designs/Rebecca Harrison, artist

Author photo copyright: David Taylor

Published by Telemachus Press, LLC
http://www.telemachuspress.com

Visit the author website:
http://www.facebook.com/thesorcerersprophecy

ISBN: 978-1-941536-59-9 (eBook)
ISBN: 978-1-941536-60-5 (Paperback)
ISBN: 978-1-941536-85-8 (Hardback)

Version 2016.09.06

Printed in the United States of America

10 9 8 7 6 5 4 3 2 1

Dedication

To my wonderful sisters, parents, and friends who were my first editors and embarked on this journey with me. Your unconditional support made this dream possible.

THE UNKNOWN

Prologue

THE WOMAN IN front of Layna could destroy her life and everything she held dear, and yet she was oddly calm. Layna came here knowing the outcome, what would happen, what would have to happen. She had accepted this inevitable fact months ago. Amidst countless nights of crying, she realized she only ever had one choice.

Azlaya appraised the woman whose blond hair spilled over her shoulders, taking mental note of this strangely compliant Layna. "Sooner or later I *will* get them. You can't keep them from me forever." She paused. "And you know that."

Azlaya's words gnawed at Layna. "They don't need forever," Layna whispered more to herself than to the tall, pale woman. Layna lowered her gaze and stole a glance back toward the way she had come. Behind lay her life and where she stood . . .

Suddenly, Layna felt a sharp stab in her stomach where Azlaya had hurled a spell at her. Layna doubled over when she was hit again, and her knees collapsed. She would not raise a hand to protect herself, would not utter a counter spell, or fight back. She was gasping and on her knees as Azlaya's hands stayed raised in anticipation of throwing another spell at the crumpled woman unwilling to save herself.

"Oh, Layna," Azlaya said slowly, as if discovering she had done something unforgivable. "You are the greatest sorceress in Alagia, are you not? Rise, defend your name, your title," Azlaya taunted. Layna painstakingly rose.

The two were only a few feet apart, but the subjects of their confrontation were worlds away.

Still breathing hard, Layna responded as Azlaya inched closer to her. "You think that my fear of you will make me tell you where they are," Layna stopped to catch her breath. "But you're wrong. I love them so much more than I fear you."

A snarl ripped across Azlaya's lips at Layna's insult. Layna had her back to the jagged cliffs that lined the ocean below. Azlaya locked eyes with Layna, but found no challenge, only compliance. Azlaya would never forget seeing the calm resolution in Layna's eyes before the final curse cast her over the edge.

Numbness set over Azlaya, the strange sensation one feels after accomplishing a goal and realizing a sudden emptiness. Then the sounds of battle ended her reverie and revealed her new goal, her ultimate goal: one which kept her vehement quest to control this land alive, one that depended on what Layna Coles had died protecting.

"I will find your daughters," Azlaya whispered and returned to battle.

Chapter 1: Casey

AS I LOOK back on all that has happened, I wonder if I missed the signs that were screaming at me that this is where my life would lead. Before everything—literally everything—changed, it was hard to imagine anything that would make me hate my sister as much as I do now. My entire life she lied to me about who she really was and what she could do. But it wasn't just the lies that tore us apart, it was everything she came to believe and support ... everything I am against. Even worse, it was a piece of paper that caused all that I knew and loved to crumble around me.

I know none of this makes sense, and it's even hard for me to make sense of it. I'll start where it all began—when all the lies started to surface, when I learned the truth about my past, and when my normal life was uprooted and changed forever.

When are you going to tell her? I thought to myself as I gathered the contents of my lunch onto a tray. *What if she finds out from someone else and knows you kept it from her this whole time?* I grabbed a water bottle from a cooler and took my place in line. *She won't find out ... she can't.*

"That'll be three-fifty, honey."

I handed the lunch lady the money and headed over to the table seemingly reserved for my friends and me. I forced the worries deep into my head and rehearsed the equations I needed to memorize for my test after lunch. Before I could greet my friends huddled around the table, I was cut off by their commotion.

"How about *Old Hollywood*?"

"I like *Under the Stars*."

"No, look at this. *Disney*, that'd be cool."

"What is that?" I asked referring to the paper that had drawn a crowd.

The lunch room was bustling with people getting their lunches, and I had to raise my voice so I could be heard. My closest friends and twin sister, Kate, were all crammed around the table, leaning in to see the paper. I sat down in a chair they had saved for me, and Kate pushed the paper towards me.

She had curled her blonde hair this morning so it hung in loose loops around her lightly tanned face. She wore one of her favorite jackets, white jeans, and riding boots. Her makeup was impeccable, as usual, and her perfume wafted around her. One look at Kate and anyone knew she and fashion were inseparable. Although our sense of style was one of the many things we had in common, I could, and often did, leave the house without checking the mirror several times on the way out the door, despite the sour looks Kate would give me.

I set my salad down and grabbed the sheet of paper, which had a long list of ideas for a birthday party. All of our friends were helping us plan our seventeenth birthday that was quickly approaching, and between both of our guest lists, it seemed as though the whole school was invited. Just as my eyes scanned over *"Pretty in Pink"* someone asked, "Which theme do you like, Casey?"

"I bet I already know," Kate smirked at me.

I was so overwhelmed by the, at least, 100 choices. I was just about to set the paper down and give up when my eyes skirted across two words: *Enchanted Forest*. I could already picture the decorations coming together in my head. There would be trees arching over our heads with beautiful candles hanging from their branches. The tables would be tree trunks, the chairs little toadstools, and there would be a crystal blue stream with a bridge stretching above. Just as I was imagining the perfect dress, someone impatiently asked me again what theme I liked.

"*Enchanted Forest*," I answered and pointed to the line.

Suddenly, concurrence with my choice erupted from our friends as Kate blurted out, "I knew it!"

"Well, which one do you like?" I asked Kate, as I stabbed some lettuce with my fork.

"I like the *Paris* theme, but we can make our two ideas work," Kate replied.

I laughed. "It could be *Fairy Couture*," I joked.

"Or *Paris in the Woods*," Kate added with a horrible French accent. We were all laughing now, with the occasional cough, trying not to choke on our food.

One of our friends, who actually took French, said playfully, "*Vous êtes tous fous.*"

"Brenna, what on Earth does that mean?" Kate asked.

"It means you're all crazy!" She replied, and then we were laughing again. "I wonder what the guys would think."

As if on cue, three of our guy friends made their way over to our table and pulled up chairs. The tallest bent over next to Kate, placing a kiss on her cheek. His hair was dark brown and cropped short. I noticed he wore his usual attire of loose jeans and one of his many football shirts as he slid into a chair next to Kate. As soon as I saw him a creeping feeling of hate filled my gut. I knew something he had done that would crush Kate, but I banished the thought from my head; I couldn't bring myself to tell her yet. She was so evidently happy, who was I to ruin it?

"Back from Juvy already?" I asked Kate's boyfriend sharply.

"I went to *court* for a speeding ticket, not murder," he boasted as though it were something to be congratulated on. Before I could subtly throw him a nasty look, he and my sister had already locked lips.

Brenna's boyfriend, Nick, sat next to her and eyed the list across the table. A shorter, yet equally muscular guy leaned over me to see what had drawn a crowd. "I think you should do a beach theme. Then you can all wear your bikinis," Connor commented. I playfully slapped his shoulder as Jackson, Kate's boyfriend, and Nick voiced their agreement.

"Ok, we'll wear our bikinis if you guys wear your Speedos," Kate added boldly.

"I'm game. Are you guys?" Jackson asked Connor and Nick.

"Hell yeah, I'm game," Connor shouted a little too loudly.

"Me too," Nick answered.

My eyebrows perked, and then we were all laughing. In the midst of it, I caught Kate giving me one of her "what can you do" glances. I smiled mildly, shoveled some salad into my mouth and pulled my physics binder from my bag. Suddenly the attention in the room was drawn by an uproar of protests from our friends.

"You can't study; you two still haven't decided on a theme," Brenna whined while leaning on Nick.

"We can finish deciding later. I have a test next bell," I explained, but that was completely ignored.

"Yeah, screw this," Jackson said, grabbing the binder from my lap. I lunged forward to snatch it back, but he kept it out of reach and taunted me with it. "Physics is stupid anyway," he laughed, joined by his pack and my posse. Kate, however, was trying futilely to defend me.

"Easy for you to say. We all don't have college football scholarships to get by on. You know, some of us actually have to use our brains for things other than smashing it into other people," I snapped as I grabbed the binder from his hands. I was close enough to slap him, but doing so would only demand an explanation from Kate, and it was an explanation I wasn't ready to give.

"Well if you were as smart as you let people believe, you would know that they give us helmets to protect all of our geniusness." He slumped back in his chair and draped an arm over Kate's shoulder as she shot him an indignant look. Connor laughed nervously, trying to defuse the tension.

"Looks like your helmet hasn't done its job, or else you'd know that 'geniusness' isn't a word." A tumultuous "Oooo" erupted from our table, causing multiple heads in the room to turn towards us. I decided if I couldn't punish him physically, I would do so verbally, glad to deflate his ego whenever I got the chance. Jackson threw one of his "whatever" looks at me and pulled Kate closer to him, as if using her as a shield from our friends' banter.

I left the girls to finish debating over the theme, while I got in my last minutes of studying. Soon the bell rang and I thankfully packed my things and rushed out of the lunchroom before Kate could intercept me and force me to explain my bad behavior towards Jackson. As I walked through the hall to my class, the underclassmen would move out of my way or glance at me when they thought I wasn't looking. Kate, our friends, and I were part of the unwritten hierarchy that existed in the school. We were on the top of the food chain, and we were greeted with more envious looks than warm ones because of the social status we possessed. Of course this "fame" wasn't something we strived for; rather it was just something we learned to live with. Having everyone in school know your name isn't something I ever really wanted or was proud of, but Kate on the other hand reveled in it. Again, I could live without the popularity. I wasn't sure she could, which is why it was imperative that I kept the secret that plagued my mind. If it got out, it could—would—challenge her image.

I was so preoccupied that I couldn't focus on my test and when the bell rang for the end of class, I still had three problems to do. I huffed in defeat and turned my test in. I headed to my locker, extremely exasperated. Worrying about Kate's problems had probably just landed me a solid "C" on that test.

Kate met me at my locker. Her arms were crossed as she leaned against the locker next to mine. "What?" I asked more sharply than I'd intended. She kept her lips pursed for a second more.

"Look, I know that Jackson can be a bit of a child sometimes, but you know I don't like it when you insult him in front of everyone," she started. I shoved my books into my bag with even more annoyance and shut my locker. *If only she knew … if only I could tell her.*

"And I don't like it when he acts like a jerk, so I guess we're both unhappy," I snapped. Kate didn't even flinch, but her eyes rolled. We were used to each other's sass and the biting tones we could use.

A few people passing by stole furtive glances at us, and then hurried along. "Lately you've taken any chance you get to belittle him. Can you at least pretend to tolerate him?" Kate asked me in a hushed whisper.

"Why should I put up with his crap?" I said, a little louder than I anticipated.

Now Kate was stealing glances at onlookers. "Because he's my boyfriend, and you're my sister. Those are reasons enough," Kate responded, leaving little room for argument. "What aren't you telling me, Casey?"

she urged. She stared through me, as though searching for the secret inside.

"He's not good for you, Kate. You may not see it, but I do," I told her softly, and she broke her gaze. She narrowed her eyes as her lips parted to say something, just as our friends bombarded us and herded us off to the mall to find dresses for the party.

For the rest of the night I didn't want another confrontation, so I avoided Kate. I tried not to let Jackson consume my thoughts, but that proved difficult since he seemed to be glued to Kate's hip the whole night. He made a point of planting a fat kiss on her lips whenever I looked their way, making me roll my eyes.

After a couple hours of roaming the mall for dresses, we decided to call it a night. It was only the middle of January and our birthday wasn't until the end of March, so I was in no hurry to find something right away. Kate, on the other hand, was acting like she was in search of her wedding dress and getting married the next day. When we finally convinced her to leave and come back the next day, we headed home.

We pulled out of the parking lot in silence, so I reached over and turned the radio on. "Casey, will you at least tell me why you think he's not good for me?" Kate began, three seconds into the song.

"I can't explain it," I said through gritted teeth as I clutched the wheel and kept my eyes trained on the car ahead.

"What the hell is that supposed to mean?"

"I just heard some things," I grumbled.

"Oh, you heard some things?" she said sarcastically. "Since when did you start believing the rumors?"

"Maybe they aren't all rumors, Kate. Did you think of that?" I snapped. I heard her take a breath to say something, but stopped and stayed that way for a few more uncomfortable minutes. "Maybe *you* should try talking to him."

I was so frustrated with the situation that my foot began to press harder and harder on the gas pedal. Before I knew it I was pushing fifty in a twenty-five miles per hour zone. I had one hand on the steering wheel, pushing and pulling it to turn the car smoothly around the winding road.

"Casey, slow down." It sounded more like a suggestion than a demand. I eased my foot, but it wasn't enough for her. "Slow—"

Just as the word jumped from her lips, a deer dashed across the road in front of the car. Had I been going the slightest bit faster, I would have been scraping deer guts off the windshield. I gasped in surprise, but the deer crossed the road safely and darted into the woods. "Did you see him alongside the road?" I asked Kate, my heart pounding against my chest. I glanced sideways to see if I'd have been able to spot the deer, but it was pitch black beyond where the headlights reached. Unless she had nocturnal vision, Kate shouldn't have been able to spot the deer either. Or maybe she just didn't want me speeding at this time of night with the cops keeping a keen eye out for speeders.

As if reading my mind, Kate replied, "No, I didn't want to have to explain a speeding ticket to Grandma."

I stole a glimpse at her face, but it was a firm statue, staring forward into the night. Her jaw was locked and I heard the muffled sound of her teeth grinding against each other. It annoyed me more than hurt me to keep the secret I had from Kate, but a part of me still wouldn't allow myself to tell it. I turned into our driveway more aggressively than I should have and parked the car.

Kate shoved herself half way out of the car, then turned back and said, "Please just lay off of him." I huffed and followed her inside. We dumped our bags in our rooms and went downstairs for dinner.

Our parents died when Kate and I were only a few months old, so our maternal grandmother had cared for us ever since. We didn't know who our paternal grandparents were or even if they were still alive. Much of our early life was like the sky at night: the stars were little parts that we knew about, while the majority was just black spaces, filled with untold stories and secrets never revealed by our grandmother. All families had their skeletons, and as far as our grandmother was concerned, we knew our parents had died when we were young, she raised and loved us, and that was all we needed to know.

I placed a steaming bowl of spaghetti and meatballs on the table, and Kate set down a plate of freshly buttered garlic bread. We sat, and our grandmother joined us with a pitcher of lemonade.

"What did you girls do at the mall?"

"Well I *didn't* find a dress for our party, but I did get some new perfume. And I saw these really cute boots, but they were crazy expensive," Kate replied as she scooped food onto her plate.

My grandmother turned to me expectantly. "I just got some more leggings. My other ones were thinning out."

She nodded. Our grandmother could feel the unspoken tension in the air between Kate and me, and wisely, didn't call attention to it. So we talked about the news, what was going on at school, and other trivial things.

After dinner Kate and I packed the dishwasher and then went our separate ways. Kate went to the fridge to get something to drink as I exited the room. I hesitated at the foot of the stairs, wanting to confess to her everything I knew, but I couldn't bring myself to shatter the love she thought she had with Jackson. Languidly, I climbed up to my room and curled up on my bed with my phone. I went on Twitter and Instagram for a while. As I was scrolling through the pictures on Instagram, I saw that Kate had posted a picture of her and Jackson from our trip to the mall and had already gotten over two hundred "likes". Some of the comments below read 'you two are so cute' and 'couple of the year.' I turned my phone off and tossed it to the end of my bed. I needed something to distract me, so reached under my bed and pulled out a long, plastic container. I'd found the box only a year ago in my mother's old room, and every now and then I would pull out its contents of journals and worn papers and absorb myself in the memory of her. It held just about all I had of my mother: her words. I laid one of the thicker journals with frayed pages in my lap and picked up where I had left off.

Chapter 2: Kate

"DO I EVEN want to know?" My grandmother asked me as she finished scrubbing a pot.

I sat at the island in our kitchen facing my grandmother as she worked. "She's just being annoying," I muttered as I texted.

"About what?"

"I'm not sure, but she's hiding something," I replied. I was able to sense others' feelings really well, and I knew that Casey was guilty about something. While tapping into the thoughts of others wasn't the easiest thing to do, with enough effort, I was able to. However, Casey was one of those people that was always stressed or thinking about something, so it made it more difficult to sort through what she was thinking. Doing so would take me an indefinite amount of time and, undoubtedly, leave me with a painful headache. I resolved that if Casey didn't confess tonight, I would take some painkillers and go find out for myself.

My grandmother harshly interrupted my thoughts. "Kaitlin, what have I told you about trying to read people's minds?" she asked in a stressed whisper. We had this argument often. I fought the urge to roll my eyes. "Kate … a person's thoughts are some of the only things that are private. How would you like it if I could read your mind whenever I felt like it?"

My eyes flashed to hers. "I would *like* that! Then at least I'd have someone who'd understand what it's like," I said, straining to keep my voice a whisper.

My grandmother made a sympathetic face. She opened her mouth when the phone cut her off. She answered and held up a finger to me to wait where I was. She went into the next room and I slid down from the chair and went to the couch.

I curled up on the couch, phone in my lap, and iced tea in my hand. Few things could make Casey and me this angry with each other, and Jackson was one of those. Her recent scornful appraisal infuriated me. She was my sister, and I felt like she couldn't trust the decisions I made when it came to my personal life.

I did love Jackson. I had never felt this way about any of my other boyfriends. I wanted a future with him, and the feeling was mutual. So why was Casey constantly pointing out how wrong he was for me? *She just didn't understand. She'd never understand*, I thought as I raised the iced tea to take a sip.

My phone started vibrating on my leg, and I put it to my ear. Jackson's voice flooded my thoughts. "Hey, baby, the guys and I are going into town to catch a movie. You wanna come?"

"No, I'm tired and not really in the mood," I sighed.

He paused. "Did you and Casey work out whatever you're fighting about?"

It was that obvious that Casey and I were mad at each other. Our grandmother picked up on it and now even my boyfriend could tell. "No, Babe, not yet."

"Whatever. If she wants act like this, let her. She can be a bi-"

"Jackson!" I interjected.

"Kate, you know it's true," he countered.

"Don't say that about my sister. I don't care what's going on between Casey and me, or you and me, but never say that about her," I said defiantly.

"You know what, whatever. Let me know when you're done being psychotic." I heard a click and slammed my phone down on the pillows. I was frustrated with Casey and Jackson, the two people I could always rely on.

I sat motionless, replaying our conversation in my head, forcing myself not to call him back and demand an apology. I raised my glass to sip my tea, expecting to hear the clink of ice. I suddenly recoiled, the tea burning my lips. I raced to place the glass on the table to relieve my hand of the heat. My grandmother returned from her phone call and saw the glass. "Honey, if you're drinking hot tea, put it in a mug so you don't burn yourself," she said, noticing the steam rising from the glass.

I glared at the glass. "It wasn't hot—" I began in exasperation.

"What was I saying before?" She picked her brain.

I jumped up. "Not letting Casey know, something you've told me a million times. I get it," I said as I slinked past her. She called to me, but I ignored her and climbed the steps, skipping some as I went.

Casey's door was slightly ajar. We never knocked, so I pushed my way in. She sat on her bed reading what looked like an ancient book from the library. I came into the room as she set the book down and met my gaze.

"Can we please talk?" I started. Casey straightened up on her bed. "I don't know what I did, or what Jackson did to make you suddenly hate him, but I think I deserve to know," I said.

Casey looked at me as if I hadn't said anything. Then, I saw a flicker of guilt. Normally I could easily read Casey's thoughts, and I always knew what to do and say to make her feel better, but she was too distressed for me to try to sort through her thoughts now. But as if the secret she kept were a palpable thing, I was still able to sense it.

"What?" I challenged her.

"I already told you, he's not good for you, Kate," she said.

"I know, but it's more than that; I know it is," I interjected.

"I wanted to tell you but …" her voice faded. My eyes boring into her made her stop trying to soften to blow. Casey sighed. "I heard that a girl who goes to Belleview has been seeing Jackson."

I felt my face scrunch, and my eyes narrowed on Casey. "That's not true," I said, more to myself. Anger bubbled inside me at the stupid lie Casey was trying to feed me. "That's a lie! That's a goddamn lie!" I screamed at her. I took a few steps away from her. I was afraid that if I was too close to her I would shove her, or worse.

"I wouldn't lie about this Kate … not about this," Casey spoke softly, as if trying to use her tone to prove what she said was true.

I stared at her—into her—and an image passed through my mind. It was of Jackson and a girl, with his arms wrapped around her. I know I'd just promised my grandmother I wouldn't pry into people's minds, but sometimes people's inner thoughts opened up and I couldn't stop myself.

"Where did you see that?" I asked in alarm. The picture in my head moments before vanished, replaced by anger.

Casey gazed at me in puzzlement. "See what?"

I shook my head, knowing she didn't see what I did. She never did. Ever since we turned ten, I started to notice a force inside of me that allowed me to read people's thoughts, and do other things.

I thought back to my once-iced tea from earlier. My emotions could induce these strange happenings. I had to be extremely cautious around others, because if people found out what I could do, I'd be locked away forever. I pictured myself being experimented on like an animal. It was something I didn't realize as a young child, and I thought my powers were incredible, but as I grew, I came to understand the danger they were to me and to the ones I loved. Half the time, I didn't even know what I was capable of doing, and it terrified and intrigued me at the same time. But since Casey never showed any sign of sharing these powers with me, I could never share my excitement—or fear.

I turned abruptly and stormed from the room. Casey jumped off her bed and followed me downstairs. "Kate!"

I went to the couch where I had tossed my phone. I dug through the blankets and pillows until I found it. I began to furiously dial Jackson's number.

"What's her name?" I asked sharply.

Casey was standing hesitantly in the kitchen, watching me from a distance.

"Her name—what's her name?"

"What the hell are you talking about? Whose name?"

"The girl in the picture!" I yelled, cursing to myself when the phone went to voicemail.

"What picture?" Casey asked. I could hear the fear and concern in her voice, and it made me even angrier that she didn't understand.

I saw our grandmother out of the corner of my eye, as I dialed one of Jackson's friends. "Kate, honey, calm down. What's wrong?" she called to me across the room. She knew better than to approach me when I was fired up. Casey was trying to convince our grandmother that she could handle me. My heart twisted, knowing that I was probably scaring the wits out of our grandmother. She knew from experience that I could be a ticking time bomb when I got angry. I could tell by her reluctance to leave that she was scared to leave Casey in my wake.

"Grandma," I inhaled deeply, "I'm fine," and exhaled. She still looked uneasy. I wanted to tell her that I would never hurt my sister, but in the moment, I didn't want to make any promises I might have trouble keeping.

She hesitantly climbed the stairs to her room, but not before saying, "Kate, please be careful. Please."

Casey brushed our grandmother's concern aside and yelled, "Kate, can you please talk to me!"

Finally someone picked up the phone, and I frantically asked to speak to Jackson. "What do you mean he won't talk to me?" I screeched. "Tell him he needs to stop by my house after the movie. Bye," I said curtly. The feeling I'd had earlier when holding the tea was returning, but I couldn't let the boiling sensation overcome me. Casey was too close and she couldn't know.

Casey inched closer to me and I collapsed on the couch. She sat next me and just stared. "What picture?" she asked calmly.

I breathed deeply, until I was calm enough to form words. "I meant, who is the girl from Belleview?" I asked, posing a question she understood and could answer.

Even though the question made sense, when she spoke her fear was still evident in her voice, and it pierced my heart. "Erica Reinhart."

Chapter 3: Casey

ABOUT TWO HOURS later, Jackson pulled up to the house. The street lights gave little illumination as he approached the door. I let Jackson in and led him to where Kate sat waiting.

"Just keep it down, okay. Our grandma doesn't know you're here," I told him. While I hated Jackson with a passion, it didn't make watching him and my sister fight any more enjoyable. "I'll go upstairs," I offered as I tried to slink out of the room.

"No, stay here," Kate called to me. I reluctantly came back into the room. Jackson sat across from Kate, leg propped on the coffee table.

"What's this about anyway? I'm tired and need to be home soon," Jackson said as he yawned.

"Who's Erica?" Kate asked simply. Jackson was facing me and shot me a questioning look. I shrugged, trying to minimize my involvement as much as possible.

"Well?" Kate pressed him. I could only see the back of Kate's head, but I could feel the stare that she directed at Jackson.

"She's a friend of my sister," Jackson answered nonchalantly.

I didn't want to watch Kate interrogate Jackson. Standing there was uncomfortable enough, so I turned to the cabinet to get a glass. As I filled it with ice and placed it under the water dispenser, I heard Kate say something. Suddenly they were both standing and she was harshly whispering obscenities at him and hitting him in the chest. Jackson kept grabbing her arms and trying to get her to stop, but she kept trying to shove him away.

"Guys, stop! Stop!" I tried to say in a hushed whisper. I took the glass from the dispenser to set it down, and just as I did, the glass shattered in my hand. Water, ice, and glass spewed everywhere, some of it slicing into my hand.

Jackson just stared, wide-eyed, at me as I stood gazing at them. I knew he saw the glass randomly break into a thousand pieces, and he couldn't rip his gaze from me. I suddenly felt like I was on the set of *Paranormal Activity*.

"Oh my God, are you all right?" Kate asked as she rushed over. I numbly nodded. "Your hand …" Kate gasped. I stole a glance and saw rivulets of blood trickling down my fingers.

Kate turned back to Jackson. "Just get out. I'll deal with you later!" she screamed. Jackson gratefully took his invitation to leave and hurried past us and outside to his car.

As I heard his tires skidding down the road, our grandmother came rushing into the kitchen and saw the mess. "What's going on?" she exclaimed. "What happened? Casey, your hand!"

I was speechless, unable to explain what just happened. Kate quickly covered for me, crafting a believable story. Our grandmother looked skeptical and disappointed all at once. I assumed it was because we invited a guy into the house after curfew and without her knowing, but her gaze was solely directed at Kate. She held her tongue and focused on my hand rather than questioning Kate. The two of them cleaned up the kitchen while I bandaged my hand.

When the glass and water were taken care of, Kate escorted me to bed. As she trailed me up the stairs I told her, "You don't need to walk me to bed."

She laughed half-heartedly. "I'd rather bring you to bed than get into the waiting fight downstairs," she whispered to me.

I smiled thinly. "Kate, it was my fault, too. I let him in."

I was at my door and Kate met my gaze. Her eyes looked distant, as though what I said went right through her. "My boyfriend—my fault," she replied solemnly. I tried to protest, but she remained unconvinced.

When she heard our grandmother start to come upstairs, she said, "Goodnight," and rushed into her room. Before retiring to her bed, my grandmother checked my swollen hand one last time. "Honestly, grandma, it's fine," I implored.

"What really happened, Casey? What did you see?" she asked me, sounding like she was searching for a specific answer.

"It was like Kate said, I wasn't paying attention to what I was doing and placed the glass on the edge of the counter and knocked it off, so I tried to clean it up with my hands before you came downstairs." I lied nowhere near as convincingly as Kate.

"A whole year of broken beakers in chemistry last year and you haven't learned not to clean up glass with your bare hands?" she asked me skeptically. Her eyes narrowed, but I pressed my lips together and shrugged. She gave up when she saw I wasn't going to admit anything. She kissed my cheek and returned to bed.

I was grateful after the night's frenzy to finally climb into bed, but once I did, I couldn't surrender to sleep, because my mind was buzzing. I still couldn't explain what had happened with the glass of water, or why Kate was asking about the picture with Jackson and Erica. Nor did it make sense why my grandmother was giving Kate such strange looks, or whatever fight Kate was trying to avoid. I couldn't subdue these thoughts as I tried to sleep.

I woke up in a haze the next morning after an often-recurring dream. In it, my sister and I are roaming in a thick wood. Oftentimes, a faint song can be heard among the trees. Neither of us know where we are going, but we each insist on our own path, and we always lose each other among the trees.

I stared at the ceiling, coming back to my senses. I heard a low rumble in the pit of my stomach and quickly shuffled out of bed and headed downstairs for breakfast. I trudged into the kitchen and sat down at the counter. The kitchen was one of my favorite places to be in the morning. It was so warm and open, always smelling of fresh pastries because of my grandmother's love of baking. It was rare if she wasn't in the kitchen whipping up something to eat. The chestnut cabinets smelled like the forest that blanketed most of the back yard right outside the house, and when the sun spilled into the room, it was picturesque.

I turned my attention to my grandmother, who was busily making pancakes, whistling a tune while she worked. She wore one of her purple blouses and jeans. She had taken the time to curl her graying, dusty, blonde hair.

She placed a plate stacked high with pancakes in front of me. "How's your hand?" She asked, gesturing to the gauze with her spatula. I looked down at it, forgetting the wound from last night.

"It still hurts a little, but it's better," I reassured her. Slowly, my groggy mind began to piece together the events of last night. "Where's Kate?" I searched the kitchen for her phone, because if it was there, so was she.

"Right here," Kate responded as she entered the room.

Kate was fully dressed, wearing her favorite sweater and boots. Her blond hair was curled gently and bounced on her shoulders. Her voice had a pleasant chime to it when she spoke, which meant she was going shopping. It was something only I would notice.

"Going shopping?" I asked as she went over to her phone.

"Later. I'm going to Brenna's first to work on that history project, and then we're going to run to the mall to pick up some boots she put on hold. I'm just going to browse for now," she explained, while simultaneously texting.

"You were just at the mall yesterday," our grandmother commented. Before Kate could respond, the ringing of the house phone cut her off. Our grandmother picked it up and stepped into the office adjacent to the kitchen.

As Kate stood there texting absentmindedly on her phone, I wanted to bring up last night. The strangeness of it still plagued my mind, and I wanted to make sense of it.

"Kate … about last night—" I started.

"Don't worry about it. Jackson and I will work it out; we'll be fine." I wasn't convinced because even she sounded uneasy about the future of her relationship.

I was about to argue that maybe it wasn't worth it to try and mend whatever she and Jackson had, but a car's horn interrupted me.

"That's my ride, I've got to go. Tell grandma I left," she said, looking back towards the office. I nodded.

My stomach tightened, knowing that Kate still didn't see all the bad that I saw in Jackson. I wondered how much blame I would receive for not pushing her to understand my view of the collapsing relationship as Kate collected her things and rushed outside.

My grandmother came back into the kitchen with the house phone to her ear. She said, "Goodbye," and placed it back on the receiver. "That was Charlotte."

"How is she?" I asked. She was my grandmother's best friend from college.

"She's good. She's actually in town this weekend and wants to meet for lunch," she continued, while dumping dishes into the sink. "You won't mind if I run out for a while?"

I shook my head. "I'm not five anymore, Grandma," I said playfully. "Tell her I say hi."

"Okay, honey. I have some other errands to run, too, so I'll be home a little late." She passed me and planted a kiss on my cheek, and before long she was out the door too.

I finished my pancakes and returned to my room. I threw on a green top and yoga pants, pulled my hair back into a ponytail, and started my homework. It didn't take long for me to become bored and start getting distracted by the smallest things. Eventually, I gave up and packed up my textbooks and binders.

I pulled the box from under my bed and found my mother's old journal that I was reading last night when Kate came into my room. I started where I last stopped. Though I had found the journals a year ago, I hadn't started reading them until recently.

The journals told of my mother's life before she died. She would never say specifically where she was, but only describe the scene as full of trees and nature, which could've been anywhere. However, I could tell by the way she wrote about it that she adored the forest and its beauty. It was part of the reason I wanted our party theme to incorporate the woods. In the part I was reading, she'd just met my father and the two walked along a stream. I went to turn the page when a couple pictures fell out. I set the journal down and held them up. One was photo of a woman sitting on a white bench. She resembled Kate and me so much. She had a round face, pink cheeks, freckles, and her hair was a sun-kissed blonde, like Kate's.

The next picture was of my grandmother hugging the woman in the previous picture. They both looked so happy. I looked a little closer, and noticed that the woman—my mother—was a little round in her belly. I suddenly realized it must have been when she was pregnant with Kate and me. A folded-up paper was among the pictures, and I opened it. It was a drawing of a man's profile. He had stared into the distance as someone drew him. His hair was a little shaggy, and he had hints of stubble on his chin. I knew from other descriptions in the journals that this was my father. I curled up with the journals and pictures and sleepiness slowly consumed me. I dozed off amidst things of the past.

Twigs and dried leaves crunched as we walked. We could hear the bubbling of a stream to our left. Kate and I came to a fork in the path, which branched into two identical paths. I started towards one, but Kate shook her head and pointed to the other path. We were obstinate and refused to follow one another. We both went our own way while the soft lullaby floated across the trees. Suddenly, a deep feeling of loneliness set upon me as I wondered where Kate's path had taken her.

My eyes fluttered open and I shot up. I glanced over at my clock, which read 4:00 PM. I rubbed my eyes, trying to chase the sleep away. I stood and made my way over to Kate's room, pictures in hand, to see if she was back yet. I stopped outside her door. "Kate?" I said, knowing she'd recognize my voice.

"Yeah, come in," she answered.

I slipped into the room. Kate was sitting on her bed with her computer, rapidly typing. She had papers all around her on the bed as she typed. I sat on an open space on the bed.

"English paper?"

"The one and only," she responded, not taking her eyes off of the screen. Sometimes I regretted the fact that Kate and I split into two eggs in our mother's womb. Between Kate's writing and history skills and my math and science skills, we could have easily been the smartest kid in school. "Oh, I edited your paper," she exclaimed, as she rifled through the stack that was spread haphazardly on her bed.

"How bad was it?" I cringed as I waited for her answer. I would always have her edit my English and History papers, while I would check her math homework and science labs. It was a foolproof system from which we both benefited.

"It wasn't that bad," she replied, still searching for it. "It was much better than the first draft you gave me."

"Okay, but …?" I led Kate on as she grabbed my paper from her spread.

She glanced over her edits, and her mouth twisted at one corner, so I knew she had lied. "All right, well your intro could be more compelling, your concession was a little weak, and your analysis of the author's style needs more support, textual preferably. However, I loved your conclusion," she added, and my face brightened. "But with the changes you'll have to make to your body paragraphs, the conclusion will need to change a bit too. Fix those things, a few grammatical errors, comma splices, and you're good to go," Kate chimed. I rolled my eyes and moaned.

"So it's awful. The whole thing needs to be rewritten," I concluded.

"No, no, no. The *first* draft you had me edit needed to be rewritten. This one doesn't need to be changed drastically, only tweaked. You have all the content, now it's just elaborating on it," Kate explained calmly.

"Kate, I've said it before, and I'll say it again. I'll pay you to write it for me, I swear," I pleaded.

Kate chuckled and went back to typing. "I have my own paper to write."

"Fine," I huffed. "I did figure out that math problem you asked me about the other day." Kate's eyebrows perked. "You use the cosecant first, and then you can find the cotangent using the identity properties." Kate stopped typing and looked at me as if I'd spoken Chinese. "I'll explain it later."

She nodded but her eyes were vacant. "Well … let's just hope there's not one like that on the test."

"You still don't get it do you?" I laughed, and she shrugged hopelessly. "Well, I actually wanted to show you these before I go," I said as I handed her the stack of photos I'd found in the journal.

"Who is it?" she asked, examining the first photo.

"It's our mom, before we were born. I didn't see any of our dad but there is a drawing," I told her.

Her face suddenly fell as she leafed through the photos. She missed the parents we never truly had, more than she cared to admit. The idea of having a mother was an obsession that she rarely talked about or allowed to be brought up. Yet, here I was throwing it in her face. Though I did this with no malicious intent, she was saddened either way.

"She was—beautiful," Kate said softly.

"She looks like you," I told her. Kate lifted her eyes to me, and they twinkled.

"You too," she laughed halfheartedly. I smiled mildly.

"Kate, I know I already said this, but I really am sorry about Jackson. I should've told you sooner," I said softly.

Kate smiled thinly. The wound from last night was still fresh, and the mention of him couldn't help her healing process, but I needed her to know. "I know you are," she replied sincerely.

I slid off the bed to leave. As I went to the door, I noticed something. A lava lamp that Kate had gotten years ago still sat on her desk, but there was something different about it. "Kate … I thought your lava lamp was pink?"

A blue hue was glowing from it. Kate glanced at it. "It changes color," she replied, gazing at the picture of our mother.

Not wanting an argument to erupt from something this meaningless, I left. But I knew what color that lamp was because I had helped our friends pick it out. It was pink when we got it, pink when we gave it to her, and pink every day since. Never once did it turn blue.

I started to walk back to my room, trying to clear my head of all the weird things I'd encountered in the last day. That's when I heard it. It sounded like a lullaby, but I felt like I had heard the music somewhere. I listened, and had a feeling of déjà vu. I realized it was the lullaby I heard in my dreams.

I walked down the hall and listened intently to try to discover its location. My dazed thinking was compounded because the music seemed to be coming from my mother's room. We never went in there. It was just a neglected, spare room. I stared at the door in fear and wonder. I didn't know what I should have been feeling.

I silently opened the door to the room and peered in. It appeared to be a normal bedroom with all the necessities. I was looking around the room one more time when I noticed the music's source. It emanated from a music box that had golden, intricate designs covering it, sitting on the nightstand.

I walked over and examined the music box. The lid was open and the inside was beautifully padded with red velvet cushions. I was about to close the lid of the music box, when I noticed that the figure spinning around wasn't a ballerina like most music boxes. Instead, a wolf inclined its head towards the ceiling as if it was howling. Two necklaces sat on the cushions, each with two rings joined together. I watched the wolf dance for a while; then I noticed words inscribed on the underside of the lid. The words were Latin, which I'd started taking in middle school, but knowing Latin didn't clarify the meaning of the inscription.

"Tollite me fuisse mundo in quo pauci, ubi tandem fato fieri meus." Take me to a world where few have gone, where destiny can finally become my own.

That was when it happened. The words on the lid began to glow yellow, and a flash of light momentarily blinded me.

A huge gust of wind suddenly hit me, causing me to stumble backwards into a wall. Papers from my mother's desk flew everywhere. I stared at the music box in horror as some of my mother's books began falling from their shelves. I ducked and kept my head down, wondering if Kate was hearing this, wondering if someone would come to my rescue.

I looked up; the wind had died down, and I blinked twice to make sure that I wasn't seeing things. Where the nightstand once sat now stood a thick, wooden door. It looked like the door to a castle from Victorian England. I stared wide-eyed at it, trying to anticipate the next upcoming surprise. The door started to inch open, and I began to panic. My heart was pounding against my chest. I slowly stood up, taking in what I was seeing. Two girls stepped through the door.

One girl had blonde hair and the other black. They looked no older than ten and wore short dresses that were form-fitting at the top, then fell loosely around their thin legs. However, the dresses weren't made of fabric; they were made of leaves, flowers, and vines, all twisting together to form a dress. The girls waited in the doorway for a moment, gazing around the disheveled room. Then they approached me, and I instinctively started to back away.

"Do not be afraid," the girl who had light blonde hair said softly.

I had bumped against the bedroom wall. I had nowhere else to go, and in front of me were these two girls, seemingly cut from a tree, coming towards me. I tried to open my mouth to say something, but I couldn't even form the scream building in my throat.

The girl with black hair appraised me and said, "Your arrival has been awaited for many years."

She took one of the necklaces from the music box and fastened it around my neck. "Do not lose this; it is your only way to return to this world," she said as she gestured to the jewelry she had put around my neck.

"What?" They were speaking of the necklace as if it were more than met the eye. The girls exchanged glances and smiled. Then they both turned and started leading me towards the door.

"What is this?" I yelled after them. I was praying with every ounce of my being that this was a new dream. "What are you talking about?"

"We have come to return you to the land of your birth. It is what your parents wanted," one of them said.

"My parents?" I shook my head. "They're dead."

"You will need to discover these truths on your own. Hurry, we cannot be in your world for much longer."

I was too stunned to object to anything or even decide whether I should actually follow these strange girls through this door. However, their swift, hurried movements made me panic and race to catch up with them. My breathing accelerated with every step. I closed my eyes as we walked through the door and a blinding light surrounded us.

I felt a gentle breeze brush my face. I tried to calm myself, preparing for whatever it was I was about to see. Then I slowly opened my eyes. I could feel the shock across my face as I stared at the world in front of me, the *fairytale* in front of me. Grass billowed in the wind and I could hear a rushing river nearby. A valley lined the horizon with a thick forest to the west and mountains to the east. In the distance I saw a large, dark structure. I struggled to believe that I had really just passed from my mother's bedroom into another world. It was too much to grasp, and dizziness seized my body. As I staggered, small arms steadied me.

"W-where are we?" I watched their faces as they both twisted into masks of sympathy. I was hoping their response was going to be something like, "Oh, don't worry, it's only a dream. Wake up, Casey, wake up."

"This is Alagia, the home of your birth," the one with blonde hair replied as they began to walk away.

"Alagia?" I whispered, testing the foreign word on my tongue. I tried to take in everything around me, and it wasn't until I focused on the forest again that I understood where I was. "The forest," I said, more to myself than the girls. I remembered the scenery my mother described in her journals, and the one Kate and I wandered through every night in my dreams. What I once thought was just a description of the woods behind my house, I now knew was Alagia. *It's what they would've wanted.* My parents were somehow connected to this world, and as crazy as it seemed, I somehow was, too. I knew that had it not been for my mother's journal, I would have stood there forever, begging myself to wake up. But I was there and awake and curious as ever about this world that I knew should not exist, but it did.

"All of your questions will be understood in time. I am Kyla," the girl with black hair responded. "And this is Isla." She gestured to her blonde friend.

I just looked at them, knowing their names were not enough to explain anything. "Your clothes …?" It was the only thing I could say.

Isla smiled, "We are forest Nymphs. We live among these trees and act as messengers for the Hunters."

"Who are—" I tried to say, but was immediately cut off by a loud horn that echoed through the trees. I turned to look towards the sound, soon followed by the girls.

Kyla gasped, "She knows." Their eyes filled with fear.

I was going to ask what they were talking about, but I didn't have the nerve to listen to a long explanation, nor did I think I would get one. The girls looked in the direction of the horn again, and then focused back on me.

"We must go. Come with me," Isla said urgently.

Kyla took out what looked like a wooden whistle and blew into it. No sound came from it, but suddenly, wolves began emerging from the forest and into the clearing.

Confusion and anxiety gripped my insides as Isla pulled me through the wall of wolves. Kyla was screaming orders to the wolves in a language incomprehensible to me. After being instructed, the wolves raced into the forest. Isla clung to me for another couple of feet until I yanked myself free of her grasp.

"Where are you taking me?" I screeched, as fear began to settle in.

"Casey, you must trust me. Kyla cannot hold off those trackers for long."

"What are you talking about? What trackers? None of this is making sense!" I yelled.

"It is imperative that you are safe, and here you are not. You must find a sea of tents. There you will find The Mistress of the Hunt, Kyraine Redding. She waits for you. I must go help Kyla. Go!" She gave me a little shove and ran off in the other direction.

I looked back just as I saw the Nymph girl dart through several trees as though she were a ghost. I stared, trying to decide if what I'd seen was real.

When I heard a wolf's cry of pain, I started running.

Chapter 4: Kate

MY TEAR-STREAKED FACE stared back at me in a mirror across my room. My eyes were red, and I looked miserable. The pillow that I clung to was soaked. After Casey left, I couldn't keep them from spilling. I know Casey didn't give me the pictures with the intention of making me cry, but that didn't stop me either way.

My mother and I were similar in so many ways when it came to our appearance. We both had golden, blonde hair, caramel eyes, round lips, and lightly tanned skin. We were creatures of the day, while Casey and my father seemed to be creatures of the night. Their hair was dark brown, their eyes were a silver-blue color, and their skin didn't hold much of the sun's rays. I smiled faintly at the thought of a family picture with my mother and me looking like we lived in the sun, while my father and Casey looked like they lived in its shadow.

I gathered myself and slid off my bed. I went to the mirror and admired the pictures of my sister and me when we were younger. We didn't realize at that age what it meant to have a mother or a father. Toddlers couldn't tell the difference between the people feeding and clothing them, but over ten years had passed since that time. Noticing the difference was almost too easy, because everything changes with time.

I sighed inwardly and made my way downstairs. Casey's sourness towards Jackson caused me to jump to conclusions while I was trying to read his mind. I think I was too scared to discover the truth for myself, so I decided it would just be easier to listen to Casey and accuse him of cheating.

My frustration with the whole situation caused Casey's glass to explode. I didn't even have to turn to know that it was my doing. I could see the shock all over Casey and Jackson's faces, but I couldn't explain to them that I had caused it. If I did, then I'd surely be checked into a government laboratory.

Just when I got to the foot of the stairs, my phone buzzed in my hand. A text message from Jackson read 'Come to the front door.' I stood frozen, glancing from the door to my phone for a few drawn-out seconds. I was a little ashamed of how I'd treated him the night before and knew I owed him an apology. Jackson stood idly, leaning against my porch with his back to me. When he heard the door open he spun around, and I saw that he held a bouquet of flowers in his hand.

My words caught in my throat at the sight. "Kate, whatever happened last night, can we just forget about it?" he said smoothly.

I sighed, knowing that I judged him prematurely the night before. "I'd like that," I replied softly. He started to approach me, but I held up a finger, gesturing for him to wait, slipped back inside and pulled on some shoes and a coat. It hadn't snowed in a while, but the air was still frigid at night. I returned to the porch where Jackson waited.

I took the flowers he held out to me and led him down the porch and around my house. There was a trail that snaked through the woods in our backyard that Casey and I liked to walk on and pretend we were explorers when we were younger. I yearned for privacy, and not what a locked door could give, but rather what the forest offered. As we walked, I snuggled into Jackson's thick winter coat, inhaling his smell deeply.

"I'm sorry," I whispered.

He planted a kiss on the crown on my head. "I know you are. Casey got you worked up; it's not your fault." I would have gone to my sister's defense, but I was too drugged by his presence to say anything.

We came to a bend in the path, and on its edge sat a wide tree stump that had been chopped down years ago. Jackson sat down and promptly pulled me into his lap. I buried my chin into the crook of his neck and fought the urge to fall asleep.

"Remember the first time we met?" I asked him.

"Mmhmm," he replied greedily.

We were at a summer concert and while I was dancing with my old boyfriend, who was basically indifferent towards me at the time, I felt someone's thoughts. They were so forward and direct that it caught my attention right away. I searched for who they came from and my eyes landed on Jackson. He was tall, fit, and tan, and everything my old boyfriend was not. He was two years older than me, which seemed more a challenge than a deterrent. *"Damn, who is that?"* he had said. I flashed him a bright smile and found myself dancing inches from his face for the rest of the night. Needless to say, my old boyfriend and I broke up very quickly after that.

"I can't wait for the concerts this summer," I said wistfully. I also couldn't wait for warmer weather that invited shorts and tank tops.

"You know what I can't wait for?" I peeled back from him to gaze into his eyes. "Longer summer nights, so I can kiss you—" he kissed me, "all—" *kiss*, "night—" *kiss*, "long," *kiss*. I wrapped my arms around his neck and pulled him into me.

I had lost track of how long we were kissing, when he finally pulled away from me. "As much as I love sitting here on this stump, I'd much rather do this back at your place." I caught a glimpse of him imagining us entwined under my bed covers. I was so lost in the moment that I couldn't find the power to say no.

"Do you really love me that much?" I asked seductively. He pulled my lips to him again. *I do love you this much. I love you, your ears, your eyes, your nose, your cheeks*, he thought as he kissed each place. *And I love it when you wear this perfume—*

I jerked away from him, and he looked puzzled.

"You like my perfume?" I asked innocently.

Jackson still looked confused. "Of course, I love it when you wear that one."

I slid down from his lap. "I just bought this yesterday. This is the first time I'm wearing it, yet you're familiar with its smell," I spoke slowly, piecing together the parts of a puzzle.

"Kate, you have so many perfumes, I probably mixed it up with another one. What's the big deal?"

"Erica wears this perfume, doesn't she?"

"Are we back on her again?" He asked as he closed the distance between us. "Kate," he whispered as he moved to place his hands on my hips.

He had let his mental defenses down while we were kissing, and they hadn't fully been restored. I peered into his thoughts and found the evidence that I had searched for the previous night. "Get the hell away from me!" I screamed and shoved him back.

His expression changed from annoyance, to anger, to fear in seconds. I glanced down and saw that my hands were starting to glow. He was turning as if preparing to dart.

"Don't move," I commanded through clenched teeth. He started to panic as my powers entrapped him as though he were tied up in rope. I felt as though someone had released a wild, burning hatred inside me. The boiling in my stomach was beginning to build, and I knew exactly what that meant: I was about to become very dangerous.

"Kate, what is this? What're you doing?" he cried frantically.

"You goddamn asshole," I said breathlessly. The flowers I had clutched in my hand wilted and were reduced to a hideous black and grey color. I threw them away from me and approached Jackson, who still wriggled helplessly. "I trusted you! Casey was right all along and I trusted you!" I jabbed a finger in his direction.

"Kate," he gasped.

"To think I was about to lose my virginity to *you*!" I spat.

"Breathe—I can't—breathe—"

"You're a lying, cheating asshole—," Jackson inhaled desperately, "and I never want to see you again!"

Then he exploded into thin air, as though he never existed. Jackson dissipated into ash and dust around me. My chest rose and fell rapidly as I stared in awe where he once stood. I glanced around and realized that my fit had leveled an area the size of several houses. Twigs and leaves fell around me, as the sound of groaning bark surrounded me.

I remember the first time the sensation came over me; I was ten. Looking back, I don't even remember what it was that made me angry, but I remember the room being tossed around as though a typhoon had rampaged through. Books and toys were thrown everywhere, posters and pictures had fallen to the ground, my windows had shattered, and my dresser collapsed on itself. It wasn't until I stopped crying and found my grand-mother staring wildly at me, that I realized that the supernatural occurrence was my doing.

She approached me cautiously, and once she decided I was calm enough, she scooped me into her arms and told me not to worry. Casey was thankfully out of the house at soccer practice and came home to contrac-tors and plumbers filling the cracks in my walls and fixing the shattered windows. My grandmother crafted a story to tell the workers and Casey and left no room for people to question her, despite the obvious peculiarities.

That night, she brought me into her room and told me everything. She explained that my "powers" were not unique, and that my mother pos-sessed the same ones. However, my mother was much older than I when she discovered them and could therefore control them better. She explained that as I became more acquainted with them and their ties to my emotions, I would be able to control them as well. As a ten year old, most of it went over my head, and I didn't understand the enormity of what I could do, or what could happen to others as a consequence of that. The one thing I did understand was the promise that I swore to my grandmother to keep: Casey must never know.

At first, it was exciting to have a secret all my own, one that I could call mine and smile about without anyone else knowing why. However, as the years wore on and I felt my powers growing and my discipline weaken-ing, I wished I could confide in Casey about the secret I held. I asked my grandmother often why Casey had to be left in the dark, and my grand-mother always explained that it would keep her safe, and in time, I realized it was only ever to protect Casey from me. It was hard to comprehend that at ten years old, but now I knew better, and when I felt my control slipping, I had to get away. But I hadn't. I stayed and now Jackson had gotten what he deserved.

My head was throbbing, and my vision was getting blurry. My mind couldn't catch up with what I had just done. My legs buckled and miserable sobs racked my body. I wasn't sure if I cried for me or for what I had done. I trembled as I tried to banish the picture of Jackson bursting into dust.

You just killed someone. He deserved it, after what he did to you. You loved him. You can't love someone who would hurt you like that. You're a murderer. You couldn't control it. You're a monster. He wasn't innocent, he deserved it. You're still a monster.

I stayed that way, at war with myself, until my entire body went numb and limp from the cold. I stared blankly at the desolation I had caused. Despair closed in. I could feel a sudden loneliness descend upon me. There was no escaping what I did, and no one to help me cope with the power that boiled inside, taking whatever opportunity it could to consume my body. However, as the time passed, I didn't want to be understood, or comforted. It suddenly started to feel good to have punished Jackson. And every minute I wondered about the lie that was our relationship, the love I thought I felt for him slowly faded.

My mind still raced back and forth, telling me that he deserved it, and then telling me I was a monster. I finally got up when I came to terms with the fact that I could live with knowing that Jackson did get what he deserved, and that part of me was a monster.

Chapter 5: Kyraine

I SAT HUNCHED over a map of the forest that had been my home my entire life. It showed the camp and Azlaya's castle. There were the mountains, the valleys, the ocean, and even the small streams that cut through the land. This was the only home I'd ever known, and I was losing it to a war and its orchestrator, Azlaya.

A high-pitched screech yanked me back to reality. My white, speckled owl, Izona, was impatiently waiting for something to eat. She snapped her beak at me.

"Calm yourself; I'm coming."

I lifted myself and searched my hunting bag. I grabbed a dead mouse and flung it towards Izona who scrambled after it where it fell. The sound of her breaking its neck didn't faze me.

I was just about to sit back down and stare at the map, when Gwendolyn Stone, my most trusted Hunter and second-in-command, entered my tent. Her red hair was pulled back, but small wisps still framed her lightly freckled face. She wore tall brown boots that laced up to her knees, a green tunic, and a cloak.

"My apologies for the interruption, Kyraine," Gwen said. She seemed unusually fidgety.

"What has happened?"

"I've just received reports that Sagen have been spotted probing at our perimeter defenses again." I still wasn't sure why she seemed so anxious. "And the forest Nymphs said that a young girl appeared in a clearing."

My eyes doubled in size. "You should have led with that." I quickly snatched my bow and arrows, knocking over Izona in the process. As the owl tried to retaliate, I rushed past and followed Gwen out of the tent.

My Hunters were socializing with each other around the campground, talking about frivolous things unrelated to the war. Regardless of all the armor and the toughness they portrayed beneath their fearsome exterior, they were still just girls. If we were going after the Sagen, I needed my best archers. I called forth the girls who I knew had the best aim and combat skills. One would think those girls were being starved and I was about to give them food by the way they jumped up and followed me into the trees. I was sure they were restless from the little activity these last few weeks, and when this opportunity came along they couldn't contain themselves.

As we were about to leave I noticed that one of the girls I called was missing. I turned to Gwen and asked where the girl, Veronica, was. Gwen shrugged. We had no time to wait or wonder.

For weeks now, Azlaya had been sending Sagen into the forest. It was as if they were waiting for something, and it seemed whatever it was had finally arrived. We darted in the direction Gwen pointed and were on our way to—well, I wasn't sure yet.

Chapter 6: Azlaya

"A STRANGE GIRL just appeared in the forest," my spy had told me.

Within minutes, I had sent the Sagen out to retrieve this girl, paid my spy, and waited. I suddenly got goose bumps on my arms, and a shiver ran through me. This had to be it. This had to be them. One of Layna Coles' daughters had finally arrived.

I hoped Kyraine was clueless about the events transpiring. As my eagerness grew, I could sense the uneasiness of the servants nearby. I turned and went to the balcony and looked out into the maze of trees that stretched out for miles. All those battles that had been fought would be meaningless, because I was about to win the war.

Layna, you fool. Your sacrifice was for nothing. You could never keep them away.

I began to drum my fingers on the stone banister, the galloping sound only heightening my anticipation. I'd been waiting for this moment since Layna died, and now it was here and in my grasp. I could taste victory on the tip of my tongue, and feel my grip tightening over this land.

Chapter 7: Casey

THIS NEW WORLD I was in was all in my mother's journals. I remembered reading about the vast, untamed forest, the towering mountains, the rushing rivers and streams. It was all in front of me as if I'd stepped into one of my mother's stories. While I initially thought she wrote about a glorified version of the woods behind my house, after seeing this new world spread before me, I knew this was the place she constantly wrote about. Except this wasn't a story. This was real, and scary, and dangerous.

As I ran deeper into the trees, I worried for the girls who were protecting me from something or someone catching me. The forest was thick and hard to run through, due to the roots that protruded out of the ground. When breathing began to hurt and my throat was unable to retain any moisture, I came to a stop, hoping that I had gotten far enough away to be safe. While I was catching my breath, I heard a rustle from a bush behind me.

It all happened so fast, I couldn't tell what hit me at first. Suddenly, I was on my back, and I'd cracked my head against a root. I propped myself up on my forearms and rubbed the back of my head. I looked up and saw a man standing over me. He was easily six feet tall, and he had his sword's tip at my chest. His stance was tense. His skin was dark and he smelled of dirt and moss. His hair was tied in a knot at the back of his head. On either side of him stood two ferocious wolves that moaned and growled impatiently, clearly waiting for the order to kill.

"Who are you," he demanded, "and why have you trespassed on Hunter lands?"

"I—I'm—" but I couldn't choke a word out while this giant and his beasts stood over me.

"Answer me!" He commanded.

"Kyraine," I said, struggling with her name. "I need to see her," I finally managed to blurt out.

"I'll be the judge of who you need to see. Who sent you into the forest?"

I stole glances at the still-growling wolves. "Nymphs—from the forest ... Kyla and Isla," I decided to leave the part out where I came through a mysterious door, but I figured my clothes gave me away. "I was in a field with them when we heard a horn. They called wolves from the trees, and they told me to go into the forest and run. I was looking for a campsite when you—" I broke off suddenly when I heard the horn for the second time. I turned my head towards the echoing sound.

"Sagen," the man said under his breath.

"What?" I asked, but my question was waved aside.

The man fell silent, and I followed his gaze to where he stared. I looked down and saw the necklace hanging haphazardly against my chest.

"Are you a daughter of Aaron and Layna Coles?" I just stared at the man wondering if he was someone I shouldn't trust. My gut said otherwise.

"Yes."

The man looked stunned, but quickly recovered. Unceremoniously, he yanked me to my feet and pulled me through some underbrush. There stood his bronze stallion, as well as four other horses with men astride. They all looked to be a couple years older than me. As I was studying them, I was flung onto the horse, and the man jumped up behind me.

The man whistled to the wolves, who took off. "What's happening? Caden, who is that?" one of the other men asked.

"We must take her to Kyraine," the man, Caden, said.

"That's in the opposite direction of where we're headed," the man pointed out to Caden.

"We don't have a choice," Caden responded firmly. My chest tightened. The four men exchanged puzzled glances but obeyed their master.

My heart was pounding as I searched the shaded forest for whoever was pursuing us. Then, all five horses raced through the labyrinth of trees as we sped through the forest.

On either side, shadows began to appear alongside us, tracking our progress. We rode for a few more feet, when an arrow flew through the trees. The animal, sensing the danger, reared back and just missed being pierced by the arrow, but Caden and I were thrown to the ground. The pain throbbed from my head, but I held back a whimper, knowing that now probably wasn't the time to show weakness.

I lay on my side and sat up. Caden and the other four men were already standing protectively in front of me, swords at the ready. I stared at the part in the trees where they seemed to be concentrating their attention. As I watched the darkness that was shed over the forest, men in black cloaks started to materialize. The five men tensed in front of me and tightened their grips on the swords, preparing for what seemed to be an imminent fight. I painfully rose to my feet, but when I looked at the oncoming men again, I noticed that all of their weapons were pointed at me.

"Stay behind me," Caden muttered under his breath. I obeyed, but searched my mind for reasons someone might have to kill me. I couldn't think of any.

I stared at the cloaked men surrounding us, eyeing their weapons the whole time. Then a figure came through the trees; the smug grin on his face was noticeable, even from where I stood across the narrow clearing. The nearing figure had pale skin and light, tousled hair. Everything he wore, from his boots, to his pants, to his cloak, was black, much like the other hooded figures that surrounded us. He seemed disappointed, while at the same time amused.

"Caden, I must thank you for bringing her to me," said the pale-skinned man. He looked Caden right in the eyes and said, "Your efforts, though brave, are futile. Now, give her to me." I bit my lip to keep it from trembling.

"You'll have to kill me." My eyes widened significantly at Caden's declaration. This man and his companions only knew me as a stranger, yet now they all stood defiantly, protecting me from these people who apparently wanted me dead. Still, I had no idea why.

The leader snapped his fingers, and the hooded men changed positions, training their weapons on Caden. Suddenly, the four men at Caden's side appeared extremely uneasy.

"Don't tempt me."

"I'd like to see you try, Logan," Caden spat at him. The man, Logan, stopped and turned towards us; victory danced in his eyes.

"Unfortunately, I don't do my own dirty work." He turned and walked back to the rest of his men. He got on his horse and gave his last command before riding off. "Kill them, but bring the girl to me." Then he was gone.

I shrunk back behind Caden, waiting for the approaching hooded men. I counted fifteen, and knowing that we were outnumbered, silently told my grandmother and sister that I loved them. Five hooded figures, which I realized must have been the Sagen that Caden had referred to, rushed forward. Two of Caden's men moved to intercept them. I flinched from the sound of metal striking metal.

Caden shoved me backwards, away from an advancing Sagen. As he and the Sagen battled, I inched away from them, debating whether or not I should take my chances and run for it. I was so busy contemplating that I didn't realize that a Sagen warrior stood behind me. Suddenly, I felt a cold, bony grip on my wrist. I gasped in surprise, and tried to twist away. One of Caden's men noticed, and darted over to help. He swung his sword up, slicing the Sagen's arm cleanly through. A horrible hissing sound came from the Sagen, who tried to retaliate, but Caden's warrior was quicker and decapitated the hooded figure. I jumped back as the Sagen crumbled into ashes.

My eyes shot up to the man who had saved me. "Look out!" I yelled, but I was too late. A Sagen warrior had driven its long sword into the man's back and through his chest. I couldn't stop my hand from flying to my mouth. He shuddered, and I watched as the life drained from his eyes. A scream caught in my throat.

The Sagen pulled its sword from the young man's body, which fell to the ground in a bloody heap. My feet were unsure of what to do, while my mind and heart were racing. I heard rustling to my left and saw Caden rushing towards me.

"Duck!" he called. I immediately dropped to the forest floor, as Caden launched his sword into the Sagen. I heard the same hissing scream as the Sagen disintegrated into ashes. I remained in my crouched position, watching the horror unfold. Caden's men fought hard, but the Sagen's numbers were too much, and they were beginning to retreat. Caden pulled me to my feet and quickly examined the battle.

Suddenly, I heard something whiz by my ear, followed by a shriek. I twisted my head around and saw one of the hooded soldiers crumple to the ground. An arrow protruded from his side.

More hissing cries of pain filled the clearing as the hooded men tried to fight back against their invisible attackers, but it was pointless. Caden stayed by my side while his two remaining men helped finish off the Sagen. All around me, the hooded, ghostlike men fell to the ground and diminished to dust. Once I'd witnessed all I could take, I turned away, only to find the attackers had shed their invisibility and were slowly approaching.

Chapter 8: Kyraine

WHEN WE SAW Caden's wolves barking madly in the forest, we knew something unusual was definitely happening. We rushed to where the wolves led us and found exactly what the forest Nymphs had warned us of.

My girls' arrows met their targets swiftly and with deadly precision. The Sagen could only be truly killed when in the sunlight. If killed in the shadow or in the dark, they disappeared, only to return again. Thankfully, the sun was high in the sky and the clearing allowed for plenty of light.

When I finally had the chance to see who was in the middle of this battle, it wasn't at all who I was expecting to find. First of all, Caden was present, as well as Brennon and Mason, two of my dear friends from the Huntsmen.

I had not seen them in months, yet their expressions showed nothing amiss, as if meeting this way was not unusual. I was so focused on Caden that I didn't notice the girl standing behind him. Her clothes were unlike anything I'd seen in Alagia, and her panic-filled eyes told me that she had never seen what death looked like, or what an arrow could do to a person.

But her face was painfully familiar; so familiar that it hurt me not to recognize who she was right away. *No—but it couldn't be. After all this time—it couldn't be her, it was …*

"Impossible …"

Chapter 9: Casey

CADEN MUST HAVE felt my sudden movement and turned, too. I stole a glance at his face, only to see a smile of relief spread across it. I noticed the other two men with him were also at ease after all the Sagen were dead.

The figure approaching us was a young woman. She couldn't have been older than twenty-five years old. Her hair was a fair color of dark brown, braided down the back. She wore a forest green tunic, cloak, tall boots, and in her left hand she held a bow. Moments before she had looked fierce and frightening, but as she came closer I noticed that her face relaxed into someone beautiful. Her face was lean, and her features were soft, making her huge, brown eyes stand out even more.

She approached me hesitantly, as if deciding whether she should stop advancing. She narrowed her eyes, and suddenly a wave of shock came over her when she recognized me. When she was within touching distance of me, she looked at Caden, astonished.

"It's been too long," she greeted Caden and the other two. Caden had nudged me aside to speak with the girl. "How ...?" she began.

She looked like she wanted to say something more, but was, again, lost for words. Her eyes never left my face, and she slowly shook her head in disbelief. It was as if she was trying to convince herself that this was happening. I was trying to do the same thing.

"Is this ... are you ... Layna Coles' daughter?" I hesitantly nodded my head. After already witnessing what the mention of my name did to Caden,

I was nervous to see her reaction. Her lips stayed parted for a moment. "Cassia Coles?"

"Just Casey," I told the shaken girl.

"Casey," she said thoughtfully, trying the word on her tongue. "Your mother always told me that her daughters would return, but … I began to doubt it would happen," she said. She might as well have been speaking Greek, and the look on my face must've given me away. "I will explain everything later. I understand you are unfamiliar with this world, but all your questions will be answered. Please, allow me to introduce myself. I am Kyraine Redding, Mistress of the Hunt." As she said this, she bowed politely. I could only manage a weak smile back in her direction.

It had taken me way too long to realize that this complete stranger in this fantasy world knew my name and my mother. Logic was screaming *dream* in my head, but something about Kyraine's demeanor made me want to believe the truth in her words.

"How do you know my name? And how did you know my mother?" I asked, flicking my eyes to Caden, too. I could hear the fear in my voice slowly returning. Kyraine must've heard it, too, because instantly she stopped staring at me so intensely.

"I knew your parents a long time ago, and I met you when you were only a baby," Kyraine tried to explain, but I was only more confused. "As I said, this will all be explained when we get back to camp."

I nodded numbly, not sure if I believed this world was real, if Kyraine's words were truthful, or if I was just being compliant to keep from getting even more confused. When Kyraine spoke again, the numbness instantly vanished, and my attention was hers again.

"Kaitlin, is she here as well?" Kyraine asked, looking past me. She spun quickly, her eyes darting across the small battlefield.

"How do you know about my sister?" I asked in alarm.

"I told you, I knew you both when you were young, too young to remember," Kyraine said.

She turned to the empty trees surrounding us and gestured for someone to come forward. At first, all I could see were shadows moving through the trees. Then I saw nine girls emerge from the forest, each holding a bow and arrow identical to Kyraine's. Each wore a tunic and cloak, all of them in green. Kyraine turned back to me, but found that I had backed away from her.

My breathing was picking up again as the archers neared me. Kyraine held up a hand and the girls stopped emerging from where they hid. "What's going on?" I asked frantically.

"Don't be afraid. We're here to protect you," Kyraine tried to assure softly.

"We all are," Caden added.

I kept shaking my head and backing away. "This isn't real. None of this is real. It's a dream—it's all a dream," I said to myself. My legs crumpled under me, and I buried my head in my arms and whispered to myself to wake up, over and over again.

I thought it was working until I felt a hand on my shoulder. I jolted and recoiled from it. "Casey, you do not need to be afraid. I promised your parents, Layna and Aaron, that I would protect you. You must come with us back to the camp to keep you safe from the people who were trying to take you. Please," Kyraine whispered so as not to startle me.

I glanced past her at the patient girls, Caden, and his friends. They all watched me silently. One of the girls carefully picked her way across the clearing to come over to us. My ragged breathing accelerated as she knelt down beside me. She looked me in the eyes, and I tried to shrink away from her as she placed a warm hand on my cheek.

"Shhh," she hushed me. "Just relax."

As though I'd been drugged, my eyelids suddenly felt heavy, and I was fighting to keep them open. When I finally gave in, I felt someone pull me into their arms. I couldn't open my eyes or my mouth to protest. Before long, I couldn't even remember what was happening, until finally, blackness consumed the world.

Chapter 10: Kyraine

CADEN BALANCED LAYNA'S daughter in his arms as he rode back to the Hunters' camp. The girls and I led the small group of horses back, and when we arrived, I estimated that around sixty girls had come to greet us. They emerged from tents, or peeled away from their various conversations or training sessions to see what newcomers had arrived. Even some of our many wolves abandoned their lounging to see what disturbed the peace. Their ear-splitting barks erupted through the trees as they noticed the stranger among their midst. They were hurriedly quieted by some of the onlooking girls.

Many of the Hunters only knew about Layna, and the legacy she left behind, from stories. Though few knew her personally, nearly everyone in Alagia was familiar with what her daughters meant to this land and to their future freedom. Some of the girls in the crowd were present in the battle when Layna died, and they remembered watching Aaron's heart break at the realization of his wife's death and his daughters' absence.

Caden handed Casey to me and started to rub down his horse. I carried Casey into Layna's old tent. In sleep, she seemed so calm, unlike earlier when her fear made her heart nearly leap from her chest. All the terror that engulfed her before hadn't left a single trace on her face as she rested soundly.

Gwen entered the tent with Veronica on her heel. I turned away from Casey and gave Veronica a questioning look, so she could explain the reason for her absence earlier. "Three Hunters have been injured and two

Huntsmen are dead. The time we spent looking for you cost lives. Where were you?"

She wouldn't look me in the eye and her voice wavered. "I was hunting."

I made an incredulous sound. "Well since you seem to value that so much, you'll be on hunting patrol for the next month. I expect enough meat to feed this entire camp."

Veronica crossed her arms and trained her gaze on the ground. "Fine," she grumbled. I returned my attention to Casey. "Who is she?" She evidently didn't understand our reactions.

Before I could answer, Gwen responded, "She is one of Layna Coles' daughters, Cassia," Gwen explained. I still hadn't completely convinced myself that this was real—that *she* was real.

"All right … and …?" Veronica continued.

"She is one of the girls from the prophecy," I told her.

"Which means she could end up being our enemy," Veronica pointed out wittily.

I made an exasperated sound. "Get out," I ordered.

Gwen ushered Veronica outside. "Return to training, Veronica," Gwen said. I followed them outside, and they went their separate ways. I pushed aside the flap of my tent to escape the hot sun. As I was pulling my cloak off, I saw silhouettes in the tent flap.

"May we come in?" a deep voice said.

"Yes," I responded as Caden, Mason, and Brennon entered.

All of their eyes looked tired and the way Caden's shoulders sagged in exhaustion told me they had been traveling for days with little rest. Their rigid movements were evidence that their bodies were racked with soreness from sitting in a saddle for days. I motioned for them to sit and they all gratefully collapsed onto stools around the wooden table with the map.

Caden was the leader of the Huntsmen, our counterpart. While the Hunters were female warriors, the Huntsmen were all male. The Hunters and the Huntsmen were ancient clans that had been a part of Alagia since the beginning of time. While we had no allegiance to any of the kingdoms, it was our responsibility to keep peace among them. Those who joined had to relinquish any ties to their old life and fully commit themselves to their duty as a protector of peace. Once this duty was fulfilled, the leaders of the respective groups would grant them half immortality. The new recruits would stop aging; however, death was not inescapable, as Hunters and Huntsmen could still die from mortal wounds. The two warrior clans were seen as the ancient protectors of Alagia in time of turmoil, and as Azlaya and the Sagen grew as a threat, we were being called upon again.

I called to one of the attendants outside to fix my old friends plates of food and drinks, which were quickly delivered. They were silent while they ate, and I waited patiently. I could tell by the looks on their faces when they swallowed that they were starving. I rolled up the map and stored it away as they finished their last bites, and then sat at the fourth stool at the table.

"I'm sorry about the two men you lost today," I broke the silence. "I wish we had arrived sooner."

When you're Master or Mistress of the Hunt, as Caden and I are, death of a friend becomes commonplace. "Thank you, Kyraine. We are grateful that you came at all, otherwise the outcome would have been very different."

"What brought you this far east?" I asked.

"We were riding to Canabar," Mason answered. He had thick, wavy hair that reached his shoulders, and his face was narrow, much like his figure. His heavy travel cloak made him seem much larger and broader than he actually was. Brennon had blonde hair that was just as wavy but cut shorter. He, on the other hand, was taller and had more muscle mass than Mason.

"For what purpose?" I already knew the answer.

Brennon and Mason's eyes shifted to their leader to explain. "Kyraine, there is a war coming, far larger than we had anticipated. We fear that the four kingdoms will be brought into this conflict, and we must be sure that they ally with us," Caden said.

Alagia was divided into four kingdoms: Calem, Eileen, Canabar, and Aerilon. Currently, two queens and two kings sat on their respective thrones. Queen Amelia ruled Calem, Queen Gisele ruled Eileen, King Mathias ruled Canabar, and King Nathaniel ruled Aerilon. If any of the kingdoms turned against us, Caden and I knew that winning the war would be practically impossible.

"We are going to speak with King Mathias to make sure his allegiance is still with us," Brennon added. I met his gaze, but dropped it quickly.

"Who else would it be with?" I asked.

"Azlaya. She's already made an agreement with Queen Gisele of Eileen to keep them out of the war, so I want to be sure that King Mathias will be ready to enter this war if and when the time comes. Security, Kyraine, that's all," Caden said in a reassuring voice.

Too many priorities were battling for attention inside my head. I couldn't stop thinking about Casey, her mother, the Kings and Queens, royal politics, and now I had to think about our defensive skirmishes evolving into a war greater than the one the Hunters were already involved in.

"Queen Amelia sends her regards," Caden said, interrupting my thoughts. I looked up.

"What's happening in Eileen?" I regretted asking because I didn't want to hear the answer. Gisele's kingdom was unstable, and if her people revolted, then the Huntsmen and Hunters would need to intervene to maintain control. My fear was that if and when that happened, the Hunters and I wouldn't be able to provide help if we were already battling Azlaya and the Sagen.

"Conditions are not ideal, but it's nothing you need to trouble yourself with. You must focus on the girl and defeating Azlaya," Caden said.

I nodded numbly.

"She will need to be trained to prepare her for what's to come."

"I'll train her in archery. Myra will handle sorcery," I told him. Myra was a forest Nymph and a great sorceress who had taught Layna Coles everything she knew. She had trained Layna and now she would train her daughter.

"Does she even possess her mother's gifts?" Mason asked.

"They must have been passed on to her," Caden answered before I could say I didn't know. His confidence was reassuring. "But what of other defensive skills, such as swordsmanship?"

"I'll admit I'm not a master." My eyes flicked to Brennon for a second. "But I can try to teach her what I know."

"Don't worry. When we return home I'll send someone to you," Caden offered.

"I can stay," Brennon said abruptly. He turned to Caden, who just looked at him, puzzled. I probably had the same look on my face. Brennon was the most skilled swordsman other than Caden, and even though I wanted him to stay, there was a sharp warning in my head telling me that this wasn't a good idea.

"I'll send someone when we return," Caden reiterated.

"Yes, I would hate to make your already small traveling party smaller," I interjected.

"It'll be fine. Besides, it doesn't make sense to delay the girl's training. I'm here now, I'll work with her," Brennon said convincingly. I opened my mouth to object, but he had a point. "You won't have time to train her," he said to me, "and I'm the next best thing," he added with the hint of joking I was used to.

"All right, fine," Caden conceded.

"I'll send some Hunters with you to make sure you arrive in Canabar safely," I told Caden. He nodded his thanks. Then we all rose and exited the tent.

I called for six of my best archers to assist Caden and Mason on their journey to Canabar. We supplied them with food and water that would last them until their arrival. Mason and Caden mounted their horses, and my warriors mounted their own. Caden thanked us, waved his goodbye, called his wolves, and set off with Mason and the Hunters in tow.

I walked over to Brennon, who was removing his belongings from his saddle. "Leave your horse here; a stable hand will take care of him. Follow me," I told him, then turned and led him to his tent.

Our tents spread out for what seemed like miles. They covered a huge clearing and a little beyond that as well. I let Brennon use a tent close to mine, and held the flap aside as he entered. Inside sat a bed, a short bedside table, and a larger one with a few stools. Across from the bed, a wide wooden chest would serve as his dresser.

"Nice place," Brennon said looking around, "Especially when compared to my recent accommodations."

I stood aside as he unpacked his things. "Most of us eat as the sun rises. You can eat lunch when it suits you. Since midday is when the patrol shifts change, the Hunters eat when they get the chance. Dinner is after evening training, and—"

"Kyraine," he cut in. I made a small noise in my throat. "It's good to see you."

I pressed my lips together, the warning signals in my head were returning. I nodded stiffly. "It's good to see you, too." Brennon set what he was holding down and started to move towards me. "While you are here I was wondering if you would teach some advanced sword lesson to the Hunters," I quickly added.

"I'd be happy to," he said. I was nodding frantically without even realizing it.

I angled my body away from him and changed the subject. "Who were you traveling with?" I asked, referring to the two men that were killed in the battle earlier.

"Cody Smith and Gunnar Peck," Brennon replied solemnly. "I'd like to bury them."

"Of course. I'll come with you."

He smiled and followed me from his tent. Brennon and I mounted two horses tied to a post and returned to where his friends had died. When we arrived at the clearing, two forest Nymphs stepped out from a tree.

"Kyraine!" one called out. "We tried to hold them off for as long as we could."

"I know, Isla," I comforted the young Nymph. "Can you help us bury these Huntsmen?"

Using their powers, the Nymphs were able to quickly dig two holes in the ground. Brennon and I carefully placed his friends into each hole and stepped back. Brennon mumbled a short incantation that is said to all Huntsmen when they are laid to rest. When he finished, I put two fingers to my lips, and gently touched each eyelid of the Huntsmen. "You fought courageously, died honorably, now rest peacefully," I whispered to each body.

I moved to stand next to Brennon again, and signaled to the Nymphs that they could cover the bodies. They waved their hands and we watched as thick roots began to grow from the ground and close over the open holes, creating a thick protective covering for the Huntsmen underneath.

"They were promising soldiers," Brennon said as the roots finished growing.

I sighed deeply, "They always are." We met each other's gazes. We spoke at the same time.

"I've missed you," he said

"I should get back to Casey."

He gestured for me to go on. As I was leaving I just caught a glimpse of his crooked smile that he used to give me all the time. But that was years ago. I thanked Kyla and Isla before quickly departing. I sped through the forest and jumped from the horse's back before it had fully stopped when I saw the tent Casey rested in.

As I entered, I tried to piece together how I would answer the countless questions she surely had. But I couldn't focus my mind. She was here. One of the daughters from the prophecy was here. I felt a small bubble of elation form in my chest, but where was her sister? Casey's arrival was a sign that maybe there was an end to this war and a new beginning for this land.

Chapter 11: Casey

I TRIED TO open my eyes, but it felt like they'd been glued shut. I couldn't feel my arms, legs, fingers—even my toes were dead. I felt so weak that it was worrisome. As I struggled to regain some strength, I heard voices nearby. I started to panic, wondering if Logan and his men had captured me. But that couldn't have happened. I was rescued by someone—a girl. I could only remember that she wore green.

I futilely tried to remember what had happened before I passed out, but my mind wouldn't recall those memories. The voices neared me and with all the strength I had left, my eyes fluttered open.

My surroundings weren't what I was expecting. I was on a bed sitting not very high off the ground. I noticed a side table with water and a piece of bread. I looked down at myself and saw a warm blanket had been laid over me. A wooden, cushioned chair rested near the tent's flap.

I heard a swift movement and my head snapped up. I suddenly remembered the girl's name: Kyraine. She walked in quietly, looking worn and tired. She sat in the cushioned chair and waited a moment before she spoke.

"How do you feel?" She made a sympathetic face.

"What happened?" I studied Kyraine's eyes.

"I'm sorry, but you were so panicked that I knew I wouldn't be able to convince you to come with us."

My eyebrows furrowed together as I tried to figure out what she meant, until I thought of the girl placing her warm hand on my cheek and slipping into darkness. "You drugged me?"

"No it was a—" Kyraine caught herself, as if deciding whether or not to tell me. "It was a spell that she used."

"A what?" I asked incredulously. "Oh, now I know this isn't real," I said to myself, throwing my arm over my eyes.

"Casey, please listen. I assure you this is real, and there are things you must know," Kyraine pressed on.

I lowered my arm. "What are you talking about? What is this place? One minute I was standing in my mother's room and the next I'm here. And why are my mother's journals full of stories about this place?"

"Because your mother could travel between our two worlds," Kyraine spoke softly.

"What?" I stared at her as though she had grown a second head.

Kyraine sighed deeply. "Since the beginning of our time, we have lived by a prophecy foretelling that someone from your world would bring peace to ours. Your mother found a doorway into our world and the prophecy began to come true. She became the greatest sorceress in the land, and here is where she met your father, Aaron. Soon, you and your sister were born, but your mother couldn't keep you safe here."

"A powerful sorceress, Azlaya, has thrown this land into turmoil. Her influence and power continues to grow, and she wants to control everything and everyone, and in accordance with the prophecy, she needs either you or your sister to accomplish this. When you were only a few months old, Azlaya came to capture one of you in hopes of raising you as her own and beginning her conquest. But your mother sent you two back to her world— your world—to be safe, along with the doorway back," Kyraine said, gesturing to the chain around my neck. I remembered the Nymphs telling me that the necklace was my only way back home. "She told us that the only way you two would return would be on your own. No amount of magic or power would be able to bring you back. You and your sister would have to find this place on your own … and you did."

I wanted to tell her that this was all a lie, and that this couldn't be real, but her story was matching up with much of what my mother had written in her journals. When I'd first found the journals, out of habit, I flipped to the last page of each one. Kyraine's story triggered a memory of one of my mother's last entries. It ended with one line: *She's coming, and I'm afraid that it'll be soon.*

"What happened to her—my mom?" I asked her, staring blankly ahead.

"Right after your mother sent you two away, Azlaya came. There was a battle between the Hunters and the Sagen. Azlaya and your mother engaged in their own fight … and your mother was killed. We started getting overwhelmed by Sagen, and in the chaos, Azlaya took your father as her prisoner. Since then we've waited for you and your sister's return."

"I read about the prophecy in her journals," I said absentmindedly. "She wasn't crafting stories … it was her life …"

"Before you and Kate were born, your mother knew you two were going to impact Alagia. She knew that this prophecy would endanger your lives. That's why she sent you back to her world—to your world. The prophecy says that you and Kaitlin would make a decision between good and evil. One of you would choose wrong, the other right."

I looked up at her, meeting her gaze. "Can I see it?" I wanted to read with my own eyes this "prophecy" that somehow bound my sister and me to this land, a land where my father was from and where I was born, yet which I didn't know existed until today.

Kyraine stood and kneeled next to a chest in a corner of the tent. I sat up to watch as she dug around on the inside. She finally pulled out a worn book and opened the yellowed pages. A crumpled paper fell out, which she picked up and held out to me.

I took the paper and unfolded it, and what I found on the page looked like a poem. The paper was yellowed too and the edges were crumbling. I held it up very gently. It read:

> *The one who brings prosperity and peace*
> *Who overcomes obstacles*
> *Must come to terms with others' needs*
> *Her two girls born on a March night*
> *Bound by one choice*

One will choose wrong, the other right
Once the choice is made one will be called
By a force of evil
The path to triumph is to prevail over all
Relationships will burn
Friendships will die
Who rises from the ashes
This land will see in time.

As I was flipping the paper over to read the remaining lines, Kyraine snatched the paper before I could read the last part of the prophecy.

"What about the part on the back?" I asked her.

"You don't need to know about that yet." She looked nervous when she finally glanced back at me.

I studied her face for a minute then asked, "Azlaya is the evil force?" Kyraine nodded. "But what does she want with us?"

"She needs one of you to aid her in conquering this world. Your mother was such a powerful sorceress, and her skills also reside in you and your sister. By indoctrinating one of you and developing your potential, Azlaya could become unstoppable."

"Well, do you know which one of us is going to join her?" I asked. Panic crept into my voice when I realized her next words could be my name.

"No. Not even your mother knew. She did tell me that when the choice is made, we will know," Kyraine told me softly.

"But I can't wait for that to happen, I have to go back home. I've been gone for hours and my grandmother is probably worried sick," I said frantically. She had probably called the police, the FBI, and the National Guard by now, especially if she saw the state of my mother's room.

"But you must stay!" Kyraine exclaimed. "Once either of you joins Azlaya, the other must be present to stop her and the ruin of this world."

"I can't wait forever. I have a life back in my world. I have friends and school ... I can't just stay here waiting," I reminded her.

"When one comes, the other will follow," Kyraine added. I looked at her in puzzlement. "Your mother told me that. You won't wait long, Casey,

I promise. If you leave now, there's little hope this world—this world that is a part of you—will survive," Kyraine added.

I dropped my gaze from hers. "You don't even know if I'll side with you."

A thick silence fell between us. It was weighing on Kyraine and whatever she was about to say, because she couldn't quite make herself say it. But if everything she was telling me was true, I had a point, and she knew it.

"You're right ... but I have a strange feeling that ..." she smiled reassuringly. "Let's not worry about that just yet."

"All right, fine, but what about my grandmother? I can't just continue to be missing," I remarked.

"She's known about this world since your mother began to travel here. If she doesn't know now that this is where you are, she will. Besides, the times in our two worlds are different, too. Being here for a couple of days would amount to much less time back in your world," Kyraine reassured me.

"All right," I sighed, having a little more piece of mind. "One more question."

"Anything," Kyraine agreed.

I started, "Since I'm accepting the possibility that I'm not dreaming—"

"You're not," Kyraine interjected.

"And considering that this place is real—"

"It is." I gave her a look which made her press her lips together.

"And assuming that your story is true—"

"It *is*." I looked at her again. "I'm sorry, but what is your point?"

"Why is it I'm almost seventeen, and I'm just learning my life story?"

Kyraine studied me for a moment before answering. By the looks of it, she was thinking and choosing her words very carefully.

"Your grandmother lost her only daughter to this world," Kyraine gestured around her. "I can't imagine she'd want to lose her granddaughters to it as well. Besides, she didn't have to tell you about it, you found it because it is part of who you are."

"So she lied to us all these years?" I asked. Feelings of anger and betrayal crept into my gut, and I couldn't dismiss them.

"There is a difference between lying for oneself and lying to protect others," Kyraine said softly, as if trying to gently push the idea on to me.

"Is there?" I said a little more venomously than I intended.

"Yes. It's a fine line, but it exists," she said firmly.

I sat in silence. Everything I thought I knew was instantly snatched from me and returned in a whole new perspective. One word just changed my life forever: Alagia.

Kyraine stood and walked over to the bed and bent down on her knees. She reached under the bed and pulled out another, shorter chest. She lifted the lid and inside lay a light green tunic with a golden embroidered hem. Kyraine removed it from the box while I stood and gazed at the dress. She held it up in front of me as if testing the size.

"This should do," she said as she handed the garment to me. "It was your mother's, and you seem to be the same size. It's not as long as it looks," she added as I eyed the garment disapprovingly.

"My clothes are fine," I began to protest.

"No, they are not. They stand out and it will be easy for suspicious eyes to spot you. We are safe here, but travelers do pass through this camp from time to time."

She placed the tunic in my hands, and I held it against my body as Kyraine drew more things from the chest. "Here is a cloak and shoes," she said to me as she placed them on the bed. "Get dressed. I'll be waiting outside."

Kyraine exited the tent and left me to change. I pulled off my clothes and slipped on the tunic. The sleeves were just past my shoulders while the hem fell just below my knees. A belt had been coiled up and thrown into the chest. I used it to wrap around my waist as I'd seen many of the Hunters do.

I pulled on the shoes that resembled the Sperrys I had in my closet, but were softer and felt more like a snug sock. I folded my other clothes, and tucked them under the bed. When I stood up, I felt something cold bump against my chest and my hand flew to what hung in place. It was the necklace that the Nymphs had placed around my neck and had branded me as Layna Coles' daughter. I held the two rings in my hands and rubbed my thumb and finger against them. It *was* a beautiful piece of jewelry, I thought, as I tucked it into the tunic. Finally, I tied the cloak around my shoulders.

I walked out of the tent only to find myself within a maze of other tents. I stood and stared in awe at the hundreds of tents spreading for what seemed like miles. I was immediately reminded of the circus my sister and I went to see every year as children. The memory made my stomach lurch with homesickness.

A voice startled me until I remembered that Kyraine was waiting for me. She was beckoning me to follow her. There were Hunters carrying game and platters of food, blacksmiths working, and horses and carts passing by. It was like a small bustling city, but Kyraine cut effectively through the commotion. I noticed the sun had sunk low in the sky when we reached our destination.

There was a large area with tree stumps scattered about. Girls of similar age as Kyraine walked and sat about calmly. They all wore green tunics, cloaks, and either shoes like mine or tall riding boots. Suddenly, I recalled all the stories of the Hunters in my mother's journals. However innocent and harmless they looked, my mother described them as nothing of the sort when it came to battle. Efficient killers, she had called them. Silent and deadly when they had to be, or fiercely defiant warriors that charged boldly into battle. I noticed that each of them had a weapon or several weapons on them.

Alongside many of the girls, wolves roamed about. Some sat next to girls, begging for scraps of food; others flanked girls as they strolled, and some even basked in the setting sun. Many also sat against trees, gnawing on bones, bark, and branches. The beasts were beautiful shades of grey, brown, and sand. Not only were they gorgeous, but also in comparison to me, huge. The wolves' heads easily reached the torso of my 5'4" frame.

In the middle of everything, a fire pit roared. The smells of grilling caressed my nose, as I realized I was starving. Kyraine noticed my eagerness to eat and led me to a tree stump.

Girls who were grilling in the fire pit began to pass out plates, heaped high with steaming food. Suddenly, a huge crowd began to withdraw from the trees as dinner readied. The atmosphere was friendly, warm, and inviting. I was handed a plate and immediately began to eat. As I was taking a bite of my bread, Kyraine stood up and addressed everyone.

"Hunters, may I have your attention?" Kyraine called out. She waited for silence. "Tonight, one of Layna Coles' daughters dines with us. This is her first time here, so please be welcoming to her."

I felt as though I'd won an award when they all began applauding. I debated whether I should stand, but decided against it. I just quietly thanked them for their hospitality.

In the crowd, a figure began to make its way towards Kyraine and me. Her hair was bleached blonde and was intricately braided around her head and down her back. She wore several rings on her fingers and had flowers twisted in her hair. Her skin was pale, which made her pink lips and grey-green eyes stand out that much more. All of her facial features were soft, and it seemed like she was carefully considering something all the time. What demanded the most attention though, was her dress, which reminded me of the dresses the Nymphs I had met earlier wore. That's when it struck me that she was probably one, too.

"Myra!" Kyraine exclaimed as she jumped up to greet the girl. She and Kyraine seemed to be close in age.

I was distracted by her effortless grace and beauty, and Kyraine had to call me twice to get my attention. "Casey, this is Myra. She will be one of your instructors," Kyraine explained to me.

I stood to greet Myra. She took my hand and gave it a small squeeze. "It's a pleasure to meet you again." She saw my confusion and explained, "I knew you briefly, as a baby."

She looked frail and petite in comparison to Kyraine, who appeared strong and fit. "Are you a—" I started to say.

"Nymph," she finished my sentence. "Yes." She held my gaze for a while. "You look so much like your parents," she added before she turned to leave.

I turned back to Kyraine, only to find her talking to the only man in the clearing. I recognized him from earlier when Caden rescued me. His hair was dirty blonde, disheveled, and hung right above his brown eyes.

The way he spoke, and the way his eyes flickered when he laughed made him seem very likable. He wore a loose-fitting, white, long-sleeved shirt under a brown vest that laced up the front, tight pants and riding boots, and around his waist was a thick, leather belt that held his sword. If I had passed him in the hallway at school, I would have glanced at him twice, meaning he was definitely attractive. Suddenly, his bright eyes fell on me. Caught gazing at him, I could only smile weakly in embarrassment.

Kyraine whirled around and introduced us. His name was Brennon Harrow and he was the most skilled swordsman in Alagia, other than Caden, who had come to help train me. I sat back down on my stump, and he lowered himself on one right next to mine.

"I was almost positive that Kaitlin was the brunette," he said, gesturing to my hair.

"No, *Kate*," I stressed her name, "is blonde. Do you know her from the prophecy, too?"

"Yes, but I was also present when you were born. Kyraine asked for extra protection when you were born so I came with some other Huntsmen. I was standing right outside the tent. I remember now ... you were always the quieter one, your sister on the other hand ..." his voice trailed off. I chuckled.

"But how were you there when I was born?" I looked at Brennon. He couldn't be more than five years older than me. He couldn't look that young after sixteen years.

His face lit up with realization. "Kyraine hasn't told you about people like her and me." I shrugged my shoulders. He continued. "We're not human ... entirely."

"What?"

"We don't die from aging like humans. We're called half immortals."

I stared at him incredulously, but also with amazement, my mouth partly open. He chuckled and continued.

"We can only die from physical injury. For instance, I could live for thousands of years, but I will always theoretically be and look nineteen. But if someone stabbed me with a sword, I would die, just like anyone else would."

"Wow," I breathed. Since my arrival, logic itself seemed to have no meaning or presence. "You just live forever?" He made an affirmative noise in his throat while forking meat into his mouth. I waited for him to swallow. "Is everyone here like that?"

"No, it's just the Hunters and the Huntsmen. Only the Master and the Mistress of the Hunt, Caden and Kyraine, can grant half immortality when someone joins," Brennon explained.

"And the Huntsmen are …?" I asked.

"They're the Hunters' counterpart. It's everything you see here, except they're all male."

I nodded my head in understanding. The sun had set and the only light was the fire burning brightly in the middle of the clearing. A few of the Hunters began to light torches surrounding the clearing to keep the darkness at bay. "So once you join you start to live forever?"

"It's not quite that simple, but basically, after years of training, that is the end result," Brennon affirmed.

"Not dying sounds pretty immortal to me," I replied.

"Being immortal is being free from death. We are not," Brennon said with solemnity. The talk of death seemed to cause his mind to wander. I had learned very quickly that Alagia was a violent world, and Brennon's serious expression reminded me of the look I would see on Kate's face when she thought of our parents.

"It would be hard," I added, trying to sympathize, "to outlive the people around you." He smiled at my effort, but it didn't reach his eyes. I remembered the sword strapped to his hip and glanced down to marvel at its size. Trying to change the subject, I said politely, "Well, I hope you're a good teacher," looking at his weapon.

He followed my gaze and cracked a crooked, but genuine, smile. "A good teacher," he scoffed, "Would be the understatement of the century."

Chapter 12: Myra

SHE IS HERE. Those words kept replaying in my head. My apprentice's daughter had finally arrived. Many thought this day was legend. The idea of Azlaya's defeat and the war's end seemed impossible, but the prophecy was right. Now, it was only a matter of how its foretelling would unfold.

I left Kyraine and Casey to their meals and wandered to the edge of the clearing where my home stood. Being a forest Nymph, I felt a strong bond to nature. Rather than living in a tent, I grew a massive oak tree, furnished the inside, and carved a door. Around the tree's roots, there was a small area of soil where I had planted a small pink flower. That single flower meant more to me than all my belongings combined.

I lifted my chin to the sky and saw ominous clouds, pregnant with rain, rolling along the horizon. The thought of a storm returned me to a rainy and cold summer afternoon a long time ago. I was sitting under a willow tree on the banks of a pond. At the time, Kyraine traveled west to train the Huntsmen in archery and had convinced me to join her.

I watched them shoot at targets in a vast field of foxtails. Kyraine would demonstrate, striking each target in the center, making the surrounding Huntsmen gawk at her. I was reading a potion book when an arrow lodged into the tree a couple inches above my head.

I was ready to turn the imbecile who had nearly hit me into a rat, but then I saw him. He was fairly muscular and his dark, tousled hair was wild and dripping with the rain. My head was screaming at me to utter the spell, but then I saw his eyes. They were big, round, brown marbles of joy. He didn't have to smile; his eyes did it for him.

He came up to me and looked down. His face was expectant, as though he wanted me to jump up and introduce myself. When I didn't, he did.

"Hello, Miss. My name is Alexander Cane."

"Myra," I said coldly. I jabbed a finger in the direction of the arrow. "Does this belong to you?"

He suppressed a laugh and apologized. "I'm sorry; I was just trying to get your attention." He took notice of my hair and wiped water from his eyes. "Myra, how are you staying dry?" He asked me. In spite of all the precipitation, I hadn't gotten the least bit wet. He studied me for a moment longer and a realization hit him. "You're a fairy?"

"Nymph," I corrected him, "is the socially accepted term. Shouldn't you be practicing?" I glanced over his shoulder at his friends shooting into the field. "Based on your last shot," I said, glancing at the arrow, "you'll need one hundred years of practice before you'll be useful on the battle field."

He shrugged off my playful insult. "I've been training all day." I must have made a skeptical face, because he quickly added, "I'm much better with a sword anyway." My eyebrows shot up at his claim. "I really am sorry about the arrow."

My narrow eyes began to widen. "You're just lucky that I'm mellower than most Nymphs. I've known some to change travelers into toads for even passing too close to their homes."

He chuckled heartedly, "Then I'd really be in trouble." He jerked his chin towards the book I read. "What are you reading?"

"A book about turning herbs into healing teas," I answered plainly.

"That sounds awfully boring," he exclaimed.

He was cute, and his demeanor and personality were beginning to grow on me. I suppressed a smile. "It is, but not all knowledge is interesting."

Alexander glimpsed back at his friends and turned back to me. I saw a quick shiver erupt through him. Through sympathy I patted the ground next to me and he gratefully sat down. As though we sat under an awning, the rain didn't fall on us. I watched as his eyes stared in wonder. I flicked my hand and drew all the water from his clothes, letting it flow back into a nearby pond.

His shuddering instantly stopped as warmth crawled back into him. He stretched his legs out in front of him and then leaned his head against the tree. I waited for him to comment on my magic, but what he said was unexpected.

He rolled his head over so that our eyes met. "So if I get a fever out here, would you be able to cure it with one of your teas?" A smile played on my lips, and our friendship was born.

Over the next year that Kyraine and I spent with the Huntsmen, Alexander and I fell in love. At night, he would take me for walks around a lake, and I would demonstrate some of my magic. While he trained during the day, he would always steal glances in my direction. When the Huntsmen were given breaks, we would hike to a secluded valley and spend the afternoon spread out on a blanket. I would tell him stories of my early years when I began to learn magic from my elders. Then, he would match them with his adventures with the Huntsmen. Every night we would sit underneath the tree where we first met, transfixed with the countless stars hanging above us. We became inseparable.

This lasted for an entire year, and when he finally professed his love for me, I got scared, because he wanted to elope. However, members of the Hunters and Huntsmen were forbidden from marriage, because love would interfere with their loyalty and duty to their respective clan. Violators of the law were harshly punished, or killed in some instances. I tried, futilely, to convince Alexander that he wasn't thinking straight. He told me that with my magic, we could run away and escape the retaliation he'd surely receive from the Huntsmen. It took him several months to get me to accept his secret proposal, and when I was just starting to get excited about our possible future together, war broke out. The Huntsmen rushed to stop Azlaya's initial wave of advances, and Kyraine learned her Hunters were under attack and she needed to return.

Alexander gave me the flower that sits at the foot of my tree before he left for Calem, in promise of his return and of our marriage. Not a day passed when he didn't cross my mind. Then one day, two months after his departure, I learned that Alexander had been killed in a Sagen raid.

In the following days, I felt like I couldn't breathe. It was as if a huge weight pressed down on my chest, leaving me gasping for air. I felt as though I could have cried myself an ocean. Words of comfort went through me like the wind. Shortly upon returning to the Hunters' camp, I retreated into the wilderness to mend what had been broken and mourn what I'd lost. It was months before I was able to resurface.

As I watched his flower dancing in the wind, all these memories came flooding back. A tear slid down my cheek, and where it fell, tiny sprouts of Harebell plants began to sprout.

Azlaya's conquest had taken so much from everyone: Layna and Aaron Coles, Hunters, Huntsmen, and innocent lives alike. I felt it was part of my responsibility to avenge everyone who had died so far and avenge the day that Azlaya's army took Alexander from me.

A few minutes passed, and from my peripheral vision, I saw Kyraine approaching me. Recognizing her gait, I turned and smiled mildly. "Do you think this is it? She and her sister can bring an end to this war?" Kyraine asked. We both were studying Casey from afar as she spoke animatedly with the Huntsmen.

I thought about it. "Yes. Kyraine it's her. She is one of the girls from the prophecy ... we just don't know if she's going to side with us," I replied, as my concern lingered between us.

"It's been so long. I started to lose hope. I'm not completely convinced that she's real," Kyraine sighed. I could feel her anxiety. She wanted—needed—some kind of certainty that this war would end, and that all these years of fighting weren't for nothing.

"She's real. You know Azlaya. She wouldn't send a large contingent of Sagen after her otherwise."

My words of assurance softened her face. She stole a glance at the flower and placed a warm hand on my arm.

"It's the anniversary, isn't it?" She didn't have to ask. She knew that today was the anniversary of Alexander's death, but wanted to say something to fill the empty space. Despite the long and deep relationship Kyraine and I shared, I'd never told her that Alexander and I were planning to run away and marry, since it'd be a conflict of interest. But she did know that we shared strong feelings for one another, and comforted me as much as anyone could in the days after Alexander's death. Now, instead of being happily married to the man I loved, I was left to mourn the future—my future that never had a chance to bloom.

I solemnly nodded. Kyraine reached down and held my hand in hers. I was grateful for the darkness to give us some privacy. I felt a slumbering ache waking inside of me. The tears were beginning to resurface, but I choked them back. I swallowed deeply, so I could form comprehensible words. "Does she know?"

Kyraine averted her eyes to me and they reflected her answer. "I didn't let her finish reading it," she responded. My elation from Casey's arrival dampened upon realizing that she didn't know of her unavoidable fate. I wished she would never have to know.

Chapter 13: Casey

THE NEXT MORNING, Brennon pulled me out of bed early to begin my training. The sun was a faint glow on the horizon, barely giving light to the clouds overhead. Breakfast was cold oats and nuts. On our way from the thick of the forest, Brennon told me stories about Alagia and its past. I was fascinated by the history of a world I never knew existed. He told me about everything; the rulers, the land, the people. One of my favorite tales was about a king from over a hundred years ago who was a sorcerer. On one day of each year, he allowed the poorest peasants to come into his castle and used his powers to grant them one thing that would improve their lives. It was all so intriguing and I found myself embracing Alagia more and more.

Once we made it past the tree line, Brennon started my training with unsheathing the sword. It wasn't at all what I was expecting. In the movies and books, they made whipping out a sword seem so easy, but I was struggling just to lift the weapon from its casing.

I learned quickly that Brennon was a very light-hearted, carefree person. Every time I went to unsheathe the sword and failed, he laughed. It was a full, rolling laugh full of warmth and spirited fun. He wasn't laughing at me, but instead enjoying the learning process. If he was impatient with my progress he didn't show it. "You'll get used to it," he reassured me on what seemed like my one hundredth attempt. The one time I did successfully unsheathe the sword, I hadn't realized how heavy it was and almost fell under its weight. By that point, I couldn't help but laugh at myself too.

Later that day, when the Hunters had a break from training, Kyraine took me to a trading village near the Hunters' camp. The villagers lived in small wooden huts, which reminded me of the log cabins I stayed in when I went to camp as a child. Children ran around playing on the dirt pathway that ran down the middle of the houses. The women and girls wore long dresses that dragged on the ground. Most of the men were wearing attire similar to Brennon's. It was almost as though I had stepped back in time and walked among colonials.

I caught a glimpse of a couple of boys playing with wooden swords, pretending to be heroes on the battlefield. My heart ached for them once I realized that one day they could be dragged into a real war, bloody and impersonal, where wooden swords became steel ones that drew blood.

Kyraine told me these people used to live in strong, fortified villages and had enough food for their families, but now they could hardly feed half the family. Azlaya and the Sagen laid waste to the land, leaving the families to rebuild their homes and their lives. With twenty years of turmoil, they had not been able to set down roots and begin to reconstruct the villages they had lost, leaving the younger generations to become refugees with no memories of permanent or settled lives. It was easy to understand the hatred towards Azlaya after seeing how she had left an entire village to start their lives over and survive off of the little they had.

Kyraine handed me a small drawstring pouch of coins and told me to go buy myself something to eat while she spoke with the blacksmith about new swords for the Hunters. I retraced my steps back to the bakery we had passed earlier. I passed several villagers, all of whom were busy with their own errands and hustled by me. That was why I wasn't surprised when I saw a beggar huddled outside the bakery, plainly ignored by everyone that passed. She had blonde hair matted with dirt, and grime covered her face and skin. The dress she wore was torn, and its hem was fraying. She looked longingly at the people who walked past her, but no one gave her a second glance.

We both wanted the same thing—to have something to eat. However, I had the means of getting food; she did not. So, I resolved to help her, and smiled widely at her as I entered the bakery. I bought the largest loaf of bread Kyraine's money could buy and returned to the street.

The girl's eyes grew three times in size when I knelt beside her, steaming loaf in hand. I broke off a handful of bread for me and gave her the rest. "I hope this will be enough for now." She was speechless and blinked at the bread in her dirty hands.

As I turned to leave, she spoke softly, "Are you the good one?" I spun to face her. She tapped herself where the necklace hung on my chest. I fingered it, not sure how to answer her question, knowing that even I didn't know if I was the "good" sister or not. "It doesn't matter," she broke my silence. "Thank you."

A thin smile spread on my lips, when Kyraine returned and shuffled me back to the Hunters' camp. For the next couple of days, I would go into the village, buy another loaf of bread, and give the girl the larger portion. I learned that her name was Irene, but that was the only information I could coax from her as she eagerly stuffed her face with the only food she received all day.

One afternoon, after a morning combat session with Kyraine, I had my swordsmanship training with Brennon. We walked to the edges of the Hunters' land to help condition my endurance and stamina, a trek that took between two and three hours each way. Not only was Brennon my teacher, but he was also my fitness coach. Since I had already had combat skills training with Kyraine, fatigue was setting in. I had been working hard, and Brennon allowed me to take a break, so we sat on a log near a river that cut through the trees.

There never seemed to be a quiet moment in the forest. Birds chirped, squirrels raced up trees, the Hunters' wolves could be heard barking in the distance, and even the wind constantly rustled the leaves. Nevertheless, I found its endless chaos comforting. Part of the reason I believe I became acclimated to life in the forest so quickly was because of my love for it as a child. Kate and I always played games in the woods behind our house, and would drag sleeping bags and pots outside and pretended to be survivalists. I laughed inwardly at how I had been training myself for living with the Hunters without even knowing it.

Brennon broke our silence and asked about my life before I came to Alagia. I told him about my grandmother and how Kate and I spent almost every second together, whether it was studying, shopping, or just hanging out with our friends. He teased me lightly when I told him about my friends forcing me to choose from over one hundred themes for my birthday party. I even mentioned Jackson, hoping that Kate had realized all the flaws I saw in him. I asked Brennon about his home, and he explained how the rolling hills and vast valleys were so different from the thick forest. He told me about Calem, the kingdom where he was born, and how the Queen's castle was the most beautiful structure he'd ever seen. It was built on the edge of a cliff overlooking the ocean, and its cream color absorbed the sun when it rose and set. I enjoyed talking about my life before it was entangled with the strangeness of this world, and it made me feel like I would still be able to retain some normal part of my life.

Suddenly, Brennon turned to me with mischievousness in his eyes. "Can you keep a secret?"

My lips parted, and I eyed him suspiciously. "What kind of secret?"

He jumped to his feet, and I slowly got to mine. He pulled me deeper into the forest and farther from the Hunters' camp. I was about to ask him where he was taking me, when he turned sharply and held a finger to his lips. He pointed behind me. I craned my head and saw a patrolling Hunter picking her way through the trees. She moved gracefully and silently, and had it not been for Brennon's keen awareness, I would never have known she was there. He gestured for me to stay still and quiet, and after a few minutes passed and the Hunter was out of earshot, started to tow me along again. When he decided we were far enough away from the roaming Hunters, he stopped. Brennon lifted a hand to his mouth and whistled, blending evenly into the cacophony of the forest.

A few minutes passed as I searched for what Brennon had whistled to. Suddenly, a violent wind began to whip around above our heads. I looked up and saw a large mass descending on us. I lurched back, so as not to be crushed by whatever the thing was. When the wind stopped and I peered at what had landed, a gasp jumped off my lips.

"Oh my God!" I exclaimed as I scrambled backwards. "Is that a—"

"Dragon, yeah," Brennon chuckled casually. "His name is Danzinar," he told me as he walked over to the beast and stroked his head.

His scales were silver with scattered flecks of blue. He had spikes running from the crown of his head all the way down his neck and then resuming down his tail, which ended in three large spikes. He had two sharp horns on his head and his face almost resembled a wolf's in shape. He was no bigger than a stubby pony, but his wings were twice that of his body length when stretched. I fought the urge to run as the beast's gaze settled on me. Somehow, I felt that darting away would only make the dragon chase me as a dog would.

"You don't have dragons in your world?" Brennon joked. He clearly found my bewilderment and unease amusing.

Brennon's pet eyed me curiously, as if he were debating whether or not to eat me. Brennon noticed my anxiety growing. "Casey, stop inching backwards," he ordered. I hadn't even realized that my feet were still moving. "It's really important that you come over and greet him with me. Dragons are extremely intelligent and perceptive creatures when they are older, but Danzinar is young and hasn't made up his mind about you yet. You need to show him that you're not a threat," Brennon explained calmly.

"H-how do I do that?" Danzinar still eyed me suspiciously.

"Come here," Brennon called softly. My heart stopped, while Brennon held out a hand, beckoning me over. A wide stare was all I could return.

"I don't think he likes me, Brennon," I tried to protest.

"Casey, just come here." I nervously exchanged glances with Brennon and his scaly pet. But Brennon was insistent, so I bit down hard on my lip, and ever so slowly, picked my way over to Brennon. I heard a rumble growing in the dragon's belly as I approached. Brennon came forward to meet me and stood by my side as I neared his pet. He took a fat fowl from his game bag and placed it in my trembling hand. "Hold it out so he can sniff it."

I did as instructed. Danzinar crawled forward, and I took notice of the curled talons on his feet. He sniffed the bird, grunted, and then snatched it from my hand. I was so nervous that his quick movement made me drop the bird and leap backwards. "I think that's enough for today," I exhaled unevenly.

Brennon laughed approvingly. "The quickest way to win over a dragon is through his stomach," he patted the silver scales. I laughed nervously from what I thought was a comfortable distance between Danzinar and me.

"So ... you have a dragon," I said.

"I've had him for a few weeks. You should have seen him when he first hatched. He couldn't have been bigger than a piglet." Danzinar nudged Brennon in search of more food.

"You couldn't have introduced us when he wasn't big enough to eat me?" I scoffed. "Where have you been keeping him?"

"Out here. There are mountains about ten miles northwest of here where he stays and hunts."

"You had him even when you were travelling with Caden?"

Brennon nodded. "Well, he hadn't hatched yet, so I had his egg. I was hoping to train him once we arrived in Canabar. That's where all the dragons reside these days, in the Mountains of Canabar. But, obviously those plans changed, so he's been living out here," he told me, and gave Danzinar a loving pat.

That's when I remembered that the beast before me was a secret. "Kyraine doesn't know?" I inquired.

Brennon half shrugged, "Not yet, but he's only going to get bigger. Sooner or later she'll find out. But for now, apprentice, he's our secret. I don't need the Hunters or villagers panicking about a wild beast on the loose." He pulled another fowl from his pouch and tossed it to me.

I caught it and realized my mistake. Danzinar trained his eyes on me again, staring intently at his food. Brennon encouraged me to try feeding him again. I inched closer to the dragon with my hand outstretched, ready to tear it away when he snapped at the bird. This time, he reached out his neck, dug his teeth into the fowl, and gently pulled it from my hand.

Brennon remarked, "I told you they were smart creatures. He can tell you're afraid of him."

I didn't hear anything coming from the pit of his stomach. "No growling," I stated, relieved.

"See, he's warming up to you," Brennon exclaimed.

I grinned shyly at the dragon. "You should probably send him off before someone comes. His entrance wasn't exactly discrete."

Brennon whistled, making a different sound than before, which signaled for Danzinar to leave. Brennon pushed me back, allowing the dragon plenty of room to take flight. We both craned our necks as we watched him rocket into the sky and out of view.

"You trained him to react to different whistles?" I asked impressed.

"It took many grueling hours and even more fowls to do so."

I was about to say something when Brennon held up a hand. He looked behind where we stood. I turned, listening for another Hunter patrolling. I kept staring at the bushes when Brennon turned all the way around.

"What are you doing?" I whispered, but Brennon hardly acknowledged me as I spoke to him.

"Stay here," he said urgently while pushing some brush away.

"Where are you going?" But he kept walking.

"Just stay here. I'm going to go see something," he replied.

Suddenly, the fear of the unknown gripped me. I hadn't encountered the Sagen since my arrival and I wasn't looking forward to running into them again. "Should I go back to the camp?" I suggested. He hushed me, then pushed aside some branches and disappeared.

"Brennon … Brennon," I whispered as loudly as I thought was safe.

I chased after him through dense underbrush. I smacked into his back, throwing him off balance and into a tree, which he grabbed for support. I mouthed my apology, but he was still focused on something still invisible to us … or at least to me.

I scanned the trees when I saw a flicker of movement. Then, I saw it again. I finally understood that it was the Sagen searching the forest.

Brennon cursed under his breath, which only made my fears grow. Brennon slowly turned back to me, put a finger to his lips, and then pointed back in the direction we had come. I looked past him at the Sagen and gingerly began to move backwards. I was about to turn all the way around to go back through the underbrush, when Brennon grabbed my arm and yanked me into him.

I shot him an accusatory look, but then I understood why it didn't matter. Sagen warriors surrounded us with no way out and nowhere to run.

Chapter 14: Brennon

I REMEMBER BEING told stories about the Sagen when I first began my training as a Huntsman. They wore long, black robes with hoods. Their faces were black holes and their hands were said to be bony and cold. The Sagen were appropriately called the Shadow Warriors, because when in the sun's shadow, or in other words, darkness, they could not be killed. They came from a desolate place in the mountains near Eileen known as the Shadowlands. The Sagen were dark creatures who had the ability to drain the souls of powerful sorcerers and use their sorcery as their own. But sorcery stolen from a body becomes twisted and dangerous, resulting in Dark Magic. Anytime I faced a Sagen, I hoped that they hadn't acquired someone else's sorcery yet, because it made my odds of survival much lower.

Watching the hunting party of Sagen roam the woods, it was easy to see why they were referred to as hooded ghosts. When they moved they were silent, and the black robes they wore made them appear to float across the ground. I knew we had traveled far outside the camp's boundaries if these Sagen roamed freely. I pointed in the direction from which we had come, in hopes that we could slip back into the Hunters' territory unnoticed, but it was too late.

"Casey!" I grabbed her and yanked her towards me just as a Sagen was about to snatch her.

I unsheathed my sword and raised it to eye level. I gently pushed Casey back with my other hand. We moved cautiously away from the hooded figure, as I calculated how I was going to get Casey out safely.

More hooded figures began to descend upon us, each with four-foot long, serrated swords. The Sagen in front of us moved into a small pool of light and I seized my opportunity.

I lunged forward and drove my sword into the unsuspecting Sagen. He screeched then fell into a pile of dust. "Casey, get down!" I collected the fallen Sagen's sword, as she obediently crouched down. As I'd watched Caden do only days prior, I hurled the sword into another warrior.

"Brennon, behind you!" she screamed. I spun around and swung my sword up. An ear-piercing clang rang through the trees. I fought the Sagen that seemed to never stop coming, keeping Casey safely behind me. She had left her sword when she followed me, but I didn't think it would have been much use anyway.

I finally came to the point where I was fighting two Sagen at once. I was so occupied with them that I hadn't noticed that they had drawn me away from Casey.

I sliced one Sagen in half and tried to race back to her, but I felt a searing pain abruptly rip across my shin and I stumbled to the forest floor. I looked down and saw that a sword had cut right through my boots and to my skin.

"Brennon!" Casey cried. I searched for her in the mass of black and found her squirming in the arms of one of the Sagen.

I held my breath and reached for my sword. My fingertips brushed it when it was kicked away. A dark shadow loomed over me.

"This one seems weak," a raspy voice floated from the Sagen that restricted Casey. He now had his sword at her throat and her back against a tree. "She wants the stronger of the two to fulfill the prophecy."

The Sagen that loomed over me answered, "We'll take her to Azlaya. She can decide." He turned back to me. "But as for you," he said.

He raised his sword over his head. I heard a piercing scream from Casey. Then, out of nowhere, an arrow plunged into the black robes. The Sagen crumbled into ashes at my feet.

I leaned my head back in relief. "Your timing is impeccable."

The Hunter that saved my life rushed forward with several other Hunters that were patrolling nearby to chase the scattering Sagen. A couple had escaped, but the rest were reduced to piles of ashes.

Casey rushed across protruding roots over to me and knelt. She looked horrified when she saw my leg. "It's only a scratch," I said, trying to calm her. This wasn't my first, nor my worst, wound. "Are you all right?" Her expression looked distant. I could tell she was perturbed by the battle, my wound, and what the Sagen had said. I pulled myself upright to be eye level with her.

"What did they mean?" she asked slowly. "What did they mean about needing the stronger one to fulfill the prophecy?" While I couldn't bring myself to tell Casey the truth that had been kept from her about the prophecy, I still believed she deserved to know.

"The other day, when Kyraine showed you the prophecy, she didn't let you finish reading it, did she?" Casey shook her head languidly. "You need to," I replied. Her face grew apprehensive as her mouth slightly parted, and her pupils enlarged.

I would have told her not to worry, but I knew she definitely had reason to worry. Casey helped haul me to my feet, as a couple Hunters returned from pursuing the Sagen. One warrior helped Casey steady me as I hobbled back towards the camp, while another took off running to fetch me a horse. It took her a painful half an hour to find one and deliver it to us. I pulled myself onto the animal's back, and the Hunter helped Casey up behind me.

"I trust you can find your way back to the camp, Huntsman?" the Hunter questioned.

I nodded and thanked her before she took off to return to her post. Casey ripped some fabric from my cloak and wrapped it around my shin to slow the blood flow. "Hold on tight," I warned Casey. She clasped her hands around my waist, and I dug my heels into the horse's side. It took off, weaving between the trees. The Hunters' horses always had the best footing of any horses that I'd ridden because they constantly galloped over uneven terrain. For the sake of my leg, we thankfully made great time, and made it back to the camp in about an hour, just as the sun was setting.

Torches around the camp had been lit and the Hunters were dispersing from dinner when we rode into the mass of tents. I saw Kyraine speaking with two Hunters, but she abruptly stopped and rushed over when she saw us.

"I just heard what happened." She quickly helped Casey down from the horse and examined her. I dismounted as slowly as I could, so as not to further strain my wound.

"Kyraine." I tried to get her attention. "Kyraine!" I said more forcefully. She paused and met my gaze.

"I want to see the rest of the prophecy," Casey told her. Kyraine's eyes returned to Casey. She looked expressionless, but I'd known Kyraine long enough to know that she debated further keeping Casey in the dark or finally telling her the truth.

"Kyraine." She looked at me again. "She deserves to know."

She finally, silently agreed, and beckoned for Casey and me to follow her. I trailed behind them to Kyraine's tent. The quiet was suffocating, and even from behind, I could tell that Casey and Kyraine's minds were spinning out of control.

Kyraine held her tent flap aside as we entered, and I sat and propped my leg to slow the blood flow. Kyraine handed Casey a yellowed paper and waited.

I read the paper over Casey's shoulder, trying to distract myself from the stinging pain in my leg. It read:

One will be ended by her loving bloodline
The triumphant one will continue
And be this dying world's guide.

"What does it mean?" Casey asked, her eyes darting from Kyraine, to me, and back to Kyraine.

"It means …" I knew Kyraine was trying to euphemize the foretelling of the prophecy, but found it couldn't be done. She looked defeated when she said, "It means that in the end, either you will kill your sister, or she will kill you."

Spasms of fear, shock, and sadness crossed Casey's face. Her hand flew up to her mouth, and her breathing became uneven and jagged. "That can't be true." She said each word deliberately, but her expression was dubious, as though she knew the prophecy wasn't a piece of fiction. Kyraine pulled Casey to her feet and led her out of the tent. I watched them leave, trying to imagine how I would feel if I was told that either I had to kill my sibling or they would kill me. I couldn't do it.

Kyraine returned a few minutes later. She collapsed on a stool, folded her hands and rested her head on them. I sensed her pent-up anger about to explode.

She snapped to attention and shot daggers with her eyes at me. "What the hell were you doing in that part of the woods? Don't you know how close you were to Azlaya's territory?" She hissed at me. I wasn't taken aback. I had known Kyraine for too many years to recoil from her sudden anger towards me.

"She was training, and we just wandered a little too far off Hunter grounds," I answered. It wasn't the time to mention that the real reason we weren't within Hunter territory was so I could show Danzinar to Casey.

"You know Azlaya is scouring this forest for her, and you almost handed her right over," Kyraine scolded. "How could you have been so reckless, and stupid, and—"

"Right," I interjected.

"What?" She cut her eyes at me.

"I told you from the beginning to tell her the entire prophecy, and our little run-in with the Sagen made you do just that," I explained, while she rolled her eyes. "Granted, it wasn't the best way to tell her, but, Kyraine," she looked at me again, "you couldn't hide it from her forever. It's better that she knows now, than later."

Kyraine let my words sink in. Strands of her braided hair were falling out, and she smelled of the forest. It was a familiar smell I'd always liked.

"I just wish it hadn't happened like that," she replied sharply.

I stole a glance at her face. "I think she's a lot stronger than you think."

"But this changes everything, Brennon. She has to be convinced to give up everything and do anything in her power for the greater good. She has to separate her feelings for her sister from doing what is right. How do you explain that to a sixteen-year-old? There's just not enough time."

Kyraine's gaze was distant, though she stared right at me. I got the feeling that Kyraine wasn't just talking about Casey anymore. Her eyes had glazed over, and she was thinking about something that had consumed her mind for years. I decided to distract her from those thoughts.

"Kyraine, she doesn't know what's right and what's wrong. Give her time to think. All she needs now is to feel safe, so she can sort through it all," I calmly said. Kyraine and I locked eyes and some of the pain and anguish left her face.

She nodded lazily. "You're right," she admitted quietly.

"Sorry, I don't think I caught that," I cupped a hand around my ear jokingly and leaned in closer to her.

"Shut up! I said you are right. That's all the apology you deserve!" She pushed me away playfully.

I chuckled, "I always am, my dear. You know that."

"Come on," she said, getting to her feet. "We need to have Myra look at your leg."

I waved off her concern. "It'll be fine."

"Ah, and balance is restored to the world, because once again, you're wrong."

Chapter 15: Casey

TEARS FELL ACROSS my face as I lay in my bed. I reached up to brush them away, but I realized that I still held the crumpled piece of the prophecy in my hand. I threw it away from me, and more sobs surfaced.

I wanted to go home. I wanted to be in my bed. I wanted to make plans with Kate to go to the mall, or even to be sitting on my bed struggling through physics problems. I even wanted to see Jackson. I wanted anything that would give me some sense of normalcy in the turbulence of chaos.

According to the prophecy, Kate and I were to be enemies. We fought often, but it never got to the point of being enemies, and definitely not to the point of wanting to literally kill one another. I couldn't begin to comprehend everything that our futures held, and the worst part was I couldn't talk to Kate about it.

I ripped the blanket away from me and ran out of the tent. It was closer to the edge of the other tents, so no one saw me leave. I let my feet pound into the ground, numb from the cold. My eyes began to water, and my lungs whined for air, but I pushed on. I ran far enough away that I couldn't see the dim light of the campfire.

I was concentrating so hard on going forward, that I didn't see the river until my toes had sunken into the riverbed. It was freezing and my toes felt like they would fall off, but I just stood there, favoring that pain over what I had felt back in my tent.

I took a huge breath to prepare myself for what I was going to do next. I rushed further into the river. The iciness bit at my legs and weighed heavily on my clothes. The water was calm as I waded across, and when I made it to the other side, I started to run again.

I felt like I could have gone on forever. The stinging from my lungs and feet only made me want me to run farther and farther. As I passed a tree, I felt something tangle itself around my foot. I threw my hands out to catch myself before getting a mouth full of dirt. I twisted around and found a wire wrapped around one ankle. I reached down to try and untangle my-self, but the more I fumbled with it, the tighter it got.

I gasped in pain when the wire finally broke my skin and blood trick-led down my foot. Whatever adrenaline, or anger, had gotten me in that situation in the first place quickly disappeared when I realized that I was stranded in the woods, and no one knew where I had gone.

I sat there for a few minutes cursing myself for being so stupid. Then, I heard a rattling sound, like metal clinking against itself. I whipped my head around, but nothing appeared. I tried to calm myself, but then the noise came back. I was terrified and inched up against the tree for protection.

They're finally going to get you, I thought.

All my muscles tensed with anticipation. I bent my head low and closed my eyes as I waited for my imminent capture.

"Who's there?" The person rounded the tree and sounded puzzled. "Casey?"

I lifted my head and tried to find the voice in the darkness. I noticed a silhouette against the moonlight. She cautiously approached me, until I realized it was a Hunter. "What are you doing out here?"

She knelt down next to me. Her black hair was pulled back from her tan face. She had her bow strapped to her back, and her pouch of arrows slung over her shoulder. I didn't know her, but she obviously knew me. Then again, everyone knew me. She must have seen the blank look on my face. "I'm one of the Hunters, Veronica Velspar. What happened to you?"

"Something's caught on my foot," I told her. She dropped her gaze and laughed.

"Oh, you're caught in one of my traps I use to catch fowls." She began to undo the trap. I sucked a sharp breath as she pulled the wire off my leg. Once I was free, I thanked her, shakily.

"Why are you out here so late? And what was that sound?" I asked her. I knew I was nowhere near the boundaries of the Hunter's camp, so she couldn't have been guarding the perimeter.

My question clearly caught her by surprise as she struggled to find an answer. "I was, uh … hunting. And the sound is money," Veronica replied, giving the pouch tied to her belt a shake, as I recognized the rattling sound I heard earlier as coins.

"Why do you need money to hunt? Wouldn't the sound scare the animals away?" I inquired.

"When I go to sell my game, I may need change," she replied quickly and decided to turn the conversation back to me. "What about you? What were you doing out here?"

Just the mention of why I was out of my tent brought back the very feelings I was running from. I couldn't bring myself to look her in the eyes. "I needed to get out of there. I need to get away from everything."

Veronica tucked her legs under her so that she sat beside me. It was like she was urging me to go on. "What happened?"

I sighed, knowing I was about to tell her what she probably already knew. "I just found out that my sister or I have to die—according to the prophecy." Saying it out loud finally made me realize that I had reason to be afraid. Before, I was upset thinking that my sister and I could be separated forever. It hadn't occurred to me until then, that I could be killed.

"I'm sorry," Veronica tried to console me. I stayed silent, and she reached her hand out over my ankle. She breathed deeply. I watched in shock as my wound slowly closed up, and the cut disappeared.

"How did you do that?" I exclaimed. I touched my ankle, but the cut was gone.

"I've been trained," she answered simply. I looked at her in surprise. "There are quite a few sorceresses here. Myra trains us when we aren't working with Kyraine." I thought back to the girl who had cast a spell on me before I was brought to the Hunters' camp.

Myra had me read books about the origins of sorcery, and it was the only training in sorcery I'd received so far. The books were from centuries ago, and the language was antediluvian, making them extremely difficult to read. The thought of being able to perform sorcery excited me, but it was frustrating when I had not had any real practice with it.

"Could you teach me something?"

Veronica's mouth parted. It hung open while she contemplated her answer. "I can try." I nodded eagerly, urging her to continue. "First you need to understand that all spells, charms, and enchantments are written in the Language of Old. It's an ancient language that only sorcerers know and use. A person must learn how to reach out to the natural forces that control life in Alagia, which keep balance between good and evil. If you learn the language, and become connected to the living forces in Alagia, you can learn the spells. As you become more advanced in your skills, you may start to think the spell, rather than say it. For example …"

Veronica held her hand out and suddenly a ball of light burst from it. I had to shield my eyes, because it was so bright. She flicked the light from her so it illuminated a small radius about us. Slowly, the ball of light shriveled and died, and we were left in the dark again. I'm sure she could see my excitement as our eyes adjusted back to the night.

"Can I try?" I asked her.

"Some spells, like that one, are simple enough for sorcerers with untrained ability to perform, so we'll see. The word for light is *lux*," she told me.

I was about to attempt the spell when I stopped abruptly. "I know that word," I said more to myself than to Veronica. "*Lux* … that's Latin," I said to her.

I couldn't see the confusion on her face, but I heard it in her voice. "Latin? What is that?"

"It's an ancient language from my world too. We must call it by different names," I concluded in amazement. Here were these two worlds that I thought had nothing in common, and yet, they shared an ancient language. "I learned it in school," I explained.

Veronica nodded her understanding, and I held out my hand as she had. "*Lux*," I said. Nothing happened.

"Concentrate and visualize a small spark of light," she instructed as she moved to cup her hand under mine. I focused intently. I could feel butterflies begin to fill my stomach, and a slight humming buzzed in my head and ears. "Do you feel that? Now, visualize the light." A tingling sensation washed over my skin

A tiny ball of light flickered in my hand and died. My mouth twisted in disappointment, but Veronica encouraged me to try again. She sat with me until I could produce a light that lasted for more than a few seconds.

I began to forget why I'd run away and turned all my attention to the spell. The excitement of finally performing sorcery rekindled something deep within me. Adrenaline was coursing through my veins every time I produced a longer-lasting ball of light. Finally, Veronica decided we should return to the camp. I agreed. Veronica stood and threw her arm out as if she were tossing a ball. Again, light shot from her hand and wove in and out of the trees, leaving a glowing path behind it. "Our way home," she told me.

We followed the faint glow all the way back to the tents. Thanks to Veronica's accidental intervention, I had a newfound interest in this world. This curiosity distracted me from the prophecy, which was most likely why I never demanded to go home. Veronica walked me to my tent, and I thanked her for everything she had done for me that night. Once inside, I crawled into my bed. I didn't even notice that the tears that had soaked my pillow had dried.

The next morning, I dreaded seeing Kyraine or Myra. I figured they found out I had run away last night, but it never surfaced. I sat next to Veronica for breakfast, which earned me a curious look from Brennon. As we ate berries she had picked that morning, bread, and eggs from the village, I asked her more about the Hunters.

She explained to me that the Hunters and Huntsmen were part of Alagia since the beginning. Originally, they had been nomads of the forest. They lived independently of the kingdoms for generations, surviving on what the forest and outer lands provided. Over a thousand years ago, two powerful sorcerers decimated and laid waste to much of Alagia. The Great Sorcerer Lothian restored peace to the land. The Hunters and Huntsmen helped him prevail and were granted half immortality to be protectors of the realm in times of turmoil. Veronica told me about the four kingdoms and the kings and queens that ruled respectively. She said the Hunters and Huntsmen continue to intervene to keep the balance.

"What about you?" I cut her off as she was telling me this.

She smiled thinly, but it didn't reach her eyes. "I'll have to tell you my personal story another time."

I was about to say something when Kyraine's second in command, Gwendolyn Stone, announced for the Hunters to begin training. Veronica rose and filed in behind the other Hunters as they left the clearing. My eyes trailed Veronica, wondering what past she had kept from me.

A tap on my shoulder interrupted my thoughts, and I turned to find Myra. She had twisted her long blond hair into an intricate braid and a band of flowers wrapped around her head.

"Are you ready to begin your training?" she asked placidly, as though she'd accept a yes or a no. I nodded my head eagerly. Myra beckoned for me to follow her. I scrambled to my feet and trailed her like a dog. She brought us to the river's edge.

"Before we begin, I want to know if you have ever performed magic, maybe without even knowing it. Rapid changes in emotions oftentimes cause this to happen with inexperienced sorcerers. Have strange things ever happened when you got angry or sad? Even happy?"

I thought for a minute, but I couldn't recall anything. I shook my head, but then, a memory hit me. I couldn't believe it had slipped my mind when it had plagued it with so many questions. As if I were standing in my kitchen, I vividly remembered Kate and Jackson fighting, and the glass in my hand randomly shattering.

"Kate." Her name floated off my tongue at the thought of the memory.

"When did that happen?" Myra asked me. I looked at her in puzzlement, not sure what she was referring too. "What you were just thinking of; when did that happen?"

"Did you just read my mind?" I asked in disbelief.

She smiled warmly. "Something you'll learn later. Now, back to your memory," she urged.

"It happened the night before I came here. She was fighting with the boy—her boyfriend—and suddenly the glass shattered. She was apologizing like it was her fault but …" I had been staring into space again and looked at Myra. "Was it?"

"It appears that her anger caused the glass to break. You never knew she possessed that kind of power?"

I shook my head. "I didn't know that *kind* of power existed in our world," I replied absentmindedly.

"In the case of twins with sorcery abilities, the powers of the older twin usually develop before the younger one," Myra explained reassuringly.

I stared incredulously. My own twin sister had powers, magical powers, and I never knew. I suddenly recalled her lava lamp turning blue, realizing that her hidden powers must have caused that too. She was upset, and the lamp only reflected her emotions. "Why wouldn't she tell me?" I asked myself, more than Myra. Almost seventeen years I'd lived with Kate, and never once did she think to tell me she had these powers. Never once did she divulge her secret to me. Me, who thought I was her best friend.

"Casey, I'm sure she didn't hide this from you to keep you in the dark. Think of it from her perspective. How do you tell your sister, who hasn't shown signs of having the same powers, that you can produce sorcery?" Myra questioned me.

I nodded, realizing her point. My mind wandered to all my years with Kate, picking through every memory, any and every occurrence that was strange, that indicated Kate had powers. Myra must have felt my mind lose focus and added, "Veronica told me you can produce a light spell."

My attention snapped back into focus. I was expecting a lecture about me running away from the camp, but none came. I shrugged my shoulders. "It's not nearly as bright as hers," I admitted. "More of a quick spark than anything."

"She's been practicing for years. You may resume your practice with that spell later, but for now, I want to focus on the elements. Four elements exist, but we'll only discuss three. They are earth, air, and water. Learning to control them will be easier than learning to produce spells. Watch," she instructed.

Myra reached her hand out over the water. It began to bubble and twist up to her hand. It reminded me of a dancing cobra. Every time her hand moved, the water mirrored it. She started to gradually close her hand and the water formation spun into a sphere. I felt my mouth slowly fall open. Then, she opened her hand flat, and the water fell back into the river.

"The key is to think about how the water moves. It flows smoothly, and so your hand must move fluidly as well. Try it," Myra said.

I stepped up next to her and held my hand out as she had. I took a deep breath. I moved my hand up and down as if coaxing the water up to me. Slowly a tube of water grew from the river. I waited until it was almost as tall as me, and then with my other hand I reached into the water to make sure it was real. My wet hand recoiled and the water went splashing back into the stream. I turned around, looking shocked.

"How did I do that?"

Myra looked like she had a secret, but could only taunt me with the fact that she couldn't tell anyone. "Your mother was the most powerful sorceress that this world has seen. Her powers have been coursing through you since your birth, yearning to be developed. Now that they finally have the chance, they will mature very quickly. You were able to do that with such ease because your mother was an incredible sorceress, and soon, you will be too." She gazed at me thoughtfully, and I couldn't help but think she had looked this way when she was training my mother.

From then on, everything seemed to move faster, and the days themselves began to blur together. I felt my training with Myra and Brennon making me stronger with each session. My arms could hold the sword for longer, my swings were harder, and my footwork quicker. Oftentimes, Brennon and I would spar, and I wouldn't find myself out of breath. With Myra, I learned how to manipulate the three elements quickly. Every day she would present me with a new obstacle or task using the elements, and every day I would successfully complete it. She began to introduce me to simple spells like the one Veronica had shown me.

Slowly, time started to mean nothing to me as days went by. I began to think less and less about my grandmother and Kate. I wouldn't even entertain thoughts about the prophecy. Alagia pulled me in deeper each day, and I didn't fight it.

Chapter 16: Brennon

AFTER A DAY of relentless training with Casey, I looked forward to the cool of evening. I sat in a plush plot of grass and leaned back against my tent. The beginning of Casey's basic training was going well, but I wasn't sure if I wanted to leave when it ended. It didn't feel right to abandon the Hunters. Not with the prophecy finally transpiring and the stakes higher than ever.

I pulled out a book Myra had given me to pass time. I was skimming over the pages and words when I heard someone walking towards me. They stopped and loomed over me, casting a shadow across my book.

Her presence to me was just as familiar as her voice. "Where's Casey?" Kyraine asked.

I held up a hand to shield my eyes from the setting sun. "I think she told me she was going to work with the other sorceress with the dark hair," I replied.

"Oh, Veronica," she concluded. I shrugged my shoulders. "Well, I came to ask a favor—rather, I came to ask you to fulfill your promise."

My mouth pulled up at one corner. "Which one would that be?"

"You still owe the girls some more sword lessons." Kyraine offered her hand and pulled me to my feet. I was grateful for being pulled away from the book I wasn't really reading. I tossed it inside my tent and followed Kyraine.

She led the way to the Hunters' training ground. It was a clearing, large enough to fit all the Hunters comfortably, and still allow room for movement. Several targets were nailed onto surrounding trees and large sacks of grain hung from some branches for the girls to practice blows. In the clearing, the girls huddled in a circle, and they stepped aside to allow Kyraine and me to enter the center.

"Hunters, quiet down," Kyraine sharply addressed them. Conversations immediately stopped. "Thank you. Now, I understand that all of you are extremely skilled with your bows and arrows; however, in a real battle, you never know what may be available to you. Therefore, I want you all to be just as comfortable with a sword as you are with your arrows." Kyraine stepped back to introduce me. "For those of you who do not already know, this is Brennon Harrow from the Huntsmen. He is, arguably," she stole a look at my face, "the best swordsman in Alagia. Listen carefully to what he says, and learn well."

Kyraine motioned for me to step up and address the girls. Since I was Caden's third in command back with the Huntsmen, running drills and commanding large groups of people were things I was more than comfortable with.

"Everyone pair up and get your swords," I called out. Once they were all situated, I demonstrated some complex counter moves. I gave thorough explanations, and then I let the girls attempt the maneuvers. "Concentrate on the weakness of your opponent. See the way they move. Turn their offense into their defense," I instructed.

I wove in and out of the sparring girls, giving compliments and corrections. They were all well-trained, but some of them were slightly better than others. I could tell that some of them yearned only to shoot at targets.

I yelled out for them to put down their weapons. "Hunters, these weapons are not like your bows and your opponent is not across the field. You must react faster and attack harder, but that's not all. Most of your opponents will be men. They are bigger and stronger than you are." I heard some grumbles of disagreement, but waved them aside. "What wins close combat is anticipating your opponent's move before they even think about doing it. Would anyone like to demonstrate?" I scanned the crowd, but all the girls seemed to duck their heads and drop my gaze.

"Girls I'm disappointed," Kyraine cut in. She took a sword from someone next to her. "Never shy away from a challenge."

One of the girls tossed me a sword. I effortlessly caught it and twisted it in my hand to test for balance. Kyraine raised her own sword defensively. I sucked in a deep breath, smirked, and lifted my sword up to eye level. I began bouncing on the balls of my feet in preparation.

Whenever I sparred with someone, I shifted my movements between offense and defense to test their level of skill. Kyraine didn't fight like she was inexperienced, because I taught her most of what she knew. In fact, she fought better than most men I sparred with back home. I didn't want to hurt her, but apparently she didn't have the same concerns, and she lunged at my face.

I swung my sword up just in time to deflect her blow. I took a step back to regain my balance. Then, she thrust her sword at me, but instead of knocking it aside, I simply sidestepped out of the way. I grinned at whatever face she had made.

"Come on, Hunter. You have to be quicker," I taunted her.

She clenched her jaw then sidestepped and thrust her sword towards me. I hadn't expected her quick move, and a wave of shock and approval flashed across my face. Evidently, she didn't like that I was surprised by her aggression and lurched towards me again. Then, we both began clanging our swords with each other's. The swords' collisions were making tumultuous sounds which lasted for several minutes.

Kyraine was becoming short of breath as my eyes darted everywhere, searching for her vulnerability. The opportunity presented itself.

As she was trying to move towards me, I quickly moved forward too. She didn't even realize what was happening, until it was too late. I had grabbed the hilt of her sword, while still juggling mine, jerked it from her, and tossed it aside. At the same time, I hooked my foot around hers, making her tumble backwards into my waiting arm.

I held her a couple feet off the ground as I bent over her. Her chest rose and fell rapidly. Her eyes blazed with shock from the speed of her defeat and the quickness of my movements. I was marginally offended, but I pushed it aside. I couldn't really tell what the mood of the clearing was. All the Hunters seemed to be astonished for they rarely, if ever, saw their leader beaten.

"I win," I whispered tauntingly in her ear.

"Not quite." I felt the point of her dagger pressing against my side.

Had it been just the two of us, she would have demanded a rematch, but she forced a smile of compliance. I lifted her up and placed her firmly on her feet, and she slipped her knife back into her belt.

"Hopefully, you all learned the importance of finding your opponent's weaknesses and that is true in any aspect of battle. Now, who can tell what my weaknesses were?" When no one answered, Kyraine added, "Hunters, you know as much as I do that you can never improve if the mistakes are not corrected."

That being said, a girl with black hair and brown skin spoke up. "Your movements weren't as quick as his," she pointed out.

"Good," Kyraine approved.

Another girl with short blond hair tied back from her round face added, "Your feet came too close to his." No one added anything to the two comments.

"Is that all?" Her girls made no more moves to critique their mistress. "Fine. What were Brennon's weaknesses?"

"Does he have any weaknesses?" I heard someone mumble. Scattered chuckles erupted, but Kyraine shot them a look that silenced them.

A tall girl with bronze braided hair spoke up hesitantly. "He shifted between offense and defense too much?"

My eyes flashed to the girl who had insulted my strategy. "No," Kyraine answered.

Another Hunter said, "He didn't try to use his surroundings?"

Kyraine replied, "No, this isn't archery. Anyone else?"

She looked around at her Hunters, but none of them had the answer she searched for. For that matter, I didn't even know what answer she sought.

"He was being too careful," she said thoughtfully and looked right into my eyes. My face must have shown some wild expression, because she let out a quiet laugh. "That is until the very end, but he should have beaten me a lot sooner."

"Maybe I couldn't. I don't think you give yourself enough credit, Ms. Redding." I saw a flicker of sadness in her eyes when I addressed her by her last name. The Hunters whispered violently among them. Kyraine smiled weakly.

"Go on, girls. I want everyone practicing for at least an hour, and an hour every day for a week. Afterwards, you may have dinner." The girls took their time to disperse. As she turned back to me, her face was impossible to read.

"I meant what I said, Kyraine. You are better than most of the guys I have to spar with back home," I pointed out.

"And *I* meant what I said about you being too careful. Don't go easy on me, swordsman; you won't hurt me," she laughed and kept walking at a fast pace. I fell in step behind her, thinking about what she said. If only that were true. One wrong move, and it could result in something that I'd never be able to forgive myself for.

I let the thoughts go and jogged to catch up to her. I decided I didn't want this to be the heart of our conversation, so I let her rampage on about a new obstacle course she had set up for her Hunters.

We talked about it the whole way back to the camp. She led me into her tent and offered me some water. It seemed she had let her guard down immensely since I first arrived. She was no longer jittery and constantly avoiding my gaze, but I didn't push it and sat down a comfortable distance from her. She seemed giddier than usual and began to ask me which of the Huntsmen I thought she was better than. I laughed and wouldn't tell her, but she insisted and started to guess names.

We were both laughing and enjoying ourselves. It reminded me of the days before either of us were looked to as leaders in our respective clans, and I wished those days hadn't had to end. As she was saying something, I caught myself staring at her. She hadn't noticed so I dropped my gaze and briefly smiled to myself. It was almost as though we had traveled back in time, before everything became complicated and had spiraled out of control.

Chapter 17: Kate

I TRUDGED INTO the kitchen, dirty and tired. My tears had dried on my face and mud had found its way under my nails. I numbly climbed the stairs to my room and turned on the shower. As I peeled my clothes off, leaves and twigs fell from me as though I was shedding them. I stepped into the scalding shower and let the pain of the water distract my mind from Jackson and what had transpired in the woods behind my house. When my body was used to the water's temperature, I turned the knob again until it was as hot as it could get. When I reached that point and my mind began to wander again, I shut the water off and stepped from the shower.

I threw on some pajama pants and one of Casey's old soccer pullovers she left in my room and went downstairs. I paced the kitchen, itching for something to do, something—anything—that would get my mind off him. My eyes fell on the fridge and decided that making dinner would entertain me long enough.

I found some chicken in the bottom drawer and seasoned it using my grandmother's recipe. I rubbed it with salt, pepper, garlic, and oregano, and placed it in the oven. I grabbed a handful of broccoli and threw it in a pot of boiling water and whipped up some mashed potatoes. The entire time I was preparing the food, I was oddly calm, even though I knew Jackson was gone. I was still confused about what it was that I had done, but I was sure that he was dead. As I pulled the chicken from the oven, my grandmother walked in the door.

She held grocery bags in both hands and looked worn. "It smells good in here, Kate," she breathed deeply and then planted a kiss on my cheek. I flinched a little. "What's on the menu tonight?"

"Chicken, mashed potatoes, and broccoli. Nothing special," I replied.

I could see the excitement radiating from my grandmother coming home to a cooked meal. "It sounds great, honey. I'll put these groceries away, and then we can eat."

"Where've you been?" I asked while scooping broccoli into a serving bowl.

"I met Charlotte for lunch, and then I had to run some errands," she explained as she placed cereal boxes in the cupboard. When she was done she helped me set the table. It wasn't until I placed three plates down that I wondered where Casey was. My grandmother broke in, "Where's your sister?"

"I'm not sure," I said blankly, thinking back to when I went upstairs. I tried to remember if I saw her in her room and didn't register it, or if I'd seen any signs that she was at home. "She might be sleeping?"

My grandmother nodded. "Well, we'll let her sleep if she is. She can eat when she wakes up," she said while gathering in her arms lotion and soap bottles she'd bought. "Go ahead and start eating. I need to bring these upstairs."

As soon as she invited me to eat, I realized how hungry I was. I sat down and began to ravenously pile food onto my plate. I poured myself a glass of lemonade and just as I was about to take a bite of chicken, I heard a sharp gasp come from upstairs. I pushed myself from my seat and rushed to the foot of the stairs. "Grandma ...?" I called hesitantly. No answer.

I heard her make a small noise, as if she was trying to suck in a breath, but her throat wouldn't let her do it. Fear clenched my gut, and I skipped steps as I ran to her. I found her at the end of the hallway where our mother's old room was. My grandmother stood in front of the door, gazing in with wide eyes.

"Grandma, what is it?" I asked her nervously.

She snapped out of whatever trance she was in and averted her eyes to me. She pulled the door closed hurriedly and stared at it for a minute. "I— uh—forgot to tell the cleaning lady to come this week. There's dust everywhere in there," she spoke quickly. I could tell how unsettled she was—almost as much as I was on the inside—but thought it best not to pry into her thoughts. "Come; your delicious dinner's getting cold."

She came away from the door and directed me back to our waiting meals. I glanced at Casey's door, which was slightly agape, but still closed tight enough that I couldn't see anything inside. I wanted to peep in and make sure she really was sleeping, but I figured my grandmother had already done that. She ushered me back into the kitchen and settled into her chair and I into mine. I asked her how Charlotte was and she, in turn, asked what I did all day. My fork paused midair as I debated whether or not I could tell her what I did all day, without faltering or cracking under her gaze. She had that power over me, and she could tell right away when I was lying.

She cocked her head in questioning, just as the doorbell rang. She signaled to me that I would have to explain after she returned. She shuffled quickly to the door and pulled it open. I didn't recognize the voice, so I twisted around to see who it was.

An older gentleman with gray hair and a thick mustache stood in our doorway. He wore a navy blue uniform and hat with a gold patch on his right breast pocket. "Good evening, Ma'am," he greeted my grandmother. As anyone would when the police come knocking at your door, I assumed the worst. I shoved away from the table and came up behind my grandmother to hear what the officer had to say. "Some of your neighbors called about some strange noises in the woods earlier," he began. My heart skipped several beats in my chest. "We just wanted to let you know that we checked it out, and we're not exactly sure what happened, but it appears a large area of trees must have fallen," the officer explained. My grandmother's hand flew to her throat.

"What caused them to fall?" my grandmother asked.

"Well," he shifted his weight and I noticed that his otherwise immaculate shoes were dusted with ashes. "Like I said, we're not entirely sure, but we think it was just some old trees that knocked down a lot of the surrounding ones. As far as we can tell, all the trees that would have fallen have, so it's safe to walk back there."

"Is that all you found?" I asked, a little more frantically than I meant to. I had a creeping feeling that he was going to arrest me for Jackson's murder soon.

"Yes, Miss. Just some trees, branches, and soot from a campfire."

"All right, thank you so much officer. We appreciate it," my grandmother said as he moved away from the door.

As my grandmother closed the door, I walked briskly back to the table, hoping she wouldn't start to speculate about the fallen trees, because I knew she'd tie it back to me in a heartbeat. I had sat down and shoveled some broccoli in my mouth, when my grandmother entered the room and carefully took her seat.

"That was strange about the trees, wasn't it?" she asked.

I nodded. "Did you say Charlotte was thinking of going to Barbados for vacation?" I asked, desperately trying to change the subject. "I've heard it's beautiful there."

"Kate, I know it was you," she stated softly.

Inwardly, I was relieved, because she only knew about the trees. "I thought I was the one who could read minds."

"Honey, you left your muddy boots on the carpet. The only ones you wear when you go back into the woods," she pointed at the back door where my boots sat, caked in mud and camouflaged with dry leaves. I cursed silently. "Kate, you can't do that. You have to control it," she pleaded.

"I try to. God, I try so hard, but sometimes I can't help it. I can't hold it in all the time," I told her, knowing, once again, where this was headed.

"Kate, I know you can't, and I don't expect you to. But you need to be cognizant of the fact that what you can do would be terrifying to anyone who found out," she tried to reason. I remembered how scared Jackson had been when I had trapped him, but quickly banished the thought from my head.

"Oh, trust me. *I know.* Isn't that why I've had to hide it from Casey all this time?" I snapped harshly at her.

Her eyes glazed over with sorrow and regret, but I was too angry to take much notice. I stood, noisily dumped my dishes in the sink, and escaped to my room. In the heat of the moment, I'd completely forgotten about what was in my mother's room until I glanced at the door. As soon as my grandmother wouldn't be hovering over my shoulder, I would find out what secrets lay hidden inside

I jumped into my bed and dove under the covers, hoping to look asleep or too irritated if my grandmother came in. As I lay motionless, I could still feel my powers humming inside me, as if they wanted another opportunity to ignite. Normally after my "episodes," the tingling left behind from my powers vanished quickly, but this time was different. They had fully sparked to life, and it seemed there was no muting them now.

Chapter 18: Casey

"HOW MUCH DOES he grow each day?" I asked, shocked.

It had been a week since the last time I'd seen Danzinar, and his size had nearly doubled. Now he was about as large as an elephant. Brennon held several large geese by their legs, and periodically tossed one to Danzinar. I still stood several arms-length away from the dragon. "I have no idea. Evidently a lot, though. One day he'll be big enough to ride."

"How big will that be?" Brennon measured out Danzinar's estimated size by pointing to trees. I put the dragon's size into my own terms, and figured the beast's length would amount to the size of two school buses, with a wingspan of three, and he would be as tall as a two-story house.

Brennon threw the dragon the last goose and answered an unasked question. "Dragons used to be widespread, many, many years ago, and people called dragon riders, were just as commonplace. The pair of a dragon and its rider was used in sporting events and for entertainment. But over time, the dragons' temperament became more aggressive towards humans, so they began to get released into the wild. Now, they gather in the Mountains of Canabar. That's why I was bringing him with me to Canabar. To raise and train him around other dragons."

"Danzinar won't grow aggressive towards you though, right?"

"No. Years ago, the problem was that humans began to travel into the dragons' habitats and steal their eggs to sell. They did a poor job training and acclimating the young dragons to being around people, so they became hostile. If you train and raise them right, though, they're fine." Danzinar snapped his teeth at Brennon, searching for another goose.

"How did you come across him again?" I asked Brennon.

"I bought it from my friend's father. He said he found it in the mountains. I've always wanted a dragon, so I couldn't resist his offer. It wasn't until I got here did he actually hatch," Brennon told me. He patted Danzinar on his broad, silver neck. Then, Brennon clicked to the dragon, and he began to beat his wings and lift himself into the sky. I jumped back before I got knocked over. Once Danzinar was out of sight, Brennon called to me. "Come on, we should go. I told Kyraine I would bring you to the village."

It took us about thirty minutes to walk across the wooded glade that separated the village from the Hunters' camp. The village lay to the west of the Hunters' camp, while our meeting place with Danzinar was to the east.

When we arrived, Hunters seemed to overrun the place. They were in shops, on the streets, talking with people, and even showing kids their bows and arrows. Brennon told me that once a month, the Hunters would come here as a sort of much-deserved holiday day trip. They also restocked their supplies and traded with the villagers and travelers.

All the houses and stores looked as though they were from the medieval times. They were either one or two stories and built right next to one another. Every so often there would be a small alley between buildings to allow access to another part of town. It was quaint and quiet. By the way the villagers rushed out to greet them and how the kids seemed to idolize them, anyone could see how much the Hunters were loved.

Brennon led me over to Kyraine, who had just finished saying something to a young boy. "Good morning," she greeted us. "We missed you at breakfast," she added.

I opened my mouth to respond, but Brennon was faster. "I wanted to do a little more practicing before we came," he lied convincingly. I nodded in agreement. Apparently, Kyraine thought nothing of it, because she quickly waved aside our excuse and began lead me around. She gave me an official tour, showing me the bakery, butcher shop, blacksmith, library, and stables.

Kyraine also showed me where the Aerilon-imported fruit and vegetable carts were that fed the Hunters. As we neared the bakery, I expected to see Irene sitting outside, but she wasn't there. I was towed past it by Kyraine, but kept glancing back to make sure I didn't just miss Irene in the crowd. Walking around, I noticed that, for a rather small village that spanned only a few acres, there were larges masses of people bustling around everywhere.

At the completion of my tour, Kyraine excused herself to go order supplies and left me with Brennon. We stopped in front the bakery again, and he said he would run inside and get us his favorite thing he wanted me to try. I stayed outside and leaned against the building, watching the commotion around me, scanning for Irene. Villagers and traders haggled, horses and carts rushed by, kids chased dogs across the street, and Hunters busily browsed and shopped.

Veronica suddenly walked briskly past, clutching a fat pouch to her chest. Her lips were pursed, and her normally blank expression was replaced by one etched with anxiety. I knew from our encounter in the woods that she carried money in the pouch, but that didn't explain why she rushed into a pub with it. She had walked by me so quickly that I didn't even get the chance to greet her. I watched the doorway, waiting for her to emerge. When she finally exited the building, she looked a little less anxious. Her eyes darted erratically as she made her way down the street. When her eyes fell on me, she rigidly changed direction and came over.

Her head titled, peering at something behind me. I turned to see Irene tentatively trying to approach, but the sight of an armed Hunter must have been deterring her. Veronica expressionlessly told her, "We have no money, beggar."

Irene halted, her already grim face falling. "No, Irene, come here," I called softly. "My friend's bringing me a pastry, but you can have it, okay?" I chimed, trying to draw her closer.

"You know this child?" Veronica questioned coldly.

When she was close enough to me, I placed a warm hand around her frail shoulder. "We've been sharing lunch for the last week or so." I beamed down at Irene, who reflected my smile, but when I looked at Veronica she seemed to disapprove of the whole thing. She made a lame excuse and departed. I was about to call out to her, when a sudden uproar of excited shrieks burst into the air.

Down the dirt road, Gwen was showing her long, wooden bow to some girls staring in awe. Apparently, she had shot a bow at an apple and pierced it perfectly, as expected from a Hunter.

I knelt next to Irene to apologize for Veronica's strangely rude behavior, but I was distracted by Irene's appearance. I noticed for the first time that her hair wasn't caked in dirt and she wore a new, blue dress with a brown apron tied around her tiny waist. While her face was still sunken and malnourished, I could tell her physique had improved immensely since I first saw her.

"Irene, your clothes!" I gasped excitedly.

She grinned, showing her teeth for the first time. "I'm a delivery girl now," she squealed.

She explained that my bread gave her more energy during the day, so she asked around for work. A man at a supply store said he'd give her a few coins for every delivery she made to his customers. I couldn't stop smiling while she recounted her story.

"Where are you staying?"

"The man's letting me stay in a spare room in his store, but says once a new shipment of supplies comes in I won't be able to sleep there anymore."

"Well, why don't you stay with me?" I offered, internally kicking myself for not thinking of doing so sooner. "You can sleep in my tent and walk to your job in the morning." She seemed baffled by my offer, but finally found the power to nod and say "Okay."

I'd learned only a few days earlier that Irene had lost her parents in a Sagen raid. While she wasn't the first person I'd met who had also lost her parents to Azlaya, her matter-of-fact innocence struck a chord with me that I couldn't ignore. Suddenly, I felt the deep longing to make Azlaya regret all the damage she had caused, both in my life and the lives of the people around me.

I stood up straight, noticing that Brennon was standing behind me. He approached us with a puzzled look, holding two glazed rolls. He held mine out to me, which I passed directly to Irene, and told her that her boss may be needing her. We decided to meet at the bakery at dusk so I could bring her back to the Hunters' camp with me. Irene darted off, and Brennon cleared his throat, as if trying to remind me that he was still there.

"You had me wait in that ridiculously long line so you could hand your roll off to some beg—"

"Her name is Irene," I cut him off. He seemed confused, just as Veronica had been, that I had befriended the girl. I leaned over and snatched a bite from his roll.

"That *is* good," I laughed.

Brennon glared playfully and held his pastry at a safe distance from me. "So, what's the story with the Irene girl?"

"I saw her one day, bought her some bread, and kept buying her some for a couple days," I responded. He seemed unimpressed with my story. "And then she told me her parents were killed in a raid from Azlaya a few months ago. They destroyed her village and killed everyone, but she and some other villagers escaped to come here. I had to keep helping her," I added, and his expression changed to understanding.

"I believe it. I remember Azlaya telling me once how she'd rather kill everyone in sight than take any as prisoners."

We started strolling down the street, but I halted at his words. I snapped my head to look at his face and see if he was joking. "Azlaya—*the* Azlaya told you this?" I asked skeptically.

"Yes, but it was a long time ago." Brennon's scarce explanation made my head spin.

"How *long* ago was that? Were you two friends or something?" I asked lightly.

Brennon cleared his throat, thinking about memories, and lowered his voice to a whisper, "Casey, she used to be a Hunter."

I stared, lips parted. Azlaya, the evil sorceress that killed my mother, was once a Hunter. She once fought for peace and the balance of power, and now she tried to rule with the blatant disregard of both these things. I couldn't keep up with my thoughts, but then one crossed my mind that stopped all the others in their tracks: she was a half immortal.

"Why didn't anyone tell me?" I said, alarmed.

Brennon held his hands up as if he had nothing to do with it. "I'm not a Hunter, remember. Besides, I can't imagine it's something they want to talk about."

"Well, what happened?" I pressed him.

Brennon looked over my shoulder and nodded in that direction. "Ask her."

Myra was walking down the dirt road towards us. She carried a woven basket full of fruits and vegetables and had a green cloak made of moss fastened around her shoulders. She looked like a walking plant. She approached with a knowing look on her face. "I'm sorry, but I couldn't help but overhear."

"Azlaya used to be a Hunter," I continued what Brennon had said as a preamble to Myra's explanation.

"Yes, she was a Hunter once."

"Which means she's a half immortal too?" I impatiently prodded her on.

Myra nodded and motioned for us to walk with her as she continued her story. "She came to them when she was no older than you. She trained with them for about seven years, accepted their ways, and with her initial training complete, was granted half immortality. She was great, according to Kyraine, and she loved her duty as a Hunter. Over time, she and Kyraine became close friends. So close, that eventually, they were like sisters. Kyraine's success and triumphs seemed to weigh heavily on their bond, but not enough to sever it. They loved each other so much that it blinded them from seeing what Azlaya was becoming. When Kyraine was appointed Mistress of the Hunt, Azlaya felt as though she had been overlooked for the position. Her jealously began to control her, and she slowly began to hate the Hunters and Kyraine. Kyraine had to accept that her friend had changed. Kyraine could see Azlaya's maddening thirst for power and control would never make her the strong leader that the Hunters needed. Kyraine had the power to pass on the responsibility of Mistress of the Hunt to whomever she thought was ready, but she refused to give it to Azlaya. She realized that if Azlaya controlled the Hunters, chaos would soon follow." Myra paused for a minute, as if reminiscing about all of those bad memories. Brennon looked like he had something to add to the story, but held back. My powers had increased my perception of other's emotions, and I sensed that Brennon was really guilty about something.

"What did Azlaya do?" I asked, not sure how to mention Brennon's guilt, or even if I should at all.

He interjected, "She figured since she couldn't control the Hunters, then she would control all of Alagia. So she allied with the Sagen, built her castle, and has been there ever since."

"Essentially, yes. She is an extremely powerful sorceress who frightened some of the best sorcerers in the land. Even I was afraid of her. No one, since Kyraine, has dared to challenge her or her oppression. She must be stopped before she, and the Sagen, become strong enough to conquer everything," Myra finished, locking eyes with me.

"That's what the prophecy says?" I inquired.

Myra nodded. "It states that either you will help her in her conquest or you will fight against it." The way Myra said it, as if it sealed my fate, made me want to run away again. But I'd grown too close to the Hunters, Brennon, Myra, and Kyraine to just leave.

"And why don't the kingdoms unite and destroy her?"

"It's not that simple. For years the kingdoms viewed Azlaya as the Hunters' problem, a conflict that would never affect them. But now they are starting to realize that she is a threat to everyone."

"But they still won't join together?"

"The kings and queens that sit on the thrones are keeping their best interests in mind. They hesitate to get involved in what's being called a sorcerer's war. They feel largely unprepared to enter a war that will be decided by the side with the more powerful sorcerers. I know many of them are deciding whether it would just be a better choice politically to stay out of the war, not aid the Hunters and Huntsmen, and appease Azlaya in hopes they'll be shown mercy in the event that she wins." Myra seemed to become more peeved the more she spoke.

"It sounds like they've given up before anything has even started," I pointed out.

"Well that used to be the mentality of the kingdoms, but not anymore," Myra added.

"What's changed?"

"You," Brennon interjected.

"Me? What did I do?" My face pinched together.

Myra picked up where Brennon left off. "Word has spread that one of the girls from the prophecy is in Alagia. It's giving people, and the rulers of the four kingdoms, hope that the prophecy is unfolding and that soon someone will be fighting against Azlaya's conquest."

My feet stopped moving and I stared at Myra in awe. News of my arrival had been spread throughout Alagia and was fueling people's hope. This world was a part of me and had wrapped itself around my heart and head. I knew in that moment that I had to stand and defend it.

I wanted to ensure that Azlaya would know how much pain and suffering she put the people of this world through. I wanted her to regret ever turning on Kyraine and the Hunters and ever wanting to take over Alagia. The feeling in the pit of my stomach sparked hateful feelings towards Azlaya, and it was just one more thing that tied me to this world. It was one more reason to stay, and one more reason to fight. While I may not have been part of Alagia for long, it, and its people, had crept their way into my heart. To leave Alagia, would be like leaving my real home, and my inability to separate the two places made it that much easier to stay.

Chapter 19: Casey

A FEW DAYS had passed since Irene began to sleep with me in my tent. I had offered to request another bed be brought into my tent, but she resolved to sleep on a pile of blankets on the floor. In the morning we'd go to the fire pit to get breakfast. Sometimes Veronica would join us, but for whatever reason, she still hadn't warmed up to Irene. After I was satisfied that Irene had eaten enough to start helping her gain weight, I saw her off to the village. It was comforting to share my tent with someone, and fall asleep telling stories as I used to do with Kate when we shared a room as kids.

After Irene had departed for the day, I decided to work on some spells Myra had assigned me, and Veronica volunteered to help. Recently, it seemed we were together whenever the opportunity presented itself. I gladly accepted this and enjoyed her company. Even though I wouldn't admit it out loud, Veronica and Irene seemed to be filling in for Kate in her absence. I didn't like to think about it that way, but I couldn't deny it on the inside.

I was working on mind-reading spells as I stared intensely at Veronica. I saw glimpses of images in my head. She must have been starving, because all I kept seeing was a five-course meal laid out on a table. My concentration broke when Veronica laughed.

I looked at her, puzzled. "Don't stare at me like that. Normally people don't like it when you read their mind, so I would try to disguise the fact that you're doing it."

I chuckled at her point. I averted my eyes from her, staring at a wolf in the distance. I saw memories of Veronica playing carelessly in a field, with two younger children that resembled her. "Is that your brother and sister?" I returned my gaze to her.

"Yes. They live in Eileen. Your friend reminds me of my sister a little," she admitted. Maybe that was why she didn't love the idea of having Irene around. It made her think of her young siblings and surely caused homesickness. "Now this time, don't stare, and try to keep that constipated look off your face."

She suppressed a laugh, as I jokingly rolled my eyes and repositioned myself. I watched a tree in front of me and let my mind delve into hers. The images and feelings I'd seen and felt earlier weren't as strong, but they were still present.

"Good," she nodded with approval. "One more time."

Again, I injected myself into her thoughts, but instead of seeing food, I saw a dark silhouette among trees and the empty village. Rather than the cravings for food, I sensed feelings of guilt and remorse wash over me. They all rapidly disappeared, because Veronica blocked me out. She had more experience than I, so she could control what she wanted me to see and not see.

I whipped around to look at her, but she had already jumped to her feet. "What was that?" I asked apprehensively.

She could see, and probably feel, the fear in me, so she calmed herself to ease me. "A nightmare I had one night. It's nothing, Casey. All right? Don't worry about it."

A Hunter ran by and shouted to Veronica, "Myra wants to do a lesson with us!" I moved to follow them. "Sorry, Casey, not you. She wants you to keep practicing on your own for now." I let the disappointment show on my face.

"I'll see you at dinner," Veronica called hastily. She turned on her heel and hurriedly chased after the other girl. I tried to see into her thoughts again, but she had completely blocked me out. I probably should have pressed her further about why she felt the things she did, but at the time, I just brushed it off. I was too focused on the fact that while Myra trained the other sorcerers and Hunters in combat with their powers, I was left to read

books and perform duller spells. Every minute I spent with Veronica, I became more and more interested in the sorcery I possessed, and what I could
do with it. It excited me, and I was getting impatient with learning slowly.

For nearly an hour, I would read a spell from one of Myra's books,
and then I would try it. As I read further into the more challenging spells, I
realized I needed a guinea pig. Out of the corner of my eye, I saw a wolf
roaming around. I whistled to it. It lifted its broad head and studied me,
then deciding I wasn't a threat, walked over to me. However ferocious and
aggressive they appeared to be the first time seeing them, the wolves proved
to be tender and very loving companions for the Hunters.

The wolf sat in front of me, and his head was a few inches higher than
my own. "Can I practice something on you?" I rubbed a spot behind his
ear. He didn't run away, so I figured that was his answer. Despite the fact
that he didn't understand what I had said, I went forth with my training
anyway.

I glanced at the book in my lap, and then I looked the wolf in the eyes.
"Alligabis." *Bind.* Immediately, the wolf started to whine. The sounds from
his throat were panic-filled. His legs were frozen, but his head could still
move. He frantically swung it back and forth and looked at me with wild
eyes. "Okay, okay," I sympathized and rubbed his ear again. "Dimittam."
Release.

The wolf shot to his feet and darted away from me. I felt guilty and
made a mental note to give the wolf some of my dinner that night. But I
was also excited to see that the spell worked, and on my first try. I was
searching for another spell to test when I heard pounding feet nearby.

A Hunter I didn't recognize was sprinting in my direction. "The village
is under attack," she called as she raced past.

"What?" I exclaimed in alarm as I jumped to my feet. I followed
closely behind the Hunter. The camp was empty, because the Hunters were
either practicing sword moves that Brennon had assigned them, or they
were working with Myra on their sorcery skills. We wove in and out of the
tents with ease, since no one was blocking our path. We finally reached
Kyraine's tent and tore through the flap. She sat at a table, in a deep conversation with Brennon that immediately ended at the sight of two frantic
girls.

"Kyraine, the Sagen are attacking the village!" the Hunter reported.

"What?" Kyraine shot to her feet.

"Gwen already sent some girls ahead, but it's not enough."

"You two stay here," Kyraine commanded Brennon and me. "Go find Myra," she said to the Hunter. They both darted from the tent before Brennon could protest.

In all the panic, it finally struck me that Irene would be among the chaos, and I couldn't do anything to help her or any of the villagers. I darted out of the tent, despite my orders to stay where I was.

I noticed a flash from the corner of my eye. I craned my neck to the left and saw another crack of lightning split the sky. Shortly after, thunder rumbled in the distance. A small raindrop landed on my cheek. *How cliché*, I thought. More raindrops started to fall, until they all gathered into a massive thunderstorm. I stood in the monsoon, hoping the rain would slow the Sagen's attack. As my powers matured, I was able to sense people around me, rather than seeing them, and I could feel Brennon standing behind me. I stole a look at his face as he gazed apprehensively at the weather. Seeing the concern etched onto his face made my nerves worsen.

"Come on. This is our fight too," he said.

He lifted his fingers to his lips and whistled. I knew exactly what that meant, and I followed him in a dash to the edge of the trees as Danzinar rocketed out of nowhere and appeared before us. Once again, he had grown, but I didn't have time to think about it as Brennon grabbed me and unceremoniously tossed me onto the dragon's slippery back, in between two spikes that would act as my saddle. He jumped up behind me, whistled his signal to fly, and we were off.

I didn't know the exact way to the village, but the screaming was like a compass. The piercing screeches seemed to lead Danzinar, too, as he quickly found the village. The village was hard to recognize with most of the buildings either burning or on the ground in pieces. Fire licked at the stores and houses where villagers and Hunters were trying to put it out. Hunters were everywhere, shouting orders and pressing the defensive counterattack. However, most were fighting with the black-cloaked warriors I'd encountered on my first day in Alagia.

The rain helped to squelch the flames, but houses were still in pieces and families were searching frantically for young ones. I scanned the village, my eyes darting everywhere in hopes of finding Irene safe, but I was too high up. "We need to go down!" I called to Brennon over the roaring winds from Danzinar's wings. Brennon whistled to the beast again. He slowly lowered himself by the outskirts of the village. Villagers and Hunters alike looked upon the dragon with terror. Danzinar let out a tumultuous roar. Several Sagen charged the dragon as he let out a stream of fire, diminishing the Sagen to ashes.

I slid down from his back, glad to see he could take care of himself in the chaos. I sprinted away from the dragon and started to weave in and out of villagers who ran for the safety of the forest. Brennon trailed me close behind, trying to figure out where I was going. We turned onto a street where I remembered the bakery was located.

As I glanced back to see that Brennon still followed me, I saw a Sagen closing in on him. "Look out!" I screeched. My body seemed to take control and my hand shot out, sending a large chunk of the ground hurdling towards our pursuer. Brennon couldn't decide between shock and awe, but his eyes seemed to approve.

"Where are you going?" he asked in exasperation.

"I have to find Irene," I shouted as I took off again, searching for the bakery.

Brennon ran a little ahead of me as we sprinted down the road. "Casey, that way," he pointed to an alley. I looked and saw a figure dart down it with something thrown over its shoulder.

Out of nowhere, three Sagen blocked our path, and we skidded to a stop. Brennon unsheathed his sword; a venomous look was in his eyes. He had been waiting for this rematch since they attacked us in the clearing. Brennon flicked his hand, signaling me to go and leave him to handle the hissing Sagen. I hesitated, but I knew whoever had run down that alley was running from us, and they were getting away. I turned down another alley and resumed the chase.

I cut corners around buildings sharply to try to make up for lost time, but I couldn't see the person I followed. Then another shattering scream ignited a shot of adrenaline in me. My feet began to pound harder into the ground. I finally caught up with whomever I was chasing. I couldn't see who it was, but I knew from its shape and the way they moved, it wasn't a Sagen. It wore a dark cloak with the hood pulled tightly around the head. I could barely see, but I noticed that whoever I chased was carrying another person slung over a shoulder. I had to squint to realize it was Irene.

"Stop!" I yelled.

The figure turned a corner, crossed the street, and ran down another alleyway. As I was about to follow into the alley, the roof of a burning building suddenly slid down in front of me. Adrenaline or stupidity made me try to dash under it, but it fell too fast.

Burning wood came crashing down on top of me. I threw my hands up and quickly pulled some rain onto the wood to extinguish the flames, but I couldn't stop its descent.

I dropped to my knees, huddled in a ball, and clasped my hands over my neck to prevent serious injury, like I was taught to do during tornado drills in school. When the wood stopped falling, I slowly raised my head and exhaled a sigh of relief. It appeared to fall in a sort of tepee shape around me. I started to shove the wood away from me, but it was heavy and hard to move.

I heard the splashing of feet and then Brennon's familiar voice. "Casey! Casey, where are you?"

I yelled to Brennon and stuck my hand out of the wood, hoping he would see that I was trapped. Brennon grabbed my hand and gave me a reassuring squeeze. "Hold on," he called to me over the pouring rain. He wrapped his arms around a beam of wood and began to rock it. Then, he threw all his weight against it and it fell away. I helped him by pushing the wood, and soon he reached in and pulled me free. I was so relieved to see him unscathed. His wet hair hung in his eyes and his clothes clung to his body.

"You're all right?" I asked. He nodded. His breathing was heavy.

"Who was it?" He said, referring to the figure I was chasing.

I stared angrily in the direction the person had gone and shook my head. "I'm not sure; I lost them. But whoever it was, they took Irene," I spat in disgust.

My insides were churning with anger and guilt. If I had arrived at the village sooner, maybe this could have been avoided. Brennon offered me a sympathetic look. We both knew that nothing could be done now. I silently vowed that I would find the kidnapper and make him regret what he had done.

"Come on. We should see if they need our help," Brennon reminded me. We ran back to where we had left Danzinar.

Once we returned, we saw that the Sagen had retreated, and the Hunters were securing the village's perimeter. Several Hunters cautiously studied Danzinar, who watched them just as carefully. The mutual interest in each other allowed for a possible conflict to be avoided.

Kyraine managed to find us, and her alarm at our presence was evident on her face. She marched over. "Do you listen to anything I tell you?" Her question was directed towards Brennon more than me.

"You seem to forget that I don't sit out of fights," he replied sharply.

Kyraine tightened her jaw. "She could have been taken." She flicked her eyes towards me.

"She isn't helpless, Kyraine, and *I* was with her," he replied with annoyance.

Kyraine's eyes washed over me, checking for any inflicted injuries. Then, she stepped aside so she wasn't blocking our view of Danzinar. "You," she stabbed her thumb in the dragon's direction, "have some explaining to do."

Brennon lazily looked at his dragon as though its presence wasn't a surprise. "Oh, right. I have a dragon," he said casually. I could tell he was still peeved about being told to stay behind in the tent.

Kyraine's lips parted, and she cocked her head as though she'd just heard the dumbest thing in the world. "If it eats anyone—"

"Don't worry. He doesn't like how you all taste," Brennon smirked. Kyraine was too stressed and preoccupied to argue with him and stormed away to go help extinguish fires.

"Take care of that," she called pointedly at Danzinar as she departed.

Brennon and I approached Danzinar, who glanced hesitantly at the people that passed him. Brennon patted him, and I heard a low rumble in the pit of his stomach. Passing Hunters and villagers stole furtive looks at the beast, as though fearing that eye contact would result in getting torched. Brennon instructed Danzinar to leave. The dragon reluctantly beat his massive wings and lifted himself into the sky. He hovered above us for a minute, and then shot into the dark.

Brennon and I drifted around the village, offering any help we could. Several hours later, we decided that for the time being, we had done everything we could. In the morning we would return to help repair and rebuild. The Hunters, Brennon, and I returned to the camp, eager to finally go to sleep. The Hunters that had to guard the camp during the night looked enviously upon everyone else heading to bed. Brennon and I met Kyraine at her tent. She looked worn, and sleep was tugging at her eyelids.

She invited us inside and built a fire in a small pit in the center of the tent. We all sat around the fire, huddled under blankets. Kyraine quickly boiled some water, and soon we sipped hot tea. Myra had stayed behind to help villagers reunite with their families, and she joined us by the time we were on our third cups of tea. Brennon and Myra sat on chairs while Kyraine and I rested on her bed. She wrapped a blanket around her shoulders, and her head was bent low. Her arms were wrapped around her body and her legs crossed. Her gaze never faltered from the spot on the ground at which she stared. Myra was the only one brave enough to interrupt her thoughts.

"Kyraine, there was little you could do," Myra offered. She received only silence from an inconsolable Kyraine. Brennon made no attempt to console Kyraine, knowing that leaving her to her thoughts would be her best therapy.

"What was the casualty count?" I was going to tell her about Irene's kidnapping, but I held back, not wanting to drive the wrench of guilt into her any deeper.

"There were a few injured from the wreckage, some were burned, but so far the death count is zero," Myra replied. Kyraine's shoulders relaxed.

Seeing her tension lessen, I added, "There was a little girl who was kidnapped though."

"What?" Kyraine's eyes shot up from the ground. "Who was the kidnapper?"

"I didn't see who it was, but I know the girl they took," I answered softly. Kyraine swept a hand over her loose hair to push it back from her face. Her reaction was similar to what one would expect when a house of cards expectedly comes crashing down. I glanced at Brennon, who watched

Kyraine, but his expression was impossible to read. "She could still be alive," I added quickly.

"We don't know that for sure." Myra spoke softly as to not upset me. I opened my mouth to protest, but I quickly closed it, knowing she was right. We had no way of knowing. "Besides you don't know who took her or where they went."

I looked to Brennon for help. It was like I was stranded in the ocean and he held the other end of the rope I clung to, but wouldn't pull me in. His expression suggested that he agreed with Myra. There were too many unknowns. "Casey, go get some rest. It's been a long day. You're not thinking clearly right now," Brennon told me softly.

"I can't just give up on her! I thought it was our job to help these people. We can't only make the effort for a select few," I protested vehemently. I felt a stab of guilt when I saw Myra and Kyraine's stricken looks, but I tore myself away from them anyway.

I stormed out of the tent and hurriedly returned to mine. I thought about recruiting Veronica to help me go search for the kidnapper and find Irene. On the way, I passed Kyraine's second in command, Gwen. Her once-flaming hair looked muddy when it was drenched. Loose strands stuck to her face, and I saw a shiver erupt through her from her soaked clothes.

"Have you seen Veronica?" She asked.

"No, the last time I saw her she was heading off to training." I suddenly recalled the image I'd seen while reading Veronica's mind: a silhouette standing in the empty village. Maybe, despite the strange jitters, it was she trying to warn me. "She wasn't in the village?" I asked Gwen.

"I didn't see her, but I'll check again. If you do see her, tell her she's supposed to be on night patrol," Gwen informed me before leaving to continue her inspection of the camp's security.

I rushed inside my tent and changed into a warmer tunic. I climbed into bed and thought about how I was going to find Irene. I tried to connect what I'd seen in Veronica's mind to the events that transpired, but all my efforts amounted to nothing. After having no luck, I let my mind drift to home. It was slowly starting to become an imaginary place. I couldn't even remember how long I had been in Alagia; I just hoped that it wasn't a significant amount of time back home.

As my mind buzzed, I fell into a deep sleep, and the dreams descended on me. It began with a tumultuous summer party with all my friends, and then shifted to my Grandmother and me. I was eight, and we were baking cookies. As I was going to lick cookie dough off a beater, I was abruptly torn away and thrown into the forest surrounding the village.

I looked around, trying to make sense of everything. From the corner of my eye, I saw a figure running off into the woods. My curiosity forced me to follow the figure to the village where I saw it slink behind one of the houses. I quickly ran to the side of the house and peered around the corner. Irene sat in the grass and played animatedly with her dolls and a friend. She looked just as I remembered her.

I scanned the area for the person I had followed. As if it melted out of the trees, the figure surreptitiously approached the girls. I watched carefully and strained to hear what was said. Try as I might, I couldn't make out the words that passed over their lips. Whenever someone spoke, I only heard a faint sound resembling the wind rustling through the trees. Suddenly, both girls quickly scrambled to their feet and curtsied, followed by an obscure exchange of words. I still couldn't understand why they showed the hooded stranger so much respect. Irene's friend reluctantly shuffled off in the direction the stranger had pointed, glancing over her shoulder every few feet.

Once the friend was out of sight, the unexpected happened. The person grabbed Irene and twisted her around to tie her hands behind her back. Irene screamed; the scream split the air and became the only sound I could clearly make out. The hooded figure lifted a squirming Irene into his or her arms and turned. When my eyes fell on their faces, the breath was knocked out of me. Veronica stood there restraining Irene, and then fled. My feet wanted to move, but I stayed immobile, not believing, or not wanting to believe, what I had witnessed. It struck me that what I'd seen in Veronica's head wasn't what she told me was a nightmare she'd had. It was her future crime. She had been thinking about creeping into the village to kidnap Irene, and I didn't realize it.

All these thoughts flew around in my head, and before I knew what was happening, I was falling. The night air whistled past me like a train in a station. I landed with a thud. It didn't hurt, but I lay still for a minute before I finally sat up. A massive stone castle with tall, dark spires loomed over me. On one of the balconies, a slim woman with wavy black hair pulled away from her sharp eyes and face, and wearing a deep purple gown, stood watching. Her skin was pale, but her lips were the color of blood, and she grinned wickedly at me. I felt a shiver race up my spine, and even though I didn't know her, a dreadful feeling inside me screamed that the woman was Azlaya.

A voice slid through my head. It was haunting, and yet seductive, all at once. *You know where to go. Come and find her.*

I woke with a start. My breathing was fast and shallow, and I was drenched in cold sweat. Veronica had kidnapped Irene, and the voice, whether it was Azlaya's or my own conscience, was right. An ominous feeling inside me knew it had to be a trap, and that Azlaya only wanted the opportunity to claim me as her own. However, the fear would not deter me. Now I knew where to find Irene, and I would go.

Chapter 20: Kyraine

IF THE GIRL Casey spoke of really was taken by the Sagen, I had very little hope that she was still alive. Azlaya was not merciful, regardless of the fact that the girl was a child. I was still trying to understand the motives behind attacking the village when only one girl was taken. There was immense damage to buildings and, relatively speaking, minor injuries. It was a large raid in size and distance for so little in return.

"She probably sent them after Casey," Myra interjected. I was used to her adding to my internal conversations after reading my mind.

"Then why would they take a child?" I asked absentmindedly, still turning the thoughts over in my head.

Myra's mouth parted when Gwen interrupted. "Kyraine, may I enter?" She sounded short of breath. I called her in and she seemed unsettled. I stood slowly and cocked my head to the side a bit, in question.

"Yes …?"

Gwen swallowed a lump in her throat. "Kyraine, a girl from the village was taken," she began.

I nodded. "I know, Gwen," I replied tiredly, but her anxiety didn't lessen. "What?" I asked, more harshly than I should have.

"It was Veronica," Gwen said quietly.

"How do you know Veronica was taken? Casey believes the girl was Irene," Myra questioned her.

"No, Veronica kidnapped the girl!"

My face twisted in confusion and disbelief. I started to shake my head, "No, it had to have been the Sagen."

"Kyraine, she's gone. I can't find her anywhere," Gwen answered.

I didn't want to believe her. One of my best archers was a traitor? A sadly familiar pang in my gut made my breathing accelerate. It seemed as though Azlaya's betrayal was repeating itself. The feelings I felt then were ones I'd hoped to never experience again. Yet, they were, once again, coursing through my veins. Myra moved to sit next to me and rested a hand on my arm to calm me, but whatever spell she tried was useless.

"Why would she do it?" I said more pointedly, to Myra.

"She was working with Azlaya." Before I could object, Myra continued, "That is what Casey saw in her dream, I just caught a glimpse of it," she concluded with certainty.

"Where is Casey?" I asked Gwen.

"She's outside, but Kyraine …" her voice trailed off and her eyes flitted towards the tent flap. I dropped the blanket from my shoulders and pushed aside the flap. I was startled to find a large gathering of the Hunters waiting anxiously for answers. They had managed to creep around my tent and overhear our conversation. Gwen and Myra slowly followed behind me.

"Kyraine, is it true?" someone called out.

"Tell us, did she do it?"

"Are there other traitors among us?"

"She must have sold her soul to the Sagen and that's why she's working with Azlaya," another stated accusingly. Conversation and arguments erupted among the girls.

"Enough!" I silenced them. I glanced at Myra who nodded, agreeing with the thought in my head. "It was Veronica." More mumbles. "But we will find her." I stressed each word.

Eerily, the silence remained. It was as if they didn't want to believe it either, and gossiping about it made it less plausible. I thought about how I had said these exact words not too long ago. Some girls who stood before me had heard me say it then and would hear me say it again. "She may have betrayed us, but we must move on. It is not the first time that this has happened. We recovered then, and we'll recover now. I cannot tell you Azlaya's intentions for doing this. But we can't let it distract us and lose our trust in one another. If we do, then this war will be lost before it begins." I paused, letting my words sink in. "It's been a very long day. Now go," I ordered tiredly. The girls never saw me this way and wisely chose to return quietly to their tents or other duties.

I turned to Gwen. She had a grim look on her face. "Get some sleep, Kyraine. We'll worry about this tomorrow." She departed from us, shooing stragglers as she went. Myra said her goodbye, too, and returned to her tree. A lone person leaned against a tree, staring blankly into the forest. I slowly approached. As I got closer, I realized it was Casey.

Until I saw her, I had forgotten that Veronica and Casey had become close friends. They ate together, read together, and spent hours developing their powers together. Only from past experience did I understand how much she hurt on the inside. I imagined that I looked similar, if not worse, when Azlaya had left me.

"I thought she was my friend," she whispered to me, and at the same time to no one.

Her words hung heavily between us. I thought about what I would say to my old self in this moment. "I know this hurts right now, and that you'll wonder for the rest of your life whether all those moments you shared were real. And I know that no matter what anyone says, it's still going to be painful, but soon, you'll look back on this and be grateful it happened. Veronica would not intend for this to happen, but this feeling inside of you," I placed a hand on her shoulder and gave her a reassuring squeeze, "I promise it makes you stronger."

She wouldn't tear her eyes from the trees. She was so shaken that she couldn't even turn to face me. I offered to take her back to her tent, but she declined, saying she wanted to stay and think. I knew how her insides ate away at her and that space was what she needed. So, I left her to deal with her feelings however she saw fit.

I returned to my tent, my head humming. Azlaya knew that a storm brewed. A fight lay on the horizon, and she was prepared to twist the minds of my Hunters before it happened. An army is easily beaten when its soldiers cannot trust each other. My Hunters were on edge and nervous. I tried to predict her next move, but those thoughts left me sleepless and apprehensive.

I lay awake most of the night, deeply concerned about what else might come from Azlaya. The person I had spent countless hours training, because I saw her potential. The person I came to love and view as a sister. The person who grew jealous of me and the things I had, stabbed me in the back, and twisted the knife. Ever since, I'd been struggling to breathe from the betrayal that left me broken. She had abandoned me, my heart torn out, and she was the one who ripped it from me.

You can't forget those memories, just like you can't forget the scars they leave behind. My heart suddenly swelled for Casey. It struck me that this wasn't going to be her last time experiencing those feelings. Even worse, when it happened again, it would be her sister holding the knife.

Chapter 21: Casey

THE HUNTERS AND villagers were all on edge once the news of Veronica's betrayal became public. Side glances were more common, and the whispers grew quieter. Even though Kyraine said no more traitors were among them, it had happened twice now, and no one was entirely convinced. If Azlaya successfully turned them against one another, even I knew that all hope would be lost.

I visited the village a few days after the attack, and unlike before, children weren't out playing. It was eerily quiet and empty. Seeing what the once-lively village was reduced to was like sharp daggers of guilt to my heart. I wish I had protected the villagers better, but as Brennon consistently reminded me, there was little that I could have done.

During my archery training, Brennon said, "You can't keep blaming yourself for things out of your control." My training with Kyraine was temporarily suspended. I told her to spend as much time as she could with the Hunters, sensing they needed her more than I did. Until she felt the Hunters' minds were sound again, Brennon took over my archery training. He transitioned me from basic, stationary targets to moving ones.

"It happened because of me," I said, frustrated. I lowered the bow that was poised to fire.

"Casey, we'll find them. And when we do, Veronica is going to regret ever joining Azlaya," Brennon reassured me. I smiled grimly at his efforts to cheer me up. He closed the distance between us and raised my arms again. He lined my body up with a target.

"Hold the string and only pull it taught when you're ready to shoot," he instructed as he laid his hands over mine, guiding the right movements. With his added help, we easily drew the string as far as it could go. Brennon backed away, leaving me a clear shot of the target.

"And release," he whispered gently in my ear.

My fingers uncurled, and the arrow shot from us and straight into the target. It didn't strike the center, but it was close enough for me. I stared excitedly at the target swinging from the tree. I whipped around and our eyes met. My eyes were full of joy, his of mild approval.

"Good," he said.

We stared into each other's eyes for a few seconds, until I finally looked away and stepped back from him. "Can I ask you something?" He nodded. "Remember when we were in the village, and you told me that Azlaya was a Hunter once?" His eyebrows furrowed. I recalled sensing feelings of guilt within him when he spoke of Azlaya's past with the Hunters. While my mindreading skills weren't fully developed, I was able to pick up on his emotions. "What was your connection to her?"

Brennon's gaze hung on me, as he was deciding what to say. "We were friends at one time." I remained silent, allowing him to sort through his thoughts and continue. "I'll give you the quick version," he started. "Over twenty years ago, Alagia was in a time of peace, so the Hunters and Huntsmen came together for about a month of festivities. I met Azlaya there, and we became friends. She started to develop strong feelings for me, but I didn't feel the same way about her. The situation got even worse when I started to favor Azlaya's friend over her. That, coupled with her anger about not being named the next Mistress of the Hunt, caused her to turn on the Hunters."

He walked a few steps from me and lowered himself to the ground. He stretched himself out, crossed his hands behind his head, kicked one leg over the other, and closed his eyes. His shirt pulled tightly across his flat stomach, and I could see his muscles so clearly I could have traced them with a pencil. He patted the ground next to him, "Take a break, or your arms will be sore for days."

I took my place at his side and stared at the voluminous clouds, turning his story over in my head. "So, Azlaya liked you?" I said lightly, imaging the evil sorceress blushing at the sight of Brennon. "But I thought the Hunters and Huntsmen couldn't get involved in relationships?"

"Not quite. We're not forbidden from having feelings for another person, but the Master and Mistress of the Hunt are completely forbidden from love. Otherwise, their loyalty would not be solely to their clan."

I nodded in understanding. "Who was the friend?" Brennon opened his eyes and gazed sideways at me. "You know, Azlaya's friend that you liked?" I pressed.

"Think about what you just said," Brennon replied.

I replayed my words over in my head. Azlaya's friend? It struck me that in everything I'd learned about Azlaya's time as a Hunter, she seemed to only have one friend that meant a lot to her. "Kyraine," I exclaimed.

A bleak smile was stretched across Brennon's face, and instead of guilt, I could feel something much warmer floating from him.

"You love her," I whispered my realization as if to keep the conversation between us, even though we were alone. I felt his emotions shift. "But she doesn't know?"

"It doesn't matter," Brennon answered. "The Master and Mistress of the Hunt are forbidden to love, remember?"

I saw a submissive sadness in his eyes. "I'm sorry," I said gently.

Brennon smiled thinly. "Again, you're worrying about things out of your control." Brennon decided our sentimental moment was over, pulled himself to his feet, and offered me his hand. He tugged me upwards and handed me the bow.

I smiled inwardly, never having seen this side of Brennon surface before. His guarded and facetious self was the polar opposite of this sensitive and aching person. Immediately, I felt closer to him. Brennon may have been all laughs on the outside, but on the inside, his heart yearned for something it might never have.

He motioned to the target, and as quickly as he had appeared, the "other" Brennon disappeared. "Again."

Later that afternoon, Brennon needed to run an errand in the village, so I offered to feed Danzinar. Brennon regularly called the dragon to attend my sword lesson, so Danzinar and I had definitely become used to each other. I whistled for him as I'd watched Brennon do, and when the scaly beast appeared, I no longer dashed to the end of the clearing in fear. His eyes lit up with excitement when he saw that I carried food for him.

"Here," I yelled, as I tossed Danzinar a goose, upon which he extended his neck and caught it effortlessly.

Since I'd learned of Brennon's love for Kyraine, it made my heart heavy when I thought of his burden. For years he has loved her, but when she became leader of the Hunters, they could no longer acknowledge the feelings they felt for each other—or at least Kyraine couldn't.

Danzinar made impatient grumbling noises, and I set down two more geese in front of him. "That's it," I warned him as he pounced on them. After devouring the birds, he nudged me for more. "I said that was it," playfully pushing him away.

A snarl crossed his face, but then it fell off abruptly. He keenly studied a wild turkey in the distance. He was enticed by the plumpness of the bird.

He carefully rose from his lounging position. Before I could make any futile attempt to stop him, the dragon had shot with unexpected speed after the turkey. I watched him snake around trees and completely knock over other ones, his tail flicking excitedly as he went. I lost sight of him, but heard the sound of splintering bark in the distance.

When I couldn't hear Danzinar crashing through the trees anymore, I assumed he had caught the turkey and was happily gnawing on it. Then, an unfamiliar growl came from behind me. I knew it wasn't a wolf from the Hunters, because their growls were lower; and I knew Danzinar was busy with his bird. I spun around and saw a mountain lion eyeing me from his perch on a branch. I knew the large cats lived in these woods, because I'd seen Hunters using their pelts as blankets and rugs, but this was the first time I'd seen one alive.

Named mountain lions because they looked like lions, only smaller and without manes, his coat was the color of sand, and his ears were pointed, with flecks of black at the tip. He hunched over, claws and teeth bared, ready to spring. The only weapon I carried was a dagger strapped to my belt. The more the cat studied me, the worse my odds looked. I turned slowly and then darted in Danzinar's direction. My feet had grown surer of where to step as I raced over and around branches, roots, and trees. I heard the cat snarling angrily as it pursued me. The fallen trees obstructed my path.

"Danzinar!" I called through the trees. I was so focused on catching Danzinar that I didn't see the thorn bush. I had run through it, but didn't think twice about the slashes up and down my legs as I sped through the trees.

"Danzinar!" I screamed frantically. I glanced back and saw the cat closing in. I sprinted forward, following the fallen trees like breadcrumbs, not caring about knocking branches from my way. My heart skipped beats as I ran.

I was suddenly blinded by the glint of the sun off something. My foot caught a root and I tumbled to the ground, throwing my hands out to catch me. I rolled over just as the cat leaped forward. I closed my eyes and shrieked. Then, I heard jaws snapping and a cry of pain from the mountain cat. I lowered my hands from my face and opened my eyes. I breathed a shaky sigh of relief when I saw that Danzinar had caught the cat in his razor sharp teeth. Strangled sounds came from the cat, until the dragon finally ripped into his flesh.

I realized that the root I'd tripped over was actually Danzinar's tail. I pushed myself to my feet, followed by a black cloud of powdery material. I raised my hand to wipe away my sweat and noticed that my palm was black. Suddenly, I looked down and realized where I stood. A smoky smell invaded my nose, and I started to cough. I grabbed the front of my tunic and found the black dust on it too. A brown satchel I had slung across my body was also covered in the black powder. I brushed it from me, and then I gazed around at the trees in wonder. As if someone had taken a flamethrower and torched a circle in the forest, the surrounding trees were burnt to a crisp.

It couldn't have been a fire, because no forest fire burns in a circle and then stops. I looked past the charred trees and saw the normal green foliage. It was creepy and eerily quiet, other than Danzinar's chewing. Clearly something magical had happened, and I was more than scared to find out what.

I cautiously picked my way across the clearing so that I stood in the middle. It looked like the site where a bomb had detonated at my feet. Scorch marks expanded from the central point. I bent to examine it. I held my hand out and moved it in circular motions. I felt something buried in the ground, and jerked my hand up. Soot flew everywhere, sending me into another fit of coughs. I batted my hands at the ashes. Danzinar, finally finished with the cat, looked down on me and let out a huge bellow of rage. He abruptly rose and dashed towards the edge of the burnt trees. He sat frozen, looking as if he were trembling.

I gazed at him, puzzled by his reaction to mere soot. I returned my attention to the earth I had just yanked up and noticed what had surfaced. It was a wooden box that seemed to have been caught in the same inferno as the surrounding trees. On it were various scorch marks that I would have mistaken for a design, had I not known better. Inscribed on the chest was one word: *Ignis*. Fire. I glanced around me again, thinking that the box and the appearance of the trees must be connected.

"It's just a box, calm down," I called to Danzinar, who didn't seem any less nervous. I couldn't understand the reason for his fear. I turned back to the chest and opened it slightly, half expecting it to explode into flames. Nothing happened. I slid the top open and found that the contents were nothing but a red-covered book. I lifted the book out of the chest and was running my fingers over the scarred cover when something caught my eye. On the bottom of the book, I saw my mother's name in pale, gold letters: *Layna Coles*.

I opened the book, the spine making no sounds of complaint. I started to hear low growls coming from the pit of Danzinar's stomach, as if trying to warn me of something. I merely ignored him and flipped through the pages. I didn't know what he was trying to warn me of, because all the pages were blank, singed, and smelled like a bonfire. I flipped back to the first page and found writing that I had previously overlooked.

> *Fire I am strong*
> *Willing to learn your secrets*
> *But burn my hands alone*
> *I come prepared*
> *Loyal at your side*
> *IGNIS AMPLECTI ME.*

I translated the last line which meant 'fire embrace me.' I reread the little chant over and over again, until I had it memorized. I feared saying the words out loud, remembering where that had landed me last time, literally. However, knowing that my mother's name was on the cover of the book offered me some comfort. I studied the page, debating whether or not to speak the words. Curiosity overcame my fear, and I read the words.

Suddenly, a rush of pain washed over me. My hands burned as if I held them in a fire. I gasped in agony, for the pain wouldn't leave. I tried to shake and rub my hands together, hoping it would help, but it only made it worse. After only a few seconds, my hands trembled, and my breathing became unsteady. I hunched over, burying my hands in my stomach. When that didn't work, I brought them up to my eyes. What looked like small, flame tattoos burned brightly on my palms. When they were boldly noticeable, they flashed red and then disappeared, as though they never existed. The pain started to fade, along with the "brandings." I examined my hands, front and back, but the markings were gone. As I sat, staring at my hands, Danzinar carefully crept from his hiding place over to me. He nudged me in the back and then jerked away.

"What just happened?" I whispered to him. He only gazed upon me with his crimson eyes full of concern. My breathing began to even, as I curled and uncurled my fingers. My hands felt, thankfully, normal again. I scrambled to my feet, grabbed the book, and shoved it into the satchel.

"Come on. Let's get out of here."

I brushed any lingering ashes from me, and then I located the path of the fallen trees and hurriedly started navigating my way through them. Danzinar followed at a good distance behind me, not bothering to step around the trees, but rather on them. He was strangely wary of me, but I still didn't know why.

We quickly returned to the camp. Once on its edge, I clicked, signaling for Danzinar to leave. He gave me one last disconcerting look, and departed. I had started toward my tent, when a group of Hunters rushed past me. They weren't going to training, because that was in the other direction, so I followed them. I trailed them to where we ate our meals, where Hunters and wolves were already huddled around something. The crowd was too thick for me to see anything, so I began pushing my way through, trying to find Brennon.

Once I was closer to the front, I found Brennon and Myra standing next to each other. Myra's body was angled outwards as if she were preparing to run, and Brennon had his arms crossed, appraising something. Their gazes were locked on what everyone else stared at. I moved to stand next to Brennon, fearing Myra would be able to sense what I'd just done.

Kyraine advanced through the Hunters, approaching a tall man in a black cloak. As soon as I saw him and his companions, I jumped to conclusions. The Sagen had infiltrated the Hunters' camp. But then I noticed that their faces weren't black holes, and they didn't glide across the ground when they walked. The hooded figures were just humans.

"Who are they?" I said, to no one in particular.

"Tradesmen," Brennon answered, not taking his eyes off the men he studied intently. Then his face scrunched, and he wrinkled his nose. He snapped his attention to me. "Why do you smell burnt?"

He was familiar with my mannerisms when I tried to lie, so I found a sudden interest in my feet. Myra had heard what Brennon said and turned to see my response. She was about to say something when a voice, thankfully, cut her off.

"Kyraine, it's good to see you and your Hunters again," the tall man said.

"As well as you, Matthew," Kyraine responded with a curt bow. "What brings you this deep into the forest?"

"My men and I are headed back to Calem."

In the pause, we heard a faint scratching sound. Suddenly an orchestra of growls and snarls filled the air, as all the wolves bared their teeth and bent into aggressive stances. Alarmed, some Hunters tried to calm the suddenly vicious wolves. Kyraine glanced around at the animals nervously. She turned back to Matthew. "What is that?" Kyraine asked him.

"See for yourself," Matthew said, as two other men lugged out a large crate. Everyone watched with curiosity as the men opened the door of the crate and pulled out what looked like a black wolf. The animal was only a little smaller than the growling wolves. All the Hunters immediately began to speculate. Kyraine appeared to be assessing the animal, while Gwen gazed upon it with fear.

"Where did you get that?" Kyraine questioned.

"We found her in Eileen's mountains. She was roaming the woods and terrorizing a small village. So, we captured her, and we're going to sell her in Calem," he explained.

"Handle that thing with care," Kyraine warned. Suddenly, the black wolf snarled ferociously. The men restraining the wolf threw all their body weight on it. I noticed that they all wore thick, protective gloves to handle the animal. Many scared gasps filled the air. A few Hunters jumped back. "My point exactly," Kyraine added.

I cocked my head to Brennon and whispered, "What is it?"

"It's a Demon Wolf. Their sense of smell allows them to find anything, anywhere, dead or alive," he explained. "Extremely dangerous though, because they have venom in their teeth that is fatal to anyone who is bitten."

I turned my attention back to Kyraine and Matthew. "Actually, Kyraine, she could be an invaluable asset to you and the Hunters," Matthew pointed out convincingly.

"We already have the wolves, thanks," Kyraine responded sharply. Clearly, she wanted nothing to do with the Demon Wolf.

"But she is stronger, faster, smarter, and can find anything you ask her to," he claimed, as Kyraine gave him a sour look.

I suddenly thought of Irene, and my eyes seemed to grow three sizes larger. I needed a way to find her, and fate or chance presented it to me. So without thinking, I stepped forward.

"I'll take it." Everyone's attention turned to me.

"What?" Myra and Kyraine said in unison.

"How much do you want?" I asked Matthew, completely forgetting I had no money to give.

"Wait a moment," Kyraine interjected. "This isn't a pet, Casey. It could kill you—it *will* kill you."

"But it could kill anyone who attacked me. You're the one who's always worried about my safety, and Brennon won't always be with me—"

"Leave me out of this one," Brennon guffawed.

"I'd be protected, is what I'm saying," I finished.

"The Hunters aren't sufficient protection?" Myra exclaimed.

"This way I wouldn't need a bodyguard around the clock," I added, motioning to Brennon, "and the Hunters could focus on their tasks."

Kyraine and Myra exchanged looks. Kyraine appeared to be slightly convinced, but Myra still had her reservations.

"How much do you want?" I asked Matthew again, stronger this time to let him know I was serious, regardless of Kyraine and Myra's hesitations.

"Fifty gold pieces." Matthew spoke slowly, as if testing to see if I had the money. Kyraine broke in.

"Fifty?" Kyraine gasped in disbelief.

"Yes. You know how rare these animals are," Matthew pressed with a smile, knowing he had a passionate buyer.

"Thirty-five."

"Forty-five."

"Forty, or you and your caravan can be on your way now," Kyraine said sharply. She shot him a cold look, which wiped the smugness off his face. He submitted and nodded. She faced me. "Are you sure about this?" I nodded and glanced at Myra, who stared at Kyraine, horrified.

"Kyraine," Myra interjected, alarmed.

"Myra, she can control it once they've made the bond," Kyraine explained. I wasn't sure what she was talking about, but I was too focused on the black wolf to ask Brennon to clarify.

Kyraine turned to Gwen and nodded. Gwen departed and soon returned with a small green pouch. She handed it to Kyraine, who reluctantly passed it to Matthew. Matthew opened the pouch and quickly counted the contents. Satisfied, he stowed it away in his saddlebag.

"It'll be dark soon, and you definitely won't make it to Calem before then. You're welcome to stay here for the night," Kyraine offered politely.

"How gracious, Kyraine, and thank you for your business," he nodded in her direction, as she waved his comment aside.

"We'll talk about Aiden later," finished Kyraine. She briskly walked away, slowly tailed by most of the Hunters. The ones that lingered behind watched me as I cautiously approached the Demon Wolf who was still being restrained by Matthew's men. It looked like the other wolves that the Hunters owned, except for its color. I noticed with the other wolves, most of them had a white belly, but the Demon Wolf was a solid black mass. Only its eyes, two round, icy blue orbs, weren't black.

She lay on her stomach in the grass, panting from the heat. She looked up at me with curious eyes. Suddenly, that curiosity melted into aggression as she sprang forward at my face. The men grabbed the wolf by her shoulders and forced her back down.

"I *told* you she was dangerous," said Myra breathlessly.

I knelt before the wolf. "She needs a name," Brennon pointed out, "Or she'll keep trying to kill you."

"Why?" I held a hand up to block the glaring sun in order to see him.

"They feel the need to kill the person who thinks he or she can become their master. Once given a name, though, it seals some bond. It's something like that—ask Myra," Brennon responded.

Myra gave a nod of approval and added, "Brennon's right; once you give her a name, an unbreakable bond is formed. It is a connection only sorcerers can make. You will be able to communicate with her without speaking, and she will listen to you alone."

The wolf started to wriggle its way out of its restraints while the men struggled to keep her down. I racked my brain for something to call the restless wolf. Randomly, I thought of a name I had stumbled across in some reading. I had loved the way the word rolled off my tongue effortlessly and the light, winsome feeling it had.

"Preferably before she kills someone, Casey," Brennon joked, yanking me back to reality. The wolf fought hard to be freed.

"Okay, I've got one," I said.

"Hold her head down," Myra instructed the men. She turned back to me. "Place your hand on her head, tell her through your thoughts the name that you give her and that she belongs to you."

I stared at the wolf. Her eyes resembled Brennon's when he got his rematch with the Sagen in the village. A vengeance and yearning to kill pierced through her irises. I reached a nervous hand out. Matthew's men pushed her snout to the ground to keep her head still. When my finger made contact with her fur, she calmed slightly. *I give you the name Adalia, and now you belong to me.*

Instantly, her struggling ceased. Matthew's men jumped back from the wolf and retreated. The charcoal-colored wolf stood, and our eyes were level from where I knelt. All her desires to rip me apart ebbed away. She held my gaze, and then deliberately bowed her head. It looked like she bent her head only to sniff the ground, but I knew it must have been her surrender to my command.

"Come here," I beckoned softly. The wolf raised her head and carefully approached me. *No one here is a threat*, I told her. *No biting, understand?* I held my hand out, and I could hear Myra suck in a sharp breath. Adalia licked it gently.

I smiled and ran a hand over her head and down her spine. Her body began to shake, side to side. I peered behind her and saw her tail wagging. Brennon and I laughed, and he joined me, rubbing Adalia all over. I wondered how the now amiable wolf still possessed the power to kill. As long as she helped me find Irene, though, I didn't care what she could do.

Now that Adalia and I were bonded, Myra knew she wouldn't try to kill me, and I was safe again. "I'll leave you three," Myra said before departing. Matthew and his men had been watching from a safe distance and started to pitch their tents.

"What's it like in Eileen?" I asked, trying to start a conversation with Matthew.

"It's very different from here. It's cold most of the year, and the ice and snow rarely melts. The people are not friendly at all, and food is awfully bland in comparison to that in the other kingdoms." From his brief description, I didn't like the sounds of Eileen.

Matthew was pounding stakes in the ground when he asked, "What's your name, Hunter?"

"Casey Coles, and I'm actually not a Hunter," I answered blankly, and then cursed under my breath. The attention my name garnered was like the equivalent of introducing myself as Oprah Winfrey back home. Everyone's eyes grew larger and their mouths hung open at the sound of it.

"Ah," he sighed rather calmly. "You're the girl from the prophecy."

"One of them," I responded flatly. My unenthusiastic attitude silenced Matthew. Brennon noticed, but made no remark. Feeling guilty about my sour attitude, I redirected the conversation. "Who's Aiden?"

"One of Kyraine's brothers," Matthew responded as he moved around the tent, still hammering the stakes.

"I didn't know she had brothers." I glanced at Brennon. "Where are they?"

"Well, one of them, Aiden, is in Calem," Matthew responded.

"With the Huntsmen," I concluded, remembering Brennon had told me that the Huntsmen lived between the kingdoms of Calem and Aerilon.

"No, not with them. He works for the Queen of Calem, Queen Amelia," Matthew answered.

"You never told me she had a brother," I said pointedly to Brennon. "What about the other one?"

"He died in the early years of the war," Brennon replied softly. He shoved his hands into his pants' pockets and shrugged. "She doesn't like to talk about it."

I nodded. "But why isn't Aiden with the Huntsmen?"

"It's not a lifestyle for everyone, Casey," Brennon said languidly, as though the topic bored him. "I'm hungry. Are you coming?"

I shook my head. "I'll meet you there." Brennon turned to leave. I repeated my question to Matthew.

"As a boy, he trained for it his entire childhood. He and his siblings did. They were all promising recruits for the Hunters and the Huntsmen. But when Aiden became a half immortal, he was seventeen, and he decided he didn't want to be a warrior of the Huntsmen anymore," Matthew explained to me.

"What changed his mind?"

"Who knows? Like your friend said, it's not a life for everyone to lead," Matthew shrugged.

"What does he do for the Queen?"

"Various things, but mainly he steals information," he replied.

"What do you mean?"

The men traveling with Matthew interrupted us. "Matthew, could you help us with this tent?"

"Yes, I'll be right over." He turned back to me and said, "He's the Queen's right-hand man." He rose to leave, but I was still confused. "He's her spy. Keep an eye on that one," he said pointedly to Adalia.

Later that night, we had a feast to treat the Queen's tradesmen. A vast selection of meats, breads, and fruits was our dinner, and the tradesmen were more than happy to help the Hunters drain their stored wine. Adalia lay at my feet, gnawing on a bone while I ate. I had given my leftover dinner to the wolf on which I had practiced my sorcery the other day.

I had dropped my bag, with the book I'd found in the burned trees, in my tent on the way to dinner. Knowing that I didn't carry the evidence of my "discovery," lifted a huge weight from my chest.

After dinner, Kyraine pulled Matthew aside, and they wandered into the woods. Curious to know more about Kyraine's brother, I conjured a spell to enhance my hearing, and I eavesdropped on Kyraine and Matthew's conversation.

"How is he?" Kyraine asked. I heard concern waver in her voice.

"He's fine. He's been in Calem for weeks now, doing some simple errands for the Queen's court." He paused. "Queen Amelia is worried, Kyraine. She believes that being a part of your war is inevitable. Everyone is beginning to fortify their defenses. Rumor has it that Aerilon is building up its army and Canabar has already increased its naval fleet."

Kyraine paused and contemplated what Matthew had said. When she spoke again she was off the subject, clearly not wanting to bother with it tonight. "I know, Matthew." Kyraine stole a glance at me, and I quickly turned my head away. "Tell her we have one of the two ... hopefully this conflict will not stray from between the Hunters and Azlaya, but that's, unfortunately, not a promise."

Chapter 22: Casey

THAT NIGHT, AS I lay in my tent, I waited for the tradesmen's lights to extinguish and for Kyraine and Myra to go to bed. I'd waited long enough to rescue Irene, and now that I had Adalia, I decided I would go after her tonight. Once I was sure Kyraine and Myra had retired for the night, I jumped up, closely followed by Adalia, who had been sleeping at the foot of my bed. I grabbed a black cloak, threw it on, and slipped into the chilled night, tailed silently by Adalia. The sky was, I saw gratefully, vacant. In the moon's absence and under the cover of darkness, hopefully I would be a ghost.

We quietly snuck through the sleeping camp. The Hunters boarded their horses in stables at the village, but I had never been. I silently thanked Matthew for bringing Adalia and I together as she confidently led the way, after getting a small whiff of the horses. I trailed her as she kept her head bent low and followed an invisible path to the village. I estimated the village being about a mile from the camp, and soon, we arrived. Even in the dark, I could still make out fallen structures from the fires.

Once at the stables, the smell of horses and soiled hay filled my nose. One horse, who looked darker than all the others, raised his head to look at me when I walked by. He whinnied and I tried to hush him, but to no avail. The horse was restless and his noise was beginning to disturb the other horses, so I grabbed the harness around his face and pulled him forward. A saddle sat on the floor of his stable, and I threw it on, which instantly silenced him. For as long as I could remember, I had loved horses and riding, so saddling up the animal was a comforting familiarity. I mounted the horse, placed my boots in the stirrups, and tightened the reins. Adalia waited patiently, until I motioned to her. Finally, we were off, racing through the trees towards Azlaya's castle.

As I rode, I tried to strategize the best way to get in and out of the castle without getting caught. I only had until morning before someone would notice I wasn't in my tent. I guessed it was a little past midnight, which gave me at least six hours before the Hunters would wake. Of course, that didn't take into account any complications. I thought through this during my ride.

As I bounced around on the horse's back, my bottom was numbing, and my fingers ached from clutching the reins for so long. The tress that flew by made me realize that if I ever got lost in these woods, I would never find my way back to the Hunters' camp.

I was about to stop to allow Adalia and the horse to rest, when Azlaya's castle rose up in the distance. The castle was huge, even more so than I had imagined. As I got closer, I could see a wide moat circling the entire castle. The water looked like tar, black and thick. Beyond the moat stood a huge, walled fortress that separated the water from the stone castle. Lit lanterns and red banners with black dragons lined the wall, and inside that was the castle. It looked like the castles of the medieval ages: dark stone, large cylindrical towers, and flat roofs. I looked closer and saw Sagen positioned along the wall too, watching the silent night.

As I rode towards the castle, I searched for an opening where I wouldn't be seen. The castle had a drawbridge, however it was heavily guarded. I slowed the horse to a walk and slid from his back. I found a tree, far enough from the castle, and tied the horse to it. I prayed that while I was gone, he would behave himself and remain quiet.

My one advantage was that no one had reason to expect an attack on the castle. My disadvantages were that I didn't know anything about the interior of the castle. It occurred to me that I was walking right into a trap. Irene was taken as bait, and I was obediently trying to save her, but even with that realization, I didn't care. I had a responsibility to these people, and I wasn't prepared to fail an innocent girl.

I approached the murky water and studied it, dreading everything I would have to do to get past the exterior wall. I hated swimming in anything but a pool, and I still wasn't even used to bathing in the stream. Oceans are full of things with teeth, and moats are famously known to contain alligators. I breathed deeply, trying desperately to calm myself.

"Let's go," I whispered to Adalia. One wrong move and we would be caught. I approached the water where the light from two lanterns didn't reach. It was a blind spot. I stopped at the water and reluctantly slipped into its icy clutches. I walked for a couple feet, then my feet hit nothing, and my head ducked under the surface. I sprang up and heard Adalia whimpering frantically at my sudden disappearance.

I'm fine. I thought in my head. She immediately stopped whining, and I remembered Myra telling me that Adalia could hear and respond to my thoughts. *Come on, girl. Be careful, it's deep.*

Adalia looked at me, and I could see in her eyes she understood. Together, we quickly swam through the dark water. Whenever something slimy slid along my arms or legs, I recoiled in fear, but I had to contain myself because splashes would only call attention to us.

After crossing the moat, we finally pulled ourselves ashore. I saw Adalia begin to shake the water from her soaking coat, but I held my hands up to stop her and shook my head vigorously. She gazed at me curiously as I drained all the water from my clothes and her fur and directed it to flow silently back into the moat. I pulled myself to my feet and scanned the wall. There had to be a way for people to enter and exit the exterior wall without always lowering the drawbridge. I placed my hand on the chilled, stone wall, but I knew it was too thick for me to penetrate, and trying it would be too loud for the Sagen not to notice.

I walked along the wall, my hand guiding me rather than my eyes. Finally, I swept over a rough surface and froze. I lifted my eyes to what my fingers rested on and found I had happened upon a door. I went to open it, already knowing it would be locked. It didn't budge. For the second time that night, I internally thanked someone for helping me prepare for that moment. "*Reserare*," I whispered the spell Myra had taught me: *Unlock*.

I slowly pulled the door open, and Adalia and I rushed through before any of the guards could look over and see us. On the other side of the door, a tunnel stretched into nothingness. I couldn't even see my hand in front of my face as I advanced forward. I walked until I stubbed my toe on something. I realized it was another door. I twisted the handle and, strangely, it was unlocked.

Before going through the door, I knelt next to the silhouette of Adalia. *Adalia, attack only threats, no one else.* I didn't, nor couldn't, check to see if she understood, but she had already proven earlier that she did. I inched the door open, and we slipped in.

It looked as though we had stepped into a Spanish courtyard. A huge, grassy area spread out, and around it doors lined the walls circling the opening. Several stories were stacked on one another and a couple balconies were scattered about each story. Sagen floated aimlessly around the open area until our sudden entrance caught their attention. They rushed towards us, and I felt my heart rate burst into a gallop. I quickly noticed the ground under them was dirt, and despite the chaos going on around me and the growling at my feet, I concentrated. I jerked my hand down, causing the ground underneath the approaching Sagen to collapse. They toppled over each other in the new ditch in the ground. While it didn't stop them, it slowed them down and gave me time to run.

Sagen above us aimed their cross bows at Adalia and me. We raced along the wall where a small awning offered a little protection. I reached another door and wrenched it open, hoping we wouldn't come face to face with more Sagen.

I slammed the door behind me and uttered a locking spell. Adalia and I raced through the quiet corridors of the castle. Banners like the dragon ones on the exterior wall hung inside the castle, too. Dark windows stretched tall, as high as the walls, and they were all stained glass, each depicting the black dragon doing different tasks. On some windows, dragon's fire burned entire cities; on other windows it flew over a land shrouded by the dragon's shadow. I assumed the dragon represented Azlaya. I vaguely thought about her narcissism, but quickly pushed the thought aside.

The sound of my shoes and Adalia's paws echoed off the walls, but no soldiers or guards had discovered where we had gone. It was eerie running through the castle of the woman who killed my mother.

I chased Adalia deeper into the castle. She brought me to a staircase that led to a lower level. The air floating up from below was frigid and goose bumps erupted on my arms. I walked cautiously down the slippery stairs, which spilled into a dimly lit room. Thick, wooden doors surrounded the tight space; each had a window with bars. Adalia pawed at one, and I rushed over to her. I stood on my toes and peered inside.

It was a room so small that you could only take a couple steps in each direction before hitting another wall. Hay had been strewn about and some was piled in a corner, serving as a bed. A ragged blanket sat on top of the hay, and I saw a small tin can acting as a toilet in the corner. Sitting inside the prison cell was Irene. Her skin was pale, and she had a cut across her cheek, and her hair was tangled and matted. Her dress was covered in dirt, and she clutched her knees. She leaned against the damp wall and hummed somberly to herself. I whispered the unlocking spell and threw the door open.

At first, Irene was startled, and it took her a few moments to realize who I was. Then, her eyes melted into pure joy and relief. "I'm so sorry, Irene," I whispered to her as she collapsed into my arms. I gave her a quick squeeze, and then remembered the danger we were still in. "Someone must've heard that," I said, referring to the loud creak of the cell door.

I took Irene's frail hand, and we tore out of the room with Adalia leading us. The corridors were no longer empty, and raspy orders filled and bounced off the walls. We turned a corner and ran into a group of Sagen. They all angled their cross bows at us, and I pushed Irene behind me, as Caden had once done for me. One man standing in the middle of all the Sagen was someone I could only hope to forget. Logan stared at us with his arms crossed over his chest, looking smug. Irene clutched painfully tight to my hand, clearly horrified by the arrows poised for fire.

"Casey, we've been expecting you," Logan said as he clasped his hands.

Chapter 23: Kate

THE WAY MY grandmother had behaved outside my mother's room
left me disturbed. Rarely did I ever see her upset or scared—really scared.
The way she looked at Casey's hand the night the glass cut her didn't even
compare to the terror etched into her face earlier. But when she spun
around, she tried to hide what she had seen in a bleak smile and quickly
shuffled me away.

I lay awake for hours, staring at my clock, turning thoughts over and
over in my head. Whenever I closed my eyes, my grandmother's face would
meet me on the edges of sleep, and I'd jump awake. Exhausted and impatient, I tossed the blanket from me and tiptoed over to Casey's room. I
paused at her door, which was still ajar. I thought it strange that I never
heard her get up to go eat dinner; despite the late hour, it was unlike her to
skip a meal. The lights were off, so I assumed she was still sleeping. Then it
occurred to me that this was even more unusual than Casey missing dinner,
because I knew she never slept with her door open. I hesitantly pushed my
way in and scanned the dark room, but it was empty.

I squinted as I gazed around the room, and it appeared she had been
reading the old book again and became distracted, because it was thrown
haphazardly on the bed. Her phone sat idly on the nightstand, and her set
of car keys was on her desk. A deep feeling of dread hung in the pit of my
stomach as reality settled in. It was the early hours of morning and Casey
was nowhere to be found. I backed out of the room and closed the door
soundlessly. I could feel my heart start to race faster with each passing

second. Had I made Casey disappear too? I turned to go wake up my grandmother, when my eyes fell on the cause of my paranoia.

The mystery of the door to my mother's room seemed to lure me in. I felt as though I were in a trance as my feet began to move forward. I stopped in front of the door, when suddenly I could hear a faint noise coming from inside—a song. I rested an ear on the door to listen, when I felt my body fall forward. I regained my balance and realized that the door had somehow fallen open. I was too curious to leave, and I slipped inside and pulled the door closed behind me.

My eyes slowly adjusted to the darkness. I looked around, but I couldn't make sense of what I saw. The room was a wreck, as though someone had gone through and thrown things everywhere. Books, paper, and furniture were scattered around the room chaotically as though a tornado had passed through. Even the blankets and sheets were askew. I couldn't understand why the disorderly room had made my grandmother act as though she had seen a ghost.

Too drained to search further, I turned to leave, when I heard the song again. It was music—a song—coming from within the room. The eeriness of my situation made me panic and produce a ball of light in my hand. My grandmother would lock me in my room for weeks if she saw me using my powers this freely. A small orb, the size of a golf ball, formed in my hand, as I picked my way across the room. I approached an almost-empty bookshelf, knelt down next to a pile of books, and pushed some aside to find a small box buried beneath. I lifted it onto a shelf, shed light on it, and flipped the lid open.

Whatever I expected to see wasn't what I saw. A wolf, seemingly howling, twirled as the music played. I waited for the clockworks inside the box to stop, but the contraption continued endlessly. A silver chain with two interlocked rings rested peacefully on the plush cushion inside. I figured it belonged to my mother as I gazed at them. Holding the orb of light closer, I saw something glint off the underside of the lid. I drew my face in and saw gold, spirally writing.

It was a language I didn't recognize, but I tried to read it anyway. So, slowly and uncertainly, I whispered, *"Tollite me fuisse mundo in quo pauci, ubi tandem fato fieri meus."*

As if I had said the magic word that sent the world spinning in a movie, wind began to whip around me. As more things flew around, I finally understood why the room was in its current state.

I was scared, but only momentarily, because exhilaration and amazement consumed my thoughts. A door began to materialize into view, and once it didn't appear to be transparent, it swung open. Light flooded into the room, and I threw my hand up to shield my eyes. I couldn't begin to imagine the look on my grandmother's or Casey's face if either of them had walked in at that moment. The light dimmed, and I lowered my arm. Adrenaline coursed through my veins as my feet began to tug my body forward.

I couldn't explain it, but something beyond the door called to me and yearned for me to enter. It was as if each step forward was another step to something I'd been waiting for my whole life. I could feel energy beyond the door that was similar to the energy I felt from my powers. In the chaos of the moment, I felt oddly at peace, as though all the fights I'd had with my grandmother about my abilities, and all the times I'd wanted to admit my secret to Casey didn't matter anymore. I felt free and limitless, as if whatever beckoned me forward was opening my eyes to a new perspective, one that didn't involve hiding. With these feelings of exhilaration bubbling in my chest, and without even thinking about Casey or my grandmother, I walked through the threshold.

I heard crickets chirping, and the sound of trees rustling in a faint wind. Immediately, I thought that I had ended up in the forest behind my house, but when I turned, my house wasn't there. It was dark and I couldn't see too far into the distance, but I could see the boundaries of a clearing and trees stretching beyond. I heard the rushing of water over stones, and felt grass licking at my legs. Everything seemed to beckon me to travel deeper, but I could only stare and take in the sights around me.

I wanted to see more—I had to see more. With no one to stop me, I produced another ball of light and tossed it into the air. My powers sparked to life much more freely, and I didn't feel a heavy guilt weighing on me. At its peak, the light exploded and fanned out around me, shedding light onto more things in the distance. A laugh filled my chest and burst off my lips. I felt so alive, and something inside me screamed that this is where I belonged. For years I'd been terrified of my powers and where they came from, but in that moment, I knew that this was where I got them, and the thought of them didn't scare me anymore.

The light that fell around me faded into the night and I heard the sound of pounding hooves. I turned in the direction they came from and waited. Thoughts of American Indians and cowboys crossed my mind as I watched the untamed forest, but nothing of the sort burst through the trees. Rather, dark horses with hooded riders approached me. They stopped a couple feet away, and one of the riders floated down from his mount. He closed the distance between us and slightly bowed his head. My eyebrows perked as I tried to catch a glimpse of his face. When he raised his head, I saw that his face was only a black hole. He wore a black cloak with the hood pulled around his head, looking like a black, cloaked ghost. I wanted to ask him who he was—what he was—and why he had come, and I figured he wanted to know the same things from me.

Then, a raspy, hissing voice halted the words in my throat. "Kaitlin Coles, we have been expecting you."

The voice sent chills down my spine, not from fear, but from excitement. This thing—this creature—had been waiting for me, and I felt like I had been waiting to be found.

I smirked thinly. "I guess I arrived just in time."

Chapter 24: Casey

I BIT MY lip to keep it from trembling. I refused to show Logan that I was afraid. "Let her go. I'm the one you've wanted, and now I'm here. Just let her go," I said, trying to keep my voice even.

Logan slowly walked closer to me, and when he spoke, I felt his breath tickle my face. "You may not be who Azlaya needs. It could be your sister."

I clenched my teeth in anger. My breathing was heavy and flaring through my nose. "Then let both of us go," I said deliberately, letting each poison-filled word sink in.

"That's not an option either. It makes no sense to have to find you again." My eyes flashed to his face with loathing, and in my anger, I swung my fist up to his face. His reflexes were quicker than I expected, and he snatched my wrist and gave it a violent twist. I twisted my arm unnaturally to keep my wrist from snapping.

Sagen suddenly yanked Irene away. I whipped around to grab her back, but I was also being restrained. In all the confusion, I completely forgot about an invaluable weapon. Thank goodness *it* hadn't forgotten its purpose. One Sagen holding me suddenly shrunk away from me and doubled over. Its scream sounded like a whistling kettle, then the hooded figure melted, leaving behind a pile of dust. I mentally noted that the Sagen weren't immune to Adalia, regardless of the time of day.

Adalia growled ferociously at the Sagen. I seized the opportunity and, using moves that Brennon taught me, I slammed into Logan and shoved the warrior holding Irene. He tumbled away from me. Adalia held off the rest of the Sagen who tried to approach her, but most recoiled. The few that did get too close were reduced to dust.

I spotted the door Adalia and I had entered through, and I lifted Irene into my arms and dashed towards it. Having Irene bouncing on my hip slowed me down as I ran, and I didn't even hear my pursuer. Logan snatched my cloak, and the sudden jolt digging into my neck made me drop Irene. I fell under Logan's weight and rolled over. He loomed over me, knife in hand, the blade glinting in the candlelight. I didn't want Irene to see what he was about to do.

His chest rose and fell rapidly. His breath in my face made my blood curdle, and I tried to twist away from him. "You'll have to try harder than that," he spat.

I looked past him helplessly. Adalia still fended off attacking Sagen, not allowing any of them to aid Logan. Hatred for Logan boiled in my veins. I had come too far and risked too much to be hauled off to Azlaya or thrown into a prison cell. I glared at him and felt my limbs tremble with a yearning to punch him. Logan's eyes suddenly shot open, he dropped the knife, and jumped clear from me. His hand that had pinned my arm to the ground was burned and flaring red. He flicked his eyes in horror, from his hand to me.

I had burned him. I suddenly recalled the fire that now coursed through my veins. I was so mad that my new ability to produce fire had swept over my skin. I scrambled to my feet, feeling an uncomfortable heat under me. I turned to see that where I had lain now burned with little flames. I didn't look twice; I called to Adalia, and snatched Irene again. The three of us bolted through the door. Once on the other side, I muttered another locking spell.

Adalia, Irene, and I stood on the bank of the moat. I searched hurriedly for a shallow spot, knowing I couldn't swim in deep water and keep Irene above the surface. I found none and my time was running out. Despite the spell I had cast, we still had only a few seconds before Sagen burst through the door. Adalia barked and stepped into the water, waiting for me to realize what she wanted me to do.

I laid Irene across Adalia's thin, but strong, back. She towed Irene through the icy water, and I paddled closely behind them. As we reached the other side, soldiers spilled from the door. More lowered the drawbridge and were preparing to cross it. I quickly threw a spell at the bridge, causing it to groan to a halt. I didn't take the time to dry us. I thrust Irene in my arms, and sprinted towards our means of escape.

My heart fluttered with relief when I realized that the vast forest might shield us. I searched for where the horse was tied. I was sure that Azlaya knew of my "breaking and entering," and I wanted to be far away before she joined the fight. If she found me, I had little hope Irene and I could still escape.

I finally saw the horse shifting nervously among the dark foliage. I heard shouts behind me but didn't dare to turn around. As we reached the horse, one of the Sagen shot an arrow, and it sliced me, cutting cleanly through my arm. From observing the Hunters practice, I knew it took two seconds to reload a bow, which meant I had seconds to get everyone to safety.

I threw Irene on the horse and jumped up behind her. I stole one last glance at the castle and caught sight of a figure on a balcony. Azlaya wore a dark blue gown that hung tightly to her body and then fanned out at the bottom, and her curly, dark hair was piled on her head. Her eyes were trained on me, but she remained calm and motionless. She called to no one and made no move to stop me. It struck me then that she had already given up on me. She wanted Kate, and my heart shuddered at the thought.

In my delay, more arrows sliced and whizzed through the trees. Most of them missed us, but one finally connected with the horse. It went deep into his shoulder, and he reared in horror and pain. He took off into the labyrinth of trees, and I clung to him with all the strength I had left.

We rode that way until silence was a heavy blanket on us once more. When I felt we were far enough away and that no one followed us, I jerked the horse to a halt. I dropped off his back and inspected his shoulder. I touched his skin gingerly, and he let out a pain-filled whinny. Irene stroked his mane in a soothing manner and cooed in his ear. I glanced down at Adalia, who also panted heavily, but she remained unscathed. I returned my gaze to the horse's injury. Blood pooled down his coat, making it look wet.

My knowledge of caring for animals was limited, but I guessed that pulling the arrow from the horse's shoulder would only hurt more, as well as allow for infection. Instead, I snapped the arrow in half, so it wouldn't knock against trees as he ran and further irritate the wound. I also drained the biting water from our clothes and fur coats before continuing onward. I clambered onto the horse again and eased him into a steady canter. His uneven gait under me told me that he was limping. I infused a spell into him that would numb the pain, but it was weak against the severity of the cut.

Adalia could probably sense my anxiety, so she confidently and quickly led the way back to the camp. I wanted to reach down and stroke her, but I had to balance Irene and myself on the constantly changing topography. As we neared the tents, the horse walked with his head bent low, and his limp had grown worse. Adalia's tongue bobbed limply on her lip, and Irene had fallen asleep in my arms. I had cradled her to my chest and wrapped my cloak around her, trying to keep her as warm as I could, but the cold still soaked through to her limp body. I applied pressure to my arm were it had been sliced, but the wound kept bleeding. I was exhausted, cold, injured, and with each minute that passed, I grew weaker.

We were near the camp, but I could hardly keep my eyes open. The exhaustion from riding and the previous melee had drained any adrenaline I had. My head kept dropping to my chest, then jolting up because of the horse's uneven steps.

Unexpectedly, the horse came to a halt, and his knees buckled. We slipped off his back. He snorted in pain and was very evidently tired from carrying two passengers while coping with a bad leg. Irene jumped awake, startled by my sudden absence. I grabbed the reins and tried to haul the horse back to his feet. He was a large animal, and one thing I recalled about horses was that if they lay down, sometimes they couldn't get back up, and they would die. Our horse hardly had the strength to support himself, never mind lift himself back up.

I begged the horse to stand, but to no avail, and he rolled onto his side. He was beyond the point of coaxing. Adalia watched me curiously. I dropped the reins, defeated, not knowing what else to do. Adalia must have felt sympathetic for me, and a nasty snarl rippled across her lips. The horse immediately, but still painfully, pulled himself to his feet. I rubbed Adalia in thanks and retrieved the reins.

The horse was already injured and exhausted, and I knew that not having to carry me, too, would be a great solace. I grabbed the reins and walked next to his low-bent head. I was too tired to try to track time anymore. I mindlessly walked, watching my feet fall in step, one behind the other. The hours passed by slowly. Finally, to my great relief, my eyes fell upon the camp. Just when I thought of my bed and warm tent, I heard rustling. Unready and too worn for another fight, I placed a hand on Irene's freezing leg to provide what little warmth I could.

Even Adalia was too tired to bark. Suddenly, I felt arms pulling at me and panicked shouts intruding my ears. The pain from my arm throbbed as someone wrapped it tightly with something. I tried to wriggle away, thinking someone was binding my hands. It was too dark for me to see what was happening, or who had found us. I heard Irene calling to me, but beyond that, everything else was incomprehensible.

"Don't take her," I pleaded, but I was ignored.

"Here, give her this." It was the first sensible thing I understood.

Before I knew it, someone held a cup to my lips and tried to get my mouth open. I kept my lips sealed and closed my eyes. Then, the person squeezed my cheeks to force my mouth open. They poured in a cool liquid that I refused to swallow, and I spat it back out. I held my hands in front of my face, but I was restrained and greeted with more of the fluid. Instead of letting me spit it out again, someone placed a hand over my mouth and plugged my nose. I fought and struggled to free myself of their grasp. I panicked. I couldn't breathe, and they held me tight.

In the chaos, I heard a gentle voice in the distance. "Casey, please swallow it."

The familiarity of the voice finally made me swallow whatever the liquid was, and I relaxed. My eyes fluttered open to find the person who spoke to me. I was so tired that I didn't recognize Kyraine gazing at me. I was still restrained as she glanced at my arm, which blared with aching pain.

"If she awakens," Kyraine addressed another person who was present, "Give her more. I'll speak with her later."

Then, Kyraine left my vision, so I closed my eyes again. That time, I didn't worry about opening them. I wouldn't think about Kyraine or Irene until I woke up, and I hoped that didn't happen any time soon. I had a feeling I'd been drugged once again, as I fell into a deep sleep. I welcomed it gratefully, and, despite the aches and pains all over my body, I slept.

I woke a few hours later, only to be greeted with more liquid. I gladly swallowed it and relapsed into sleep. The routine lasted throughout the night, as I kept jumping awake from nightmares. However, in the midst of all the bad dreams, one awakening wasn't the result of a dream at all. I felt a pang in my chest, as if my heart had skipped a beat. I heard a familiar voice in my head. *She's mine*, Azlaya said. I tried to respond mentally, but my eyes closed again. It was mid-morning when I finally awoke, and no liquid waited for me. Instead, it was Kyraine.

I still felt lingering soreness throughout my limbs, so I just rolled my head over to look at her. Kyraine didn't even blink, and only sat in her silence and looked away from me. When her thoughts freed her mind, she met my gaze. She opened her mouth to say something, but no words came. She pressed her lips together and dropped her head to look at her hands in her lap.

"I'm sorry," I breathed.

"Don't, you shouldn't have to be," Kyraine said gently, not lifting her head.

"What?" Confusion bit me, but guilt gnawed at Kyraine.

"You were only fulfilling the responsibility that I said you had, and had it been me, I would have done the same thing," she finished sympathetically.

"It was stupid of me to go alone. I wasn't thinking straight last night, Kyraine, I know that. I was acting on impulse." Kyraine only shook her head, refusing to let me take the fault.

"I can't blame you for wanting to protect someone," she said flatly, leaving no room for me to say anything more. Kyraine rose. "Can you stand?"

I pulled the blankets off me and languidly stood in response. The cloak I wore earlier was gone; the only clothes I wore were a blue tunic with warm leggings underneath. I slipped my chilled toes into my shoes and followed Kyraine from the tent. Myra waited for us outside. Once she saw me, she threw herself at me and embraced me in a hug. She muttered something in Latin that I didn't catch, but I think it had something to do with the fact I was unharmed. She pulled away from me and sighed in relief.

"Miss me?" I asked lightheartedly. She half smiled and rubbed my arm.

I abruptly remembered the lumbering horse I had dragged through the night. "How's the horse—"

"He didn't make it, Casey," Myra cut me off. My lips parted to apologize to Kyraine, but she waved it aside. "Come, Casey. We need to talk," Myra said. I caught a glimpse of Kyraine looking downcast as I walked away. She saw me and smiled, but it didn't reach her eyes.

Myra nudged me and motioned for me to follow her. We walked through the camp and over to the stream, and sat on a fallen tree. Myra was hesitant about something, and it worried me. Kyraine hadn't said anything about Irene yet, and I feared the worst. Maybe I hadn't gotten her back in time. Maybe she caught pneumonia from the moat water. Maybe she got frostbite from being without a coat for so long.

"No, Casey, it's not Irene," Myra interrupted my thoughts. "Something happened last night while you were away." I waited anxiously for her to continue. "It's your sister ..."

"What about her?" I tried not to sound defensive after the way Logan spoke of her as though she were Azlaya's pet.

"Casey, she's here," Myra admitted, but she didn't seem any less anxious than before.

"She is?" I gasped. "Where is she?" I asked, hurriedly looking around, half expecting her to walk out from behind a tree. However, Myra's mood didn't match my excitement, and I knew I was missing something.

"She arrived in the clearing last night, just as you had. Nearby Nymphs rushed to retrieve her, but the Sagen got to her first. Azlaya has had them waiting there since you came. The Nymphs did everything they could, but they were too late ... I'm so sorry," Myra finished heavily.

"Could we get her back?" I asked quietly, dreading the answer I already knew. My sister was at the mercy of Azlaya, and fear for her washed over me.

"No, not easily. Once Azlaya has her, she won't let her go. Casey, I want you to understand something," Myra began. "Wherever the prophecy brings you, we will not only be your protectors, but also your loyal warriors. I don't know what's going to happen from here, but you must know that Azlaya is going to do everything in her power to turn Kate against you. I know you don't want to hear that, but we can't avoid the truth anymore. Just know that wherever this fight takes you, we will be right by your side. All of us."

I leaned over and hugged her, and she squeezed me back. In that moment, she had become the comfort I desperately needed. I pulled back from her, but I couldn't bring myself to look at her and say this. My eyes fell to my feet. "I think I finally understand the prophecy now," I said, recalling last night's events. My sudden jump awake, Azlaya's voice, the pang in my chest; it wasn't from pain. "The wrong choice—it was choosing to join Azlaya and help her take over Alagia." Myra said nothing, because I was right.

That was why Azlaya let me escape so easily. She knew I was already so closely bound to the Hunters that convincing me to join her would be impossible. Saying it out loud made it no easier to come to terms with the fact that Kate—my sister—had joined the evil sorceress. What I had felt in my heart last night was a signal to me to prepare myself for everything to come. It was a warning to begin to anticipate the unknown.

Chapter 25: Azlaya

I SAT IMPATIENTLY on my throne. My throne room was my favorite place in the castle, because it symbolized my power. I sat on a dais in the center of the room, and a long red carpet stretched from it to a door across the room. Above me, and around the room, were small balconies with deep purple curtains draped on them. Kings and queens had dark stone castles that were damp and rotting. I had a chandelier of crystals from the mines of Eileen that hung over my head. It lit the entire room as candlelight glinted off the gems, and the black marble floor sparkled . On either side of me, huge stained glass windows stretched the length of the wall, and behind me on the wall, I had burned the shape of a dragon into the wood. The castle I'd created was far better than anything I could have received as Mistress of the Hunt.

Logan stood before me, muddy and burnt, as he tried to explain how Layna's daughter had escaped him again. I wasn't even listening to his incessant rambling. He has worked for me for over two decades, and his years of service were beneficial to my expansion of power, but the fact that he'd lost my opportunity to win this war, twice, sent me over the edge.

"Enough, Logan," I snapped. Several servants nearby recoiled and tried to become one with the shadows in the room. "That's two times you've let her escape."

"My Lady, I know, but—" Logan stuttered. I was irascible, and he knew it. He was opening his mouth when the door across the room creaked open.

My head inclined as Sagen warriors entered. "My Lady," one greeted me. As they floated closer, I realized why they had interrupted my meeting with Logan. My eyes trained on the girl that walked in between them. Her gaze kept darting from one thing to another as she looked from me, to the windows, to the huge ceiling hanging over her.

She wore tight, dark pants and a loose-fitting shirt that looked too big for her. Her blonde hair was tied into a ponytail, and her skin was tan, just as her mother's had been. Her face was round, as were her brown eyes, and her lips were full and pink. I didn't need to see her face to notice the great resemblance between Kaitlin Coles and her mother. She gazed about my throne room, intrigued, and already I knew she had something within her that her sister lacked.

My eyes wouldn't stray from the sight of my victory in the impending war. She was the girl who would help me bring down the four kingdoms, conquer the people of Alagia, bring the Hunters and Huntsmen to their knees, and her sister to her death.

"Take her to her room; make sure her needs are met," I ordered placidly. Kaitlin met my gaze, looked curiously at me, and then turned to leave with her escorts.

One Sagen remained and asked me, "Will that be all, My Lady?"

I nodded curtly. "Logan owes you," I added as the warrior left. Logan dropped my gaze, hanging his head in shame. I let out an exasperated sigh. "Finish cleaning up." Logan knew better than anyone that my patience and mercy were limited. To aggravate me was to ask for a death sentence, which I would easily grant. He nodded quickly and dropped to his knees to bow. I slid off the throne and swept past him. I strode down the crowded hallways as more Sagen began to reenter the castle after the commotion from earlier. When any of the Sagen saw me, they immediately stopped and bowed their heads. They respected and obeyed me.

I climbed the stairs to the bedchamber I'd had prepared for either of the Coles sisters. I still contemplated how to gain Kaitlin's trust. If she learned that her sister was there and not willing to join me, she might start to resist me. I entered the bedchamber, trying to remain as expressionless as possible. I glanced around the room. The drapes and the blankets were deep purple, and the girl stood motionless at the window. Her eyes seemed trained on something in the distance.

I carefully crossed the room, although she didn't show any signs that she was afraid. She looked restless, if anything. I sat in an armchair across from her bed. "Kaitlin," I said, only trying to get her attention.

"It's only Kaitlin when I'm in trouble. Otherwise, it's Kate," she responded. Then, she turned and slowly lifted her gaze to meet my searching eyes. "Who are you?" She didn't sound afraid or even nervous. She almost seemed eager in anticipation of my answer.

I smiled. She was bold, and her confident demeanor fed my hopes for her future. "My name is Azlaya."

"All right, Azlaya, and where exactly am I?" The way she addressed me so casually and directly made my eyebrow shift, but her face didn't waver.

"You are in Alagia, the world in which you were born. However, you will want to hear the whole story. I'll start from the beginning. Your beginning." Kate's eyes widened slightly with interest. She walked around the bed and sat to face me. "Your mother, Layna, is from your world, but your father, Aaron, is from this world, Alagia. Your mother had the ability to travel between the two worlds, just as you do, and she met your father here. You and your sister were born soon thereafter." I saw a flicker of sorrow cross Kate's face. I saw my opportunity and attacked. "You miss her, don't you?" She opened her mouth to argue, but she knew she couldn't deny it. Her eyes gave her away. "You were barely a few months old when she died." Again, nothing. "Kate, I could help you. I could bring your mother back. You would finally be able to have what you have longed for your whole life," I said slowly, enunciating each word.

I saw an inkling of doubt in her eyes. "How? She's dead," Kate responded flatly.

"You already know how," I told her, seeing if she could make the connection. I could feel her sorcery in the throne room, and as she sat before me, I could sense her powers even more. She knew of the powers she possessed, and they were strong.

"My mother is dead and has been for the last sixteen years of my life," Kate responded defiantly.

"Kate, I know what you can do." She didn't seem to understand what I meant, so I held out my hand and formed a ball of light. A spell she had used not too long ago. Her eyes lit up as she stared at my hand. The light extinguished.

"You're like me," she exclaimed.

"You and I are sorceresses, just as your mother was. Producing light is not all you can do, is it?"

"No," she shook her head. "I've taught myself to control the elements too … and sometimes I can do other things, more out of my control though," she replied softly. I caught a glimpse of her most recent fit that had caused her to decimate a boy before her very eyes.

I nodded in approval. "Water, earth, and air are the three elements that make up our world. And those other things you mentioned are spells." I delved into her mind to find more information I could use. "And it seems you have managed to teach yourself how to conjure spells without saying any incantations. Meaning, you only think the word and you can still produce the spell," I explained to her. "And as far as accidents go," she eyed me, knowing that I knew about the boy, "those can be prevented with training."

It amazed me that she didn't know about Alagia, yet she had somehow trained herself to work with the elements and magic. She seemed to have mastered all three of the elements, and the only reason she hadn't mastered fire yet was because she didn't have access to the ancient spells.

"Your sister doesn't know, does she?" I asked, already knowing the answer.

She shook her head. "No, I swore not to tell her. I noticed them when I was ten, and when I realized that she couldn't do the things I could, I kept it to myself and practiced with them." I nodded thoughtfully, showing her that I did listen to and care about what she had to say. I needed her trust in order for my plans to unfold neatly. Due to her prior experience, her training would be easier, making the darker side of magic much simpler for her to learn.

"What I said before is true," I said, reiterating my reason for her to trust me. "Help me, and I can return your mother to you."

"Help you with what?" Kate asked. She was very comfortable around me, which spoke volumes about her confidence in her powers and her inner strength. Seeing that she could cope with a strange world, converse with a stranger who knew more than she should and not be shaken, told me she was strong.

"There will be a war, Kate. My enemies, the Hunters and Huntsmen, roam these woods. They are male and female warriors that have been part of this world since its beginning. When your mother was here, they stood by and supported her. That was until they saw how powerful she was becoming. They wanted their leader, the Mistress of the Hunt, to rule the land, and to do that, they had to dispose of your mother. Your mother sensed their mutiny, so she sent you and your sister to her world to be safe. A few days later, they killed her. I knew I had to stop them from conquering the rest of this world, so I allied the Shadow Warriors, the Sagen. It has been a brutal fight, but the war has only just begun. The Hunters know that I am all that stands in their way of conquest. The Huntsmen, the Hunters' counterpart, are West of us, only waiting for the orders to attack. If the Hunters defeat me here, they will move on to claim the rest of Alagia as their own," I told her. In my head, I heavily concealed the lie I twisted into a story. If Kate was as powerful as I thought, I had to be careful with what freely passed through my mind.

"Let me get this straight," Kate began, as she lowered her gaze to the ground. "The Hunters turned on my mother so that their leader could take over in her place. Then you and the Sagen have fought them, but are now going to war with them, to keep them from taking over the land?" I nodded slowly to make it seem as though the whole thing saddened me.

"Your sister, Cassia—" Kate refocused her attention on me when I said her twin's name, "has allied herself with the Hunters."

"But they killed our mother!" Kate interrupted.

"They have led her to believe that I killed her. There's more though. A prophecy is written about you and Cassia that determines the fate of this world and the victor of this war. It says—here, I'll show you."

I rose from the chair and walked over to a desk in the corner. I had mulled over the prophecy so many times, I had memorized it. I wrote it down years ago, saving it for the girl who would join me. I returned to Kate and handed her the piece of parchment. She read it over once, and then twice. On the third round, she finally set the paper in her lap. Kate's eyes rose to meet my own. They were glossy with fear.

"What?" she asked, horrified, a hint of a whimper in her voice. I translated to avoid any confusion or misinterpretation.

"However this unfolds, you and Cassia will face each other, and one of you will die in order to bring peace to this world."

"This is crazy! I would never even think about killing Casey and neither would she," Kate said defiantly, pushing the parchment back into my hands.

"Choose your words thoughtfully, Kate. She is already here. She's been developing her sorcery and combat skills, and she wouldn't do that to pass time," I responded sharply, tossing the prophecy back into her lap.

"She's been here?" Kate asked shakily. "How?"

"The same way you came here." Kate clutched something in one hand, and her finger uncurled as she gazed at it. She turned it over in her hands and then held it up and stared at it as it swung like a pendulum. "That is the doorway between our two worlds, and your sister has access to it, too. Casey knows about the prophecy, too, and she understands what has to happen; you need to accept it, too."

"She'd never do that," Kate said, suddenly uncertain of what she said. I only had to raise my eyebrows and watch as Kate plummeted into doubt about her own sister.

"I understand this isn't easy to hear, but you need to know the truth and trust me."

"No," she clamped her hand shut. "I can't. Not if it means killing my sister," Kate said, shaking her head and crossing her arms. "I want to see her," she demanded.

I sighed with mild exasperation. "If that'll make you feel better, then go right ahead. But I'm not sure you'll get the chance to speak with her before she kills you." Kate turned my words over in her head. I watched her thoughtfully. "What do I have to do to gain your trust?"

Kate studied me. She didn't fear me; rather, she feared her future and what it held for her and her sister. Kate dropped my gaze. I could see the terror and doubt eating away at her. "I don't understand why it had to be us."

I was caught off guard. I was silent long enough for Kate to look into my eyes again. "Because, Kate, Alagia needs this. They need you to free them of the Hunters and Huntsmen."

Kate sighed, not in exasperation or relief, but in defeat. She shed her hard outer shell I'd seen earlier, allowing me to see the person she concealed on the inside. She bit her lip, and I saw tears welling up in her eyes, but she refused to let them spill.

"Help me, Kate. I *need* you," I said with such desperation I shocked myself. Until that moment, I never realized how much I really did need her. Finally having her in my grasp would rouse the Sagen to begin and end the war.

She nodded slowly. "Okay. I'll help you … but I want to do it without hurting my sister," she responded breathlessly. At that moment, I saw her flinch. She laid a hand over her heart and relief bubbled inside me. The prophecy was finally unraveling. She was mine.

"Fine, Kate. You'll realize soon enough that your sister does not share the same concerns for you," I said softly. "I'll give you more time to think about her, but for now, get some rest," I said as I departed.

As I was leaving, I caught a glimpse of Kate fastening the necklace behind her neck. I smiled to myself. I decided I couldn't leave anything to chance and would manipulate Kate's mind that night and continue to convince her to join me. I'd force her to foster hate for her sister and believe in her mother's resurrection so much that failure could not be an option.

I had one more person to see before I retired for the night. I walked briskly to the guest quarters. Few people knew that the person I sought out was still alive. That person was either going to take my news in a pleasant way or in a poor way. Either way, it would be amusing for me.

I unlocked the door, and entered. The room was lit by a few candles that cast shadows on the cold, stone walls. The bed was neatly made, and a man sat at a desk, writing. He had dark hair that was uncombed and sticking up in some places. His skin was much paler than his daughter's, and his eyes much darker. He normally wore a warm, inviting expression, but you'd never know it when he saw me. He set his quill down and stood to face me. He wore a red shirt and brown pants with boots that went up to his knees. He wore a leather vest over his shirt and had a beard of unshaven stubble rounding his chin. Once he saw me, his face fell, and his eyes immediately turned to hate.

"Azlaya," he spat. "What do you want?"

"Ah, there's the response I was expecting," I taunted him. He crossed his arms and huffed. "I know something you may want to hear." I narrowed my eyes, targeting him. The rising pitch of my voice heightened his suspicions.

"I have no interest in your problems, Azlaya. Whine to Logan; that's what he's for."

Aaron Coles was the only person in my entire castle who would dare to speak to me that way. It took much of my limited patience not to kill him every time he opened his mouth to say something rude. I crossed his room, lifted a picture from the bedside table, and studied it. I held it out to Aaron, who snatched it away from me and glared, hating me for laying eyes on it.

"It concerns that." I pointed to the picture, as a smirk played on my lips.

His eyes looked down to glimpse the picture, and then he met my gaze. The picture he held was of his wife and two daughters. It had been drawn when the girls were only a few weeks old.

"What about it?" His voice cracked a little, and his hands started to tremble with anger.

"They are here … both of them." The edge in my voice made him freeze. Aaron's mouth parted as if he was about to speak, but it just hung open. My eyes danced with the enjoyment of his surprise.

"Kate is very much like you. She has your boldness, and your stubbornness, for that matter." I stood and glided to the door, but I heard the pounding feet of Aaron behind me. I knew sooner or later he would crack.

I lifted a finger, and I controlled his body instantly. I flicked my hand, and he soared through the air. He collided with the edge of his desk and a small grunt of pain escaped from his mouth. His crumpled body lay on the floor as he raised his head from his chest and begged me with anguished eyes.

"Let me see her, please. Just let me see her one more time." The wetness on his cheeks was his sign of surrender. Victory sang in my ears.

"I can't do that; the risk it too great," I chuckled. "Besides, she looks just like her mother." My eyes motioned to the picture he still clutched.

"Heartless is too nice a word to describe you," he said with such venom that I was amused.

"No, I don't think so. I've let you live this long, so I must have some sort of heart," I said playfully. "Kate's already agreed to help me, and you'll die soon enough." Aaron's face scrunched into a questioning glare. "I'll let you live long enough to watch her help me conquer the kingdoms, and then when I'm finished with her, I'll let you watch as I plunge a dagger straight through her heart."

Aaron made a strangled sound in his throat. I exited the room, but before closing the door, I could hear the heavy sobs of a heartbroken father.

I went to my bedchamber and called for the servants to change me. They quickly untied me from the blue dress I wore and helped me step into my silk night gown. As someone rubbed scented oils into my skin, another person carefully pulled pins from my hair until it cascaded down my back again. Then, they braided it and stepped back, just as the application of the oils was finished. I glanced at myself in the mirror, nodded curtly, and shooed them away. I returned my gaze to the mirror and smiled. I climbed under the covers of my bed and stared at the ceiling.

Everything was falling into place. All I needed was to train Kate and convince her to kill her sister, which, of course, was easier said than done. I decided this was one thing I wasn't willing to leave to chance, nor time. Every day that passed was another wasted day in trying to win Kate over. I resolved to take control of the situation and from my chamber, so I stretched out my mental abilities towards Kate and slowly began to twist and mutilate any loving thoughts she had of Casey. I would force her to find reasons to despise her sister and manifest a hate so strong that she would not hesitate to kill Casey when it came time. After a few minutes, I withdrew my powers from Kate and let them continue to seep through and poison her mind. All night long, I thought about the war and the newest addition to my arsenal.

Chapter 26: Casey

AFTER LEARNING OF Kate's arrival, I began to have mixed feelings about the prophecy, the Hunters, and everything concerning my predetermined fate. Myra sensed it, and it unnerved her. If I couldn't keep my promise to protect Alagia, it would all be over. The Hunters would lose, and the people would be imprisoned by Azlaya forever.

I tried not to think about it and always searched for distractions. Oftentimes, I spent afternoons with Irene. She stayed in the camp so Myra could monitor her delicate health. Gwen, who was more than happy to do so, watched over her. Before becoming a Hunter, she had wanted a family, so being Irene's caretaker gave her a feeling of what it might have been like.

When I wasn't visiting Irene, I was training with Myra. The powers I inherited from my mother were so strong that I mastered the three elements in a matter of days. Myra still didn't know that I had the book I found in the burnt clearing, or that I could produce fire. I tried to make an effort to read the book, but couldn't bring myself to do it. Reading it would only make me think of the night I burned Logan, which would make me think of Azlaya, which would make me think of Kate—and the tsunami of guilt, fear, and betrayal would come crashing down on me again.

Instead, I rehearsed spells in my head until I fell asleep. One night, a week after I'd rescued Irene, images suddenly began flashing through my head. At first, I thought they were dreams, but I quickly realized I was horribly wrong. I saw a bloody and bruised Irene sitting in a prison cell crying out for me. Sagen overwhelmed the Hunters by their sheer numbers. A stained glass window with a dragon on it shattered. The dragon sprang to life and engulfed the world in flames. I'd already seen enough, when the last image made me scream and bolt into a sitting position. I was drenched in a cold sweat and my chest rose and fell unevenly.

Nausea swept over me, and I jumped from my bed, stepping over Adalia's tail as I passed. I had just made it to the edge of the clearing when I doubled over and vomited. Adalia stood a few feet from me, whining, not sure why I was hunched over and heaving. I heard her start barking madly as if to call for help, and then a few minutes later I felt a warm hand rubbing my back and another holding back my loose hair.

When my stomach was empty, and I felt no more bile in my throat, I shakily stood. I turned to face Brennon, who was holding a cup of water out to me. I was a little embarrassed that he had seen me get sick, but I gratefully took the cup and mouthed my thanks. I quickly drained the water and washed out my mouth. By the time I emptied the cup, Myra had arrived. Panic filled her eyes, and questions clung to her lips.

"What happened?" she asked. "Are you all right?"

I shook my head. I couldn't find the words to speak, as the last image had taken them from me: I was lying on the ground with Kate kneeling over me. She unsheathed a dagger and thrust the knife right into my heart. Blood began to pool everywhere. As Kate watched, she grinned wickedly and a chilling laugh filled the air. As I replayed the nightmare in my head, I didn't realize that I had started to shake, my eyes in a distant trance.

"Casey," Brennon called to me, as he grabbed my shoulders and gave them a quick shake. When I gave no response, Myra stepped in and led me back to my tent. She stripped me of my sweaty clothes and re-dressed me. She laid me in my bed and stayed with me through the night. When I trembled, Myra soothed me, and when I woke with a start, she hummed me back to sleep. After a few hours of that routine, my voice returned.

"What did you see?" Myra asked me.

"There were images going through my head, like in a dream—but not like a dream—at the same time. It was like nightmares come to life," I breathed. Myra's gaze didn't waver; she wanted to know exactly what I saw. "Please, just look for yourself. I don't—can't—describe them," I told her. She nodded in understanding, seeing that I was still rattled.

Myra closed her eyes. Moments later, they flew open, mad with horror. "Oh, Casey … those weren't dreams," she said sympathetically. Her expression held all the pain I felt in my head. "This is a dark form of torture. Azlaya must have taught your sister to Thought Twist. It is when a person can take images, feelings, memories, good and bad, and manipulate them into horrific things. It is a form of Dark Magic."

"Dark Magic?" I mumbled.

"Yes. Three types of magic exist. The oldest magic is that of the three elements. The forest Nymphs," she gestured to herself, "taught others how to control water, wind, and earth. The second type comes from sorcerers. They taught people how to conjure spells, charms, and enchantments which modified the physical world around us."

"The ones written in the language of Old?" I asked. Myra nodded.

"The third type of magic is from the Sagen. They have existed in Alagia for as long as the Hunters have. They introduced the darker side of sorcery, Dark Magic. It mainly preys on our emotions, thoughts, feelings, and other mental abilities."

"Is it hard to learn?" I asked.

Myra opened her mouth, then closed it. She looked thoughtfully at something behind me, then spoke. "It is easier to learn if some part of your morality has been damaged," she said each word slowly, as if making sure she picked her words perfectly.

"And you think Kate has lost her moral judgment?" I pressed her.

"Casey," she said sympathetically. "She is with Azlaya. Her influence will change your sister in ways we cannot predict or prevent, and it is something we all must accept—even you."

I swept a hand through my hair. "So, what does this mean? That I have to put up with this every night?" I knew my sanity would be at risk if those nightly terrors constantly ran through my head.

"No. I can teach you how to protect yourself, but, Casey …" Myra began. "This kind of magic can get dangerous very quickly. It's more than just trying to block someone from reading your thoughts. It's also spells and counter spells to keep them from manipulating your mind."

I thought back to the images Kate had put in my mind. If anyone were put through what I'd seen often enough, they *would* go mad. Dark Magic sounded precarious, but Kate was probably knee deep in it, which meant, I would need to be as well. I had to keep up with everything that Azlaya fed into Kate's mind, if I was to stand any chance when we encountered each other. Then, an idea invaded my mind, and I couldn't escape it. If I wanted to know the student better, then I would need to study the teacher.

"Tell me about Azlaya," I said, catching Myra off guard.

She returned a quizzical look. "We have told you about her. What more do you wish to know?"

"No. I mean everything. Not just that she wants to take over Alagia. I need to know things about her, her childhood, her parents, friends, even her time here with the Hunters." Myra was still confused. I chewed my lip, thinking how to phrase this so that she would understand. "You have to know your enemy well enough to know how to beat them, right?"

Myra's green eyes glossed over me as she contemplated. "I understand."

"So tell me everything," I repeated.

"I do have something that may be more beneficial than my recounting," Myra said tentatively. "Before she left the Hunters, she had written journals. After she betrayed them, she didn't take them with her. I think reading her words is the best way to understand her."

Myra stood and beckoned me to follow. I dragged myself from my warm bed and trailed behind her to her home. Her large oak tree stood out amongst the others, because it was the only one of its kind. The trunk was over fifteen feet thick and she had carved a door into it. Two windows were on either side of the door and lush plants circled the foot of the trunk. One flower stood out among the others. It was bright pink with yellow edges, and its petals fluttered from an invisible breeze.

I hurried inside after Myra made an impatient sound. I had never been in her home before, and yet, it didn't surprise me that it smelled of the scented oils and floral fragrances that always wafted from her. It was much bigger on the inside than it looked from the outside. The main floor had a table in one corner with a small stool, and a bookshelf and plump chair in the opposite corner. A short staircase twisted up to another floor where I assumed her bed was. She had boxes, books, notebooks, and journals scattered everywhere. Myra started rifling through a wooden trunk stacked on other trunks. When she didn't find what she sought in that one, she moved onto another one. I glanced around the room and saw at least twenty similar trunks lining the walls, and there were more books through a door that led to the kitchen.

"Do you need help?" She didn't respond. "I can help, Myra." Still, she said nothing. I left her to search and went to gaze out her window. I stared at the mysteriously beautiful flower.

"Here it is," she breathed.

"What is that flower outside?" I asked her, still looking at it.

"A man I loved gave it to me before he died." Her eyes seemed to go out of focus, but she blinked it away.

I could see the pain and hurt in her face. "I'm sorry, Myra," I whispered. A half smile, half grimace formed on her lips. She held the worn journals out to me, and I collected them in my arms.

"Casey … be careful with those," Myra warned me. "By the end, she was a troubled person with a dark past. There are things in there that even I shouldn't know," she paused as though she wanted to say more but was lost for words.

I could see in her eyes that I was going to find disturbing things. I nodded my understanding. Myra watched me intently as I left the tree. With each step I took, anxiety and worry seethed deeper into my body, but if this is what I had to do to better understand the monster that had my sister, then so be it. Besides, by learning more about Azlaya, I would learn more about the person my sister might become. I gripped the books tightly as I walked to my tent.

I placed the journals on my bed, then knelt and pulled the book of fire from under the bed. I felt like it was a school night, and I had hours of homework to do that would easily keep me up past midnight. However, it wasn't a school night, and I was tired. It was still the early hours of the morning, and I gratefully shoved all the books back under my bed and went back to sleep.

I woke as the sun crept over the horizon. Restless and unable to sleep any longer, I dressed and went to find something to eat. I went to the circle of logs, where the Hunters ate their meals. In the center, at the fireplace, I saw Gwen boiling a pot of water. Other Hunters sat around, leisurely eating. Breakfast was usually slower than other meals of the day, because everyone was scattered about doing their own thing in the morning.

I chimed a few 'good mornings' to passing Hunters and took a seat next to Gwen. She greeted me and handed me a cup of herbal tea. I thanked her and lifted the hot tea to my mouth. Regardless of the tea burning my lips, its warmth coursed through my veins, revitalizing me.

"We heard about what happened last night," Gwen said softly. I wrapped my hands tighter around the cup. Nearby Hunters surrendered their attention to us and listened. "I'm sorry," Gwen added.

I stole a glance at her face. "I guess I shouldn't expect any less," I said bitterly and took another sip.

Another Hunter broke into our conversation. "At first we did not think much of you, since we hardly knew you." I was mildly offended. "But I think I speak for everyone here when I say that now that we do know you, we all feel horrible that you have been dragged into this war, that Veronica betrayed you, and that you are losing your sister to Azlaya. We all," she said gesturing to everyone who sat nearby, "wish we could do more to help." I didn't recognize her, but I smiled, thankful for her and the others' concern.

"Thank you—all of you—but I don't think there is anything more you can do right now. Whatever fight that is about to happen is between my sister and me," I told them sounding defeated about my future. Whatever energy the tea gave me was quickly dying inside me.

"You are giving our world a chance at freedom," Gwen added. "Something we cannot begin to repay you for." I smiled meekly.

"It's not over yet," I said lightly, hoping to brighten the mood. One Hunter decided it was time to change the subject, and we all went around the circle saying something we would do after the war.

"I'm going to go climb the Great Mountains of Eileen," a blonde girl said perkily.

"I'm going to go to Calem, not worry about protecting the castle, and spend an entire day at the market and touring the kingdom!" another shouted excitedly.

"I'm going to attend a grand ball with a Huntsman!" a girl with black hair yelled. We all laughed, and it continued all morning.

When asked what I would do, I had to think about it for a while. I had never entertained the thought, so I lightheartedly said, "I think I'll eat an entire carton of Black Raspberry Chip ice cream." All the Hunters asked what ice cream was, and I spent the rest of breakfast explaining it to them.

After my explanation, I finally departed from the still-giddy Hunters. They were all so happy when talking about what they would do when the fighting ended. It gave them hope for a better future. I loved seeing them that way, because they weren't just warriors, they were also girls.

As I left the light atmosphere we created, a heavier one set in. I remembered all the reading I had to do in my tent and groaned. I went inside and decided to start with the book of fire, since I had ignored it for so long.

I pulled the book from under my bed and set it in my lap. Before I opened it, I examined my hands. The marks that appeared on them in the burnt clearing were still absent. I cautiously opened the book, greatly fearing the burning sensations would return.

The book was open and still no pain. I stopped worrying about my hands and focused on the writings. On the first page, '*Ignus*' was scrawled in gold letters. The last time I had looked in the book, it had been empty, but to my surprise, it was full of twisting and curving writing. I flipped through the book, hiding it among the sheets whenever someone passed by my tent's waving flap. I used probably the most useful spell I'd learned thus far to translate the entire book into English. The first pages told of the origins of fire and that it was the fourth element. I finally realized that Myra had left something out earlier. She told me about the three elements; however, she never once mentioned fire.

I was flipping rapidly through the pages when something caught my eye. Across the top of the page 'Lightning' was written. Beneath the title, it looked like someone had recorded a story. I curled my legs up, got comfortable, and read.

> *Long ago, before the Nymphs learned the ways of fire, the dragons were the only bearers. A boy lived in a village near the Valley of the Dragons, and he saw them flying overhead all the time. Seeing them fly past was not uncommon, but no one ever dared to seek out where they lived. Then one day the Nymph boy decided to follow a dragon he saw pass over his house. He*

tracked the beast through the mountains that hid the valley and came to find even more dragons. He found the leader of the dragons, Ander.

Ander was a cruel dragon that lived only for power. All the other dragons feared him, but the boy bravely approached him. Since people never ventured into the realm of the dragons, seeing a boy both excited and scared the beasts. They were equally as curious about him, as he was about them.

"Ander," the boy called out to the leader dragon, who lay on a bed of leaves. "King of the Fire Breathers. I have watched you for years, and now I come to you asking for something great. The Nymphs are able to control water, air, and earth; however, they have not yet been able to master the power of fire. Please, teach me your ways of bearing it," the boy said.

Ander became furious at the boy's request. He told the boy to leave the valley and never return. Disappointed, the boy had begun making his way back to his village, when a sympathetic dragon, named Neera, stopped him. She had watched the boy face Ander and thought him incredibly brave. Neera saw no evil in the boy and assumed his intentions were good. She agreed to teach the boy the dragons' ways of bearing fire.

After months of learning from Neera, the boy finally learned all the secrets of the dragons, and during that time, Neera and the boy became great friends. But one day, one of the other dragons caught Neera teaching the boy and rushed back to Ander to tell him. Ander was furious with Neera for giving away the dragons' ancient secrets. He decided that the boy would have to be killed in order to keep the dragons' secrets concealed. When Neera learned of this, she told the boy to go far from the Valley of the Dragons and to never return, for Ander would kill him. The boy did as he was told, and Neera went to face Ander.

As she stood before Ander, the other dragons jeered at her, and Ander decided her fate. "Please, Ander, leave the boy alone. Kill me instead," Neera pleaded.

Ander thought about this and said, "I'll keep you alive as long as I need you." Neera feared for the boy, hoping that he would stay away.

The boy soon learned of Neera's fate and was horrified. He refused to let his faithful friend die at the hand of the tyrant, Ander. He began to plan how he would save her. The boy knew that the dragons easily outnumbered him, so he began to strategize. Neera had once told him that lightning was derived from fire, but she never taught him how to produce it, for reasons he did not know. Despite that, he began to train himself to control it.

Lightning was something that the dragons had never learned to manipulate. It was the uncontrollable beast of nature, as the dragons referred to it. The boy knew that lightning would be his only way to pose a threat to the dragons. Once he mastered it, he was ready to face Ander.

The boy entered the Valley of the Dragons boldly. He walked straight up to Ander and demanded Neera's release. Ander laughed at the boy and told him that he could join her in death. That made the boy even angrier, and he thrust lightning from the sky and threw it at the ground. It hit right in front of Ander, who roared in fear and scrambled to get away from the foreign magic.

The boy looked at Ander's scared face and smiled. He threatened to destroy the valley unless Neera was released unharmed. Ander declined the boy's demands, so for three days, the boy would return and destroy a little more of the dragon's valley. On the fourth day, the boy came to negotiate one last time before destroying the valley completely. The boy's last threat was to take the rest of Ander's land away and kill his mate. Ander, fearful to lose his valley and mate, was forced to set Neera free.

The boy and Neera left the valley and never returned. They flew all over the world, teaching the secrets of the dragons and controlling lightning, first to the Nymphs, who passed it on to the sorcerers. Throughout the years, the art of Fire Bearing has been passed on from generation to generation, but Ander never forgot the lightning and the destruction it brought. He and his followers never managed to learn how to control lightning, so from that time on, dragons have always feared it.

I set the charred book beside me. I vividly remembered Danzinar trembling with fear when I discovered the book. He must have known that the book contained secrets of controlling what he and his kind feared most. I thought about the story and began realizing how similar it was to mine. The boy entered the strange world of the dragons, just as I had come to Alagia. He learned about fire and lightning, as I was learning about the elements and spells. The only difference between our stories was that the boy won his battle; I had no guarantee I would win mine.

I pushed the red book away and pulled some of Azlaya's journals into my lap. Dates were scribbled on the inside covers. I found the earliest one, opened the yellowed pages, and began reading. As I read, most of the entries were of Azlaya's youth or her early experiences with the Hunters. Many held little promise for use in the future. However, one stood out that would change the way I saw Azlaya forever.

Today, many years ago, was my mother's birthday. I made her favorite sweet tart and was giving her all my earnings from that month's pay, so we could have a fancy dinner that night. I walked to her room with the tart in hand and money in the other. I knocked before entering, and I heard a thud on the other side of the door and a strangled sound. Then, I heard whimpers of pain and small cries, as if of a child. I slowly inched open the door, and what I found stole the breath from me.

My mother was in a heap in a corner. Bruises covered her face and neck. I dropped what I held and rushed to her, but I hit something strong and was thrown back against the wall. It was my father, who had been in the north fighting in the war between Calem and Eileen. There was a change in power, and the cities' tensions boiled over. His long absence resulted in my mother's loneliness. He had finally returned home.

I watched, horrified, as he stood over my mother with a dagger in his hand. His face was red, but I didn't know why. My mother pressed herself into the corner, arms wrapped around her swollen stomach. My brother or sister lived inside her, and we had spent every day since we found out preparing for his or her arrival.

"I thought you loved me, Rhea!"

"I do, it was a … an accident."

He stepped away from her as she slowly and shakily rose to her feet. She winced at the pain but stared him in the eye. I loved my mother for being strong, but I still didn't know why it was necessary at that moment.

My father was absent ten of the thirteen years of my life; two from the war, but about the other eight, my mother and I had no idea. Now I knew he was out drinking until he passed out. He fathered many children with many different women. The man was more a stranger to me than a father.

Over the years, he would infrequently visit for a couple days. He expected hot breakfasts in the morning and dinners fit for a king in the evenings. He and I only talked if it was a complete necessity. I worked at the village bakery, and my earnings went towards food and taxes. My mother did all that she could to get more money as well. She was a sorceress and became the village's doctor. She cared for the sick and concocted home remedies.

When my father stayed with us, our money went straight to paying for his alcohol. Most nights, I heard my mother crying, because her husband was out drinking instead of spending what little time they had together with her. When he was home, he was a dictator. He would do as he pleased, without thoughts of my mother and me. He threatened me after the smallest acts of disobedience. I never understood why my mother, who had raised me my whole life, had no say when he was around. She lost all powers of speech, as if it was a privilege given to her that he could take away. While he seemed indifferent about my existence, I despised him.

"When did it happen?" he asked through gritted teeth.

"After the Winter Festival ..."

"Mother, what's going on?" I asked. I did not know what she was talking about. The winter festival was months ago. We went out to celebrate with the neighbors and stayed out late into the night. My mother's gaze shifted to me for the first time since I entered the room. She eyed the tart and the money on the ground, and her lips pulled up at the corners.

"Azlaya, honey. Go down to the kitchen and start dinner, all right?" From her eyes, I could tell she begged me to obey. She would often say things that only I could hear in my mind. She did that as I stood terrified, repeating to me that everything would be all right.

I nodded numbly and exited the room, with tear-filled eyes. Seeing my mother in that state was horrifying. I was halfway down the stairs when I heard her scream and collapse.

After that, I hardly remember what happened. A second later, I was at my mother's side, trying to stop the bleeding coming from the multiple stab wounds in her stomach. I cried until it hurt, and I held her hand as she told me not to worry and that I was going to be all right. She repeated the words 'I'm sorry' so many times I was beginning to think about the atrocity of her crime. Now I know that the child she carried was, indeed, not my father's. However, she didn't deserve to be murdered.

My mother kissed me right before she took her last gulps of air. It remains hard for me to put in writing what it felt like. I kissed my mother's face over and over again, caressing her cheek and rubbing her bruises. It didn't matter though; she couldn't feel it. My father came up behind me.

"Let's go. I don't want to be here when neighbors arrive. We are going north."

"NO!" I screeched. "I'm not leaving her. You're a monster; you killed her!"

"Come on," he answered, as he tucked the dagger back into its sheath.

"I'm not going anywhere with you—you murderer!"

I could feel the heat building up inside me as it boiled to the surface. Since my mother was a sorceress, she naturally passed her magical abilities on to me. My powers sparked to life as the loathing I felt towards my father took control of my body, invaded his insides, and killed him. He did not, and would never know that I was a sorceress. He collapsed, clutching himself, and tumbled onto the floor. Shock and fear twisted on his face as he died where he lay. Blood dripped from his eyes, mouth and nose. I couldn't stand in that room any longer as both of my parents lay dead.

I ran from the house, tears rolling off my face. I could not bear the thought of leaving my mother, but I had to get away. I had to get away from it all. I was terrified that I would be hauled before the royal court for murdering my parents, so I destroyed any and all evidence. I quickly set the house on fire and headed south. The smoke and fire masked the ill deeds as I fled. Along with the house burned any memories and ties that were connected to me.

Even now, as I remember what I did to my father, I feel no regrets. He tormented me my entire life, and when he took my mother away from me, I refused to let him live. There is far too much that time cannot heal. I won't speak of her anymore, but I loved my mother tremendously. She was my entire support system and loved me more than anyone could hope to be loved. Sure, you could call me disturbed or depraved, but I can truthfully say that evil is not always something a person is predetermined to be. Sometimes it is what they become because of someone else.

I read the last sentence over and over again, trying hard to picture Azlaya writing it, but from what I'd seen, I couldn't. I read on about when she and Kyraine first met and how they went on to love each other as sisters. Then came the entries about when Kyraine's trust in her started to dwindle, until finally, the last entry, detailing Azlaya leaving the Hunters.

It said that the night she planned to run away, she was going to kill Kyraine. When Azlaya approached Kyraine's tent, she heard Kyraine talking to someone about why she refused to allow Azlaya become Mistress of the Hunt.

> *"I can't just hand it over like a sword, it doesn't work that way. But she has changed. She speaks of wanting to take over the four kingdoms and ally the Sagen. I can see it in her, her cravings for power. It's driving her mad, and I can't let her lead the Hunters that way. But it's not only that; she isn't ready for the responsibility. She doesn't understand what it means to lead these girls and to devote your life to them. She won't admit it, but she is fragile, and it would break her. I've seen it happen before and I don't want it to happen to her."*

I couldn't believe that Kyraine had said those words. Saying that Azlaya was fragile was like calling stainless steel 'delicate.' It was evident though, that after Azlaya had overheard that, she realized that deep down Kyraine loved her. Azlaya recorded her last moments in the camp, and ran away with a heavy heart and fast-forming plots to gain power.

When I finished leafing through all of her journals, I had learned so much about Azlaya's life with the Hunters. I could sense her thirst for power more profoundly through her words. During the process of reading the journals, I began to see Azlaya as a person. I started to see her as a human and not just an evil tyrant out to destroy Alagia. I still couldn't picture Kate as the horrible person she was supposed to become, as described by the prophecy. To me, Kate was still my sister and very human.

Concern stirred within me. I thought back to history class, when we were studying World War I. Soldiers were told to think of their enemies as abhorrent, wretched monsters, hardly considered human. That way, when confronting their enemy on the battlefield, it would be easier to kill them with a clearer conscience. It pained my heart to think like that. Yet, no matter how hard I tried to picture it, I could never face Kate on a frontline, army behind me, ready to kill her. It was a thought that lingered in the back of my head. I always pushed it aside when it resurfaced, never wanting to confront it, but it always returned.

Chapter 27: Kate

A WATCHFUL EYE followed my every move, scrutinizing and criticizing. I maneuvered around the room with grace and ferocity. Every time I shot a spell at a Sagen, I had no hesitations. It was enough to provoke Azlaya into complementing me from her throne.

It was our nightly routine, and it always ended with the promise of the same thing the next night. I hadn't been in the castle more than a few days, but because of my earlier experience with sorcery, we moved quickly through lessons. Azlaya determined that I had mastered the three elements and simple sorcery. She and I were starting to explore Dark Magic.

"Again," Azlaya instructed firmly.

I knocked the Sagen backwards with a spell. He stood quickly and threw an enchantment at me. It hit me in the legs, causing them to lock together. I thrust a slow-motion spell at him, which he dodged. He lifted his arms, and black smoke floated out of his long sleeves. Suddenly, two more Sagen stepped out of the thick fog. I scrambled to undo the spell on my legs as one of the Sagen sent a spell hurtling at me. I skillfully redirected it back at him, and he disappeared upon contact.

Teleportation spell, I thought. I turned on the remaining two hooded ghosts. Casting a shape-shifter enchantment on one, his body began to ripple and change. He collapsed to the floor, his body jerking around as if he were having a seizure. Finally, his black cape fell away and out stepped a giant grizzly bear. I manipulated his thoughts into wanting to kill the remaining Sagen, who just stared at the beast.

The bear lunged at the Sagen, tearing him apart. When the bear was finished, all that was left was a torn cape. The bear turned, all his anger directed at me. I grinned, watching the bear thunder towards me. I raised my hand and lifted the bear from the ground. I changed the bear back into the hooded figure then, leaving him dangling in the air, I saw a sword mounted on the wall. I flicked my other hand, sending the sword piercing into the Sagen.

Because it was night and darkness flooded the room, both Sagen only disintegrated, and reappeared a few minutes later. It was one of their many defining qualities. In the dark, they could not be killed and would only reappear. Only in the light could they actually die. Azlaya informed me that we trained at night, so that I could practice on the Sagen, without killing off her army as I trained. However, I didn't know where I had sent the third Sagen using the Teleporation spell.

"Amusing." It was difficult to get approval from Azlaya, but every so often, she would nod and offer some congratulatory words. "Have you been working on the Thought Twisting spell?"

I nodded. She leaned back in her chair and gestured for me to demonstrate. I turned away from her and gazed out a window. I could feel Casey's mind somewhere in the vast forest, and I used the spell. I pulled memories and emotions from her and changed them into horrible scenes that would play across her head like a movie. At first it was easy, but then I could feel resistance against me. She was pushing me out of her mind, and that was the first time I really felt a different kind of hate towards me. Back home, we would fight and say we "hated" each other, but it was obviously never genuine hate. However, the feeling I felt from her tightened my gut and twisted my insides. I immediately stopped invading her head.

"What happened?" Azlaya asked, bored.

"She was pushing me out," I answered absentmindedly.

"Then find your way back in," Azlaya said, as though it was the most obvious answer in the world.

A maid came into the throne room and delivered crystal glasses full of water to us. As she turned to leave, Azlaya stopped her and beckoned her over. The servant girl shuffled nervously over to Azlaya. She stood at attention, and I could see sweat beads forming on her forehead.

"Get Veronica," Azlaya ordered.

The maid bowed and quickly returned with the girl. I'd never met her before, but Azlaya told me Veronica would be a powerful sorceress one day, too. She had dark hair that she tied in a braid. She wore a green tunic and tall riding boots. She stood with her arms crossed as she studied me.

"You called?" she said to Azlaya, but kept her gaze fixed on me.

"Her Thought Twisting is weak, and she needs work with breaking through barriers," Azlaya told Veronica.

"Can't you use one of the Sagen?" Veronica answered quickly, flicking her gaze to Azlaya.

"No, Veronica. Remember what I did for you. You are indebted to me, and you would be wise not to forget it. Now, shall we try this again?" Veronica didn't surrender her stance, but she shifted her eyes back to me.

"Where should we begin?" Veronica said stiffly. The standoff between the two of them made me want to grab a bowl of popcorn and sit back on a couch. Veronica studied me thoroughly before deciding. "Try to penetrate my mind," she ordered plainly. I looked at her for a moment, wondering if she really meant what she said. I thought her insane for wanting me to practice such a torturous spell on her.

"Go on," Azlaya prodded me. "Discover something interesting about her."

I angled my body to face Veronica. She was young, no more than five years older than me. Her face was pale and sleep tugged at her eyes. Casey always told me I had a gift for reading people and their emotions, and I didn't need a spell to see that something bothered her. She crossed her arms over her chest and matched my gaze. I was surprised, because in the week I had been in Alagia, I noticed that everyone shied away from me. Similar to people's reaction to Azlaya, no one dared to look me straight in the eye. Everyone, that is, except Veronica.

I began to concentrate. My eyes narrowed slightly as I tried desperately to break into Veronica's thoughts. It felt like I was trying to pry my fingers into an elevator, but no matter how hard I pulled, the doors wouldn't open.

"Well?" Azlaya coaxed me. I tilted my head curiously as I held Veronica's gaze. She didn't look smug, only bored. It was as though she knew from the beginning that I wouldn't be able to break into her thoughts.

"I ... I don't know," I said, disoriented. Azlaya's mouth pulled into a tight line.

"That means you're average. Only extraordinary sorcerers could break through my mind's defenses. I have fortified them for years," Veronica told me confidently. I was sure that Azlaya would be able to break through them, but I dismissed the thought.

Azlaya broke my silent trance. "Veronica, you will train Kate in Dark Magic and make sure she has mastered the spells." Veronica made a sour face. "I'm retiring for the night."

Veronica finally ripped her eyes away from me and called out to Azlaya. "You won't assist in her training?" Her voice peaked higher as if it were a mild challenge.

"I have a war to win," Azlaya responded coldly and then swept out of the room.

Veronica lazily walked over to Azlaya's throne. A platter of fruit lay untouched on a small side table. Veronica picked up an apple and bit into it. I asked, "So you're going to help me?" She gave me a look as though to say she didn't have a choice. "What can you teach me that I don't already know?" I asked.

Veronica's eyes flashed to me. "All right, listen carefully. It means nothing to me that you are one of the girls from the prophecy, and it means even less to me how good you believe your skills to be. In fact, until you can break into my mind and make me squirm like you do your sister, you will remain rather insignificant in my eyes." Each word she said was full of more hatred than the last one. I wasn't sure what I did to make her so angry with me, but I understood her point, and for some reason I welcomed the tension between us.

So, I kept practicing on Veronica, working tirelessly to see into her thoughts. Since no one had ever performed Thought Twisting on me, I never realized how horrible it was. I still couldn't dismiss the fact that Casey sided with the Hunters, who had killed our mother. When I needed a break from Veronica's mental defenses, I moved on to Casey's, and I was relentless with her deserved punishment. Oftentimes, I would catch her off guard so she wouldn't be able to block me as quickly, or at all. When I tortured Casey around Veronica, she would give me a look as though she felt sorry for Casey. She even gave me hints that she disapproved of what I did to my sister. I never confronted her about it, but I figured there was more to her than met the eye. That was why she needed to defend her mind so well, because of the secrets she concealed inside.

However, after all the time we ended up spending together for the next several days, she did teach me many useful dark spells that allowed me to torture the minds of my opponents and drive them to madness without so much as lifting a finger. We would do training exercises to help me react faster, anticipate my opponents' moves, and even sense what they were going to do before they even knew. Every day I grew stronger, faster, smarter, and every day was another day closer to my confrontation with Casey. I was determined to avenge our betrayed mother. And the person I once thought was my best friend, now stood in my way.

Chapter 28: Casey

MY BOTTOM WAS numb from the frigid night and from sitting on the log. I tried desperately to rub the feeling back into my arms. A fire danced in the middle of everyone attending the meeting. Adalia lay curled at my feet, nodding off to sleep every so often. Myra and Brennon sat on either side of me, and I saw shivers rack both their bodies. The wind whipped at our faces as Kyraine stood to address the crowd.

"As we all know, the Sagen are the Warriors of the Shadows, and can therefore disappear into the shadows when needed. For those who haven't witnessed it, the Sagen become less human than they already are in shade or at night. They can melt into the shadow to evade harm. However, in broad daylight, they can be killed. That is why we must attack at dawn and during the day, when shadows are scarce and the sun will become our best ally." Mumbles surfaced from the crowd, but Kyraine continued. "We all know that this fight has been long and hard. The only difference between now, and a few months ago, is that we know an end to this battle finally exists. We will finally wander through these trees without fears of a Sagen attack, and we can finally tell the people of Alagia that they do not need to fear Azlaya anymore. That day will happen, Hunters, and it's in our grasp," Kyraine looked around at those gathered, trying to make eye contact with everyone present. "I could not think of a better group of people to share in that day with."

All the Hunters let out an elated cheer and held up their bows to Kyraine. As their revelry filled the air, I felt a sensation like something was prying in my head. I blinked rapidly, and then refocused my gaze. I brushed aside the strange feeling and started to clap along with other applauding Hunters. Then, it happened again, but this time the sensation was much worse. I felt like I was in a dream, but I was awake, just in a distant state. Then, a voice intruded into my head. I immediately recognized it and felt sick.

"You're playing with fire, Casey. You're going to burn; I'll ensure it," Kate's voice rang in my ears.

Get out! I thought fiercely, my teeth clenched tight. In that moment, I felt so much hatred towards Kate that I had to remind myself that she was my sister. Yet, she constantly kept breaking into my mind and torturing me. I excused myself from the clearing and bolted away from the excited chanting.

My eyes started to blur and the world began to spin. I thought I might faint, so I stopped moving, braced myself against a tree, and trained my vision on the ground. I was hyperventilating, my breathing ragged. I had to get away, but I couldn't run from what was inside my head. My heart pounded with fear. I slid down the tree and curled into a sitting position. My head throbbed as though I had a migraine. I sat in my misery, trying to get Kate's grasp on my mind to ease. In my disorientation, I heard a barely audible noise. It was laughing, a menacing chuckle that echoed inside me. I threw my hands over my ears and buried my head between my knees.

Get the hell out of my head!

I sat in the eerie silence while the turmoil ran rampant inside me. Everything seemed and felt unreachable. A blood-curdling scream built in my throat, and then something was shaking me, as if trying to rattle me from my strange state. I moved with the speed of a cobra as I darted from whoever found me. The pain ate away at me, and I waited desperately for it to end. I was livid that I had to go through the ordeal again, but my thoughts were too scattered to try and stop it.

In my agony, a sound broke through the perturbation in my mind. Myra tried to calm me, "Casey, push her out of your mind! Concentrate and close your mind!"

I understood what she said. But understanding and doing were two completely different things in my current state. My head felt as if it were splitting in two, and my muscles burned with sharp pains. I begged incomprehensibly to be relieved of the torture. I grabbed my arm and dug my fingernails into it, trying to redirect my attention to a different pain. Cold fingers pried my own from my death-grip grasp. They finally succeeded, and copper and rusty smells wafted to my nose.

"Casey, please listen to me. She's playing with your mind. You have to lock her out from your thoughts. It's the only way, Casey, please," the earnest voice pleaded.

I tried to clear my mind and make it go blank. *Get out.* I pictured myself trying to push a door closed, while she was on the other side trying to open it. *Get out.* I bit my lip and blood spilled into my mouth. I forgot everything, and thought of serenity, refusing Kate any more access to my thoughts, memories, or emotion. *Get out!* Finally, I heard the beautiful sound of a slamming door ringing in my ears. I had won.

But, before I could celebrate my victory, I heard Kate's voice one more time. "You are strong." She sounded surprised. I could picture her face, as though she gazed upon me with slight approval.

It took me a few minutes to realize that my mind was slowly clearing itself. As quickly as she came, Kate was gone, and my splitting headache was fading. I don't know how long I sat idly, as I regained my composure. My twin sister invaded my mind and used her magic to torment me. I felt her joy in watching me squirm under her power, and that sent shivers up my spine. My *twin sister*, who had been my best friend all my life, had finally become my worst enemy. But what unnerved me the most was that she knew me better than anyone, and as I told Myra, it's easier to beat your enemy when you know them, inside and out. I didn't want to believe that Kate meant the things she did, but my doubt was replaced by the inescapable fact that she wanted to hurt me. No matter how lost Kate may have been, I could sense, so strongly, that what she did to me, pained her in the very least. Thinking about it slowly ripped the seams out of my heart.

In that moment, I wanted to walk away from everything. I wanted to leave Alagia and flee for home, but I knew that wasn't an option. Myra believed in me so much, as did Kyraine and the Hunters. They risked their lives every day protecting me, and I owed them more than abandonment. It was easier to nurture hostility towards Kate as she tried constantly to corrupt my mind. Besides, as much as I didn't want to accept it, Kate was different. She and I would never be the same again. Our futures had been destined to shape Alagia since our infancy, and it was between Kate and me to decide who would do it. I dismissed all thoughts of my childhood with Kate, of our friendship, and of our love, and focused on what lay ahead.

I slowly opened my eyes, unclenched my fists, and raised my head. Myra had half of a grimace, half of a smile spread on her face. "Are you—" she started.

"Fine," I whispered with determination.

I was through with the unexpected torture, and I finally felt I was ready to face Kate. Countless things had changed in such a small amount of time, and while I may not have been ready to face her to the death, I wanted to confront her. The burning hatred I felt towards Kate had, unbeknownst to me, turned into a real burning. Myra drew her hand away in shock. My eyes darted to her, thinking that Kate was trying to pry into Myra's mind as well. However, when she brought her gaze to mine, shock, anger, defeat, and sorrow were all reflected in her eyes. "You're a Fire Bearer?"

Chapter 29: Myra

"WHY DIDN'T YOU tell me?" Casey's breathing returned to normal, since her sister had finally retreated from Casey's mind. My hand still tingled where I burnt my hand on Casey's skin. She was intent on looking at the ground.

"I wanted to keep it to myself. I didn't know what it was," she responded, eyes still cast downward.

I sighed impatiently. I should have seen the signs before. I recalled the day Matthew and his men arrived, and Brennon had pointed out that Casey smelled of soot. I was so distracted by everything going on around me that I couldn't see what had happened right in front of me.

"How did you ... how?" I was lost for words.

Casey lifted her head, and shame plagued her eyes. "I found a clearing where everything was burnt. There was a book with my mother's name on it." She shrugged her shoulders. The result was plain to see.

I remember the day I became a Fire Bearer as if it happened yesterday. I was in Calem, training with other Nymphs my age. We all made the decision to pursue the art of fire after mastering the sorcerers' spells. But when we started the ceremony, everyone, except for me, resigned. We were all warned of the excruciating pain and told that sometimes, if you lacked worthiness, the ability wouldn't be bestowed upon you. We were even told that some people who couldn't handle or control that type of power died immediately. However, I was determined to finish my training with that last milestone. I completed the ceremony alone, and though the description of the pain was accurate, I survived. Afterwards, I became a fully realized sorceress, something only a few Nymphs had ever accomplished.

Fire was a magic that, like Dark Magic, became dangerous quickly. It was the one element that could easily escape your control. Casey told me she hadn't tried to do anything with it, and I was so relieved. However, she did read her mother's book detailing the power of the fire. Layna wrote the book shortly after her marriage. She had recently become a full-fledged sorceress and began to document all the different fields of magic. Her book of fire was one of the many books that were currently scattered throughout Alagia.

"I know about lightning, too," Casey interrupted my thoughts. I knew of the darkest magic that existed and lightning still unnerved me. I didn't know if it was due to its unpredictability, or because it's what killed Layna. Casey still didn't know how her mother died, and I wanted to keep it that way.

"I guess we can't avoid this now," I began, making Casey swell with guilt. "Lightning and fire, as I'm sure you already know, are perilous. Learning to control them takes a great deal of practice and discipline. I can teach you, but it won't be easy."

Casey averted her gaze and pursed her lips. "How fast can you teach me?"

My eyebrows furrowed. "Why?"

She let out a curt breath, "I'm done, Myra. I'm not letting Kate hurt me anymore, and I'm not going to sit around and wait for what just happened to happen again. The Hunters have been ready. So have you and Kyraine ... and now I'm ready," Casey said, so boldly and defiantly that she sounded like her mother. I smiled thinly at her sudden bravery. Internally, my heart dropped, knowing what her readiness meant in terms of the prophecy.

Casey jumped to her feet and stormed back to the Hunters with me in her wake. She burst into the clearing; Kyraine still spoke to the Hunters. Casey was at the opposite side of the clearing and shouted to Kyraine.

"Kyraine, may I speak?" Kyraine must have seen the wildness I'd seen earlier in Casey's eyes and surrendered the Hunters' attention. I exchanged glances with Kyraine, as Casey addressed the crowd. "Most of you only know me as the girl from the prophecy. Some of you know me as Layna's daughter, and others know me as Casey. But none of those titles matters to me, because there is only one thing I've come to care about in my time here, and that is all of you," Casey said boldly. She matched the girls' gazes as though she spoke to each one individually. "And I'm not going to sit here and allow Azlaya to threaten the peace of this land anymore. I'll admit that for a while I didn't know exactly whether I would follow through with a promise I made when I first came here. I thought that things were out of my control, and that I had no power to shape my future. But I've come to realize that the one thing that no one, not my sister, not even Azlaya can ever take away from me, is the power to choose. It's up to us to determine how we want this to end." Casey paused to take a breath and to let her thoughts catch up to her mouth. "And I don't know about all of you, but I know how I want this to end, and I can tell you this—it is not with Azlaya winning this war!" She stressed her last words, and a tumultuous roar erupted from the Hunters. They pumped their fists, clapped, and raised their weapons to Casey. "And Kyraine," Casey shouted over the noise, "with your permission, I'll help lead the attack on Azlaya's castle."

I saw Kyraine's eyes light up, not with the excitement about the attack, but at seeing the Hunters' morale boosted. She nodded once to Casey, granting her permission. "We'll attack in a fortnight. That will give us plenty of time to draw up offensive plans and make any final preparations," Kyraine added.

Two weeks would be enough time to train Casey in the basics of her new abilities with fire and lightning, and it also gave her more time to prepare to face Sagen warriors and her sister. Finally, our plans were no longer stagnant.

Kyraine looked to me expectantly. "I'll rally the Nymphs." The imminent fight was finally approaching.

Chapter 30: Casey

EVERY STEP I took was echoed with a crunch. The frostbitten grass made our march through the trees a little louder than we wanted, but the Hunters were masterful when it came to stealth. Kyraine was on my right and Myra on my left, and the massive army of Hunters trailed behind us. The sun began to rise from its slumber and shed a pink hue throughout the black sky.

I felt like I was repeating my first journey to the castle, and with every step closer, my adrenaline rose. Inching closer to my foretold destiny made my feet feel heavy as lead. I knew that I had to face Kate, but I hadn't thought too much about the last part of the prophecy: one will be ended by her loving bloodline. When Kate attacked my mind, I felt sudden hatred towards her as though it were a tangible thing. Whatever Azlaya had told her, it had cleared her conscience about hurting me. I wondered whether Kate's misplaced anger would be enough to make her want to kill me. I didn't think I had reached that point yet, no matter how much I despised her for the nightly tortures.

Anticipation of the impending battle tore at everyone's minds during the hours of the ascent to the castle. The Hunters wore their usual green tunics, thick belts around their waists holding a dagger and sword, and they had their bows in hand and arrows slung over their backs. They all tied their hair away from their faces, and the other sorceresses in the group drew signs on the Hunters' foreheads as a protection symbol. Once on the outskirts of the castle, about one hundred girls surrounded and secured the castle's perimeter. I stayed close to Kyraine as everyone prepared for battle.

In the silence, I heard a rustle behind me, and I whipped around and raised my hand in preparation to launch a spell. Two familiar faces emerged from the trees, and they glanced questioningly at my poised hand.

"Kyla, Isla, I haven't seen you two in a while," I greeted them.

Kyraine heard me and turned to the girls with a smile. "Hello, girls. Where are the others?" she asked, looking past them.

"They are here." Kyla gestured to the trees.

Suddenly, men, women, boys, and girl Nymphs began to walk out from the tree trunks. Their clothes were made of leaves, vines, flowers, and other plants, much like Myra's, yet each was unique. The forest Nymphs were everywhere, each surveying the scene. The waiting Hunters exchanged short glances with the Nymphs, but everyone's attention was trained on the castle.

"We couldn't resist the chance to topple Azlaya's throne," Kyla exclaimed.

"And for you, Cassia Coles, anything," Isla added, and the two bowed in unison. I thanked them, and we all turned back to the castle. On the outside, I was grateful to have more aid to face Azlaya, but on the inside, I prayed that if and when the time came, I wouldn't let all my supporters down.

"Myra said we will help hold the perimeter around the castle. We do not know what resources will be available to us once inside," Kyla explained quickly. The Nymphs could control the elements of nature, earth, water, and air, but couldn't rely on the chance that they could access them all inside the castle. Kyraine nodded, agreeing with Myra's judgment.

I watched as the Sagen began to come out of the dwindling shadows and continue guarding the doors. They floated and moved as eerily as I remembered. Everyone's eyes focused on their target and their target alone. The Hunters and Nymphs around the perimeter were to attack any Sagen on the wall, while those going inside the castle were responsible for the Sagen within. Last night, Kyraine called a meeting where we slowly went over our plan of attack, sorting through and analyzing each contingency. I was responsible for lowering the drawbridge, the Hunters would attack the

outer wall guards as they infiltrated the castle, the Nymphs would help se-
cure the perimeter, and Brennon and Danzinar were to take care of Azlaya's
dragon that was rumored to dwell within her castle. Everyone had a part
and everyone was ready.

Kyraine stared at the drawbridge as Myra beckoned me over. "On my
command," she told me. I heard the nerves in her voice, but like me, she
was ready to start the fight. I nodded my response and patiently waited for
my cue. I paused with bated breath for what seemed like an eternity, as
Kyraine signaled to the surrounding Hunters and Nymphs to prepare for
battle. Then, I heard Myra's faint whisper in my ear.

"Get ready," I said under my breath to those around me. I took one
last breath before the chaos broke out. *"Aperire."* Open.

A groaning sound resounded from the bridge. The chains jingled as
they started to wind down, lowering the bridge. Finally, when the bridge hit
the ground a massive thud made the ground tremble.

"Congelo." Freeze.

My eyes shot to where I heard a hissing cry of pain. Kyraine pierced
one of the Sagen with her arrow, and he didn't disintegrate into smoke as
he attempted to return to the shadows. The triumphant smile that spread
across Kyraine's face told me that the Sagen couldn't hide. The blinding sun
was going to be the death of them, and the Hunters knew it.

Suddenly, a shower of arrows fell upon the Sagen, and the battle began. Arrows from both sides were fired, and one by one Sagen soldiers fell
to piles of dust. The few seconds of victory were short-lived. The Sagen
threw flaming rocks at the Hunters below, easily knocking over and burning
some of the strongest trees surrounding the castle. The Hunters could do
nothing to stop the rocks and could only duck out of their way. Then, I saw
water shooting at the rocks and the Sagen on the wall. I turned, expecting
to see Myra throwing the water, but I found the Nymphs. I breathed a sigh
of relief and instructed to them to keep the rocks at bay.

A faint cry echoed through the trees and grew louder and louder until
it was ear-splitting. A huge shadow passed overhead and landed behind us.
Danzinar's massive body crushed the trees around him. Brennon slid off his
back and rushed over to me. He wore a thicker vest and pants and heavy

boots. His sword bounced on his hip and he had a dagger on his belt and one strapped to his shoe.

"Took you long enough," I greeted him and stole a glance at Danzinar, who growled at the castle.

"I'm here, aren't I?" He knocked his elbow against mine and, whether he knew it or not, it calmed me.

"We need to help get rid of the Sagen on the wall," I updated him.

"We can't do much from down here," he pointed out as he glanced at Danzinar.

The dragon had reached full size now; his body was as long as two and a half school buses and his wingspan was twice that. My gaze fell upon the dragon and something clenched around my gut. Brennon constantly rode the dragon, but I had never wanted to climb onto his scaly back. I sighed, and pushed aside my reservation. It wasn't the time to be hesitant, and I knew I had to do it. I had become used to ignoring my fears, and I stomped over to Danzinar and climbed on his back. Brennon jumped up behind me.

"Just don't let me die," I whispered to the dragon, and to no one. Brennon patted Danzinar's shoulder twice, his wings began to beat, and he began to rise into the sky. Sagen saw the huge target and began to launch the rocks of fire at us. I quickly used wind to redirect their path, but as more rocks came, I knew I wouldn't be able to deflect them all.

"Danzinar, get closer to the wall," Brennon ordered as the dragon flew as close as he could. I held my breath and jumped from his back onto the wall, trailed by Brennon. Danzinar shot away from us and took cover in the clouds above. I heard a whizzing sound soar by my ear. Hooded figures advanced on us. "You take those guys; I got these ones," Brennon called to me. I quickly nodded in agreement as he sped off.

I unsheathed my sword and drove it through the first Sagen. He collapsed in the sunlight and turned to dust as I hit the next one with the spear, square across the face and over the wall. The last Sagen threw a curse at me. I held my hand out to deflect it, but its strength slammed me into the stone wall. My head spun with dizziness, and my eyes blinked with confusion. He dropped in front of me and thrust my head against the wall and jabbed his bony, cold hand around my throat.

I clawed at his hand, and I let out a strangled whimper. I clumsily cast the first spell that came to mind. The Sagen was knocked away from me, and I scrambled to regain my balance. As I turned to run, I felt something tangle around my feet, and I already pictured the bruises before I hit the ground. I hurriedly undid the binding spell on my legs.

I tried to freeze him, but he used his own magic to prevent me from using mine. I swore as I lashed out and kicked him and rushed to get away. I flung a gust of wind at him, which knocked him backwards into several somersaults. I left him in a crumpled heap and tried to signal to the Hunters below to enter the gates. I met Kyraine's gaze and waved her forward, but she began shouting at me in alarm. Her mouth formed words I couldn't understand. I tried to tell her, but my breath was stolen by a blow from behind.

My knees crumpled under me, and I rolled over to face my attacker. I groaned from the pain. The Sagen warrior returned, and with greater ferocity. I was already so spent from before that I could barely block my midsection as he kicked me. My ears rang; I could hardly hear the tumultuous roar from Danzinar as he crashed upon the wall and snatched the Sagen in his jaws. He clamped his jaws shut, snapping the Sagen in two. Brennon rounded the corner and raced to my side. He knelt down, panic swelling in his eyes, and carefully pulled me into his arms. He climbed back onto Danzinar, who brought us back to Kyraine.

She and Myra rushed over. I groaned in such agony and pain that I was making Myra wince with every noise I made. My head, my stomach, my elbows and knees where I fell on them all hurt, but I wanted to push them all away and tell them to focus on the battle, not me.

"Stop," I objected, but I was plainly ignored. Myra used her healing skills to make the bruises and bumps less painful and fade. "I'm fine," my words slurred. I sounded drunk.

"You are *not* fine," Kyraine snapped. "Gwen, take the others through. I'll be there soon."

I studied the way Gwen and Kyraine bid what could have been their final farewells. A lot hung on Gwen and Kyraine's survival that day. If Gwen died, Kyraine would not be able to pass on her position, because none of the others Hunters were ready for the responsibility. It could take years before that happened, and that would mean more time for Brennon to wait for Kyraine. If Kyraine died, Gwen would become the Mistress of the Hunt, regardless of her readiness, and Brennon might die from his heartbreak. An unexpressed sadness lurked in their eyes, knowing that if one of them died, the other's life would change forever. Gwen departed, calling out to the Hunters to advance.

I fought to sit up straight, but my restraints weren't Myra or Kyraine; it was my own body. My abdominal area shook furiously, and I slumped onto my back.

"Casey this is going to sting," Myra warned me before she rubbed an earthy-smelling liquid over my cuts. I winced from the pain, but it was nothing unbearable. Again, I tried to lift myself. Kyraine helped pull me up.

"Kyraine, I'll be okay. Go," I pressed. She looked to Myra for any reason to stay. When she saw none, she whispered something to me, kissed my forehead, and joined her Hunters in battle. I watched her leave, a feeling of despair descending on me. Our goodbye was so brief, yet it could be the last we would ever have. I begged so earnestly on the inside that this would not be the last time I saw her alive. "What did she say to me?" I asked Myra, who was close enough to hear what Kyraine whispered into my ear.

"'*Dirige cor tuum ut te.*' It means, may your heart guide you," Myra translated.

I averted my eyes from the castle to Myra. They overflowed with apprehension, and Myra picked up on my fears right away. "What is it?"

"I'm afraid," I admitted. "I know I shouldn't be, and I'm ready because you all trained me well. I know I can do this, I know it but ..." my voice faded as I spoke.

"But what ...?"

"I'm afraid of what I might find."

"You mean you're scared to see what your sister's become?" Myra replied gently, understanding what I tried to say.

I nodded, but I couldn't let my fears get the best of me; I couldn't stop. Not when I stood on Azlaya's doorstep with Kyraine inside fighting with everything she had, knowing she might never see tomorrow.

"Casey, we all believe you can do this. We would not be here if we didn't think that. You've been through so much, and, if anything, you owe it to yourself to see what's beyond those doors." Myra was right. I owed it to myself to see what Kate truly was. Regardless of the prophecy, I wanted to see what Azlaya had done to her. I'm sure Kate wondered the same thing about me. Myra's eyes never wavered from my face. "Are you ready?" she asked.

I stood shakily and Adalia, who had been waiting in the trees with the other wolves, emerged and flanked my feet. It was enough of an answer for Myra. I forgot that Brennon had been with us the whole time, until he placed a firm hand on my arm. He gave me a reassuring squeeze and smiled. "You're ready, Casey," he said.

I returned his smile. "I'll see you later," I promised myself. Brennon nodded, and prepared to mount Danzinar and search the castle grounds for Azlaya's dragon. "All right, let's go," I said to Myra. We raced to the bridge and towards the future of Alagia.

The sounds of our pounding feet on the drawbridge were nothing in comparison to the tumultuous music of war. Shields clashed, swords swiped the air, and arrows sliced through everything. On top of that, spells were exploding all around us. Kyraine was the conductor, ordering people around while warding off attackers that threatened her. She was like a tiger, killing with brutality. The Hunters modeled their Mistress as they fought. A few windows along the walls were shattered by the Nymphs outside, allowing pools of light to flood into the rooms, making it easier to kill the Sagen. After all the weeks of rigorous training, it was finally paying off for the Hunters, who fought as fiercely as my mother's journals had described. I just hoped that when I faced Kate, I would be able to do the same.

Chapter 31: Kate

THE COURTYARD WAS a masterpiece; a chaotic, living mural of Hunters and Sagen battling. It was hard to tell who was winning, if anyone. Azlaya was right about the Hunters, though. They used their bows and arrows with frightening accuracy, easily hitting targets that were over fifty feet away. They could shoot an arrow and have a new one poised for fire within seconds.

The sound of the battle was a cacophony that strangely soothed my ears. I pulled myself away from the window and gathered a black cloak around my shoulders. I tied my hair back from my face and slipped my feet into my shoes.

The anger I felt towards Casey fueled my powers. The emotions associated with Casey bubbled forth whenever I thought about confronting her, but my hate demanded my attention.

Suddenly, years of playing dolls, chasing each other around the yard, and doing each other's hair seemed nonexistent. All those things were part of a past that was unreachable. Casey was an enemy—my enemy. Whatever love I had for her before was slipping away so quickly that thinking of her brought tastes of vinegar to my mouth. Azlaya told me something a while ago, and it wasn't until that day did I understand what she meant.

He who ceases to be a friend, never was one.

Chapter 32: Casey

ONCE OVER THE bridge, Myra and I finally spilled into the court-yard. Hunters and Sagen clashed everywhere. The clanging of swords, the slicing of the air by the arrows, and the shouting pierced my ears. I re-frained from cupping my hands to the sides of my head, because I needed my peripheral vision to keep from getting skewered by an arrow or crushed by rocks being thrown down from above.

Kyraine peeled off to help a group of trapped Hunters, as a Sagen ad-vanced on Myra and me. I reached out with my senses and hurled a solid piece of mass behind me towards the Sagen in front of us. I hit him square in the chest with the boulder pulled up from the ground. Myra shot me a look of approval. Together we fought and defended one another, each protecting the other's back. Our movements soon became entwined as we fought like two halves of a whole. Mentally, Myra reached out to me so I could have a 360° view of the battle as we fought together; it was as though we were connected, fighting as one. We maneuvered fluidly and in sync, always knowing what the other was doing.

The Sagen were becoming wary of us, but attacked nonetheless. The only magic they knew was Dark Magic, and our mental defenses were stronger. Myra did most of the attacking, while I defended with a myriad of charms and shields. Every time one of them worked, I blinked to the sky, thanking anyone who would appreciate my gratitude. For me it was trial by fire, but my mental connection to Myra helped me keep focus and clarity.

"Start moving in!" Kyraine shouted across the open area.

The Hunters began making large advancements towards the castle doors. Myra and I moved to the opposite flanks of Kyraine to support the advance. Although seemingly panic-stricken, the Sagen continued to battle. Next to me, a hooded figure collapsed and began to fade. I reached down and grabbed his sword from his wilting grasp as he disintegrated into ashes. As I lifted it to test its weight, it was knocked aside. Had I not been holding onto it tightly, it would have skidded across the floor, far from reach. I thrust it up to my face just in time to deflect another blow. I had been separated from Myra, who was across the courtyard, occupied with other Sagen. I could see their dark faces hidden behind black hoods, and where the hilts of their swords stopped, the sleeves of their cloaks started. Even though I'd seen the Sagen up close many times, they still gave me chills.

I stepped forward and swung upward. The clatter of metal-to-metal contact echoed off the walls. I sliced the sword around, hoping to catch the side of the closest Sagen, but he only moved out of the way. I tried again for his thigh, only to be disappointed as he took a step back. We continued that at a quick pace, and I was struggling to keep up. A second too late and he would inflict a nasty gash.

The Sagen jabbed his sword into the ground, just missing me, and he couldn't get it free. He reached out, his bony hand connecting with my face. I wanted to rub my stinging cheek, but I resisted the urge. This wasn't a simulation; I wasn't practicing with Myra, or training with Brennon or Kyraine. It was real, and it hurt.

I stumbled back and regained my footing. He had unstuck his sword from the ground and ran at me with the sword raised above his head. My breathing was heavy, and I didn't think I would be able to fight him off again with the sword. I spun around and saw a huge, looming window on the wall behind me. I drew my arm back and with all the power I could muster, threw the sword at the window. Shards of glass and sunlight showered down on top of both my opponent and me. A high-pitched screech came from the Sagen as he melted into ashes from the new light streaming in. Other Sagen also caught in the pool of sunlight met the same fate.

I threw my arms over my head and ducked to protect my face. When the orchestra of glass hitting the marble floor ended, I slowly rose to my feet. The glass had sliced my cloak in various places, and my arms had several cuts on them, too. I found Myra, whose attackers had been killed by the light as well. She looked at me and then at the glass. "Improvising," I shrugged, and for the first time I was able to look at the room around me.

The remaining stained glass windows shed a rainbow of colors across the marble floor. The ceiling had a beautiful, yet chilling, painting of a dragon basking in flames. A master staircase wound its way up through the center, twisting as it ascended, and banners of more dragons adorned the walls. The battle had undecorated everything else. Hunters and Sagen ran around in every direction. Myra rushed forward to help, but Adalia stayed loyally at my side, until two Sagen advanced towards us, and she shot forward to intercept them. I took my "spare" moment to search for Kate or Azlaya, knowing that finding one would lead me to the other. As I was about to follow Myra, I sensed someone behind me. I spun around and started conjuring a spell as I flung my hand out.

I watched as Veronica's limp body crumpled to the ground. I wanted to throw her into another wall as she slowly stood and regained her balance. Her face contorted, as if she didn't know whether to glare or look surprised. I noticed that she had traded her green tunic for a black one, which made me feel a little better, because I thought she was unworthy to keep wearing what the Hunters wore. She was responsible for Irene's capture and allowing paranoia to seep into the minds of the Hunters. Poisonous words flooded my mouth, but I restrained myself from having a magical outburst that I couldn't control or undo. She didn't have such worries.

Chapter 33: Brennon

I WATCHED THE Hunters push deeper into Azlaya's castle. I stayed outside, supervising the Nymphs and other Hunters protecting the perimeter. Danzinar waited impatiently, scanning the perimeter and keeping a watchful eye on the castle under siege. I wanted to be inside helping the Hunters, but Kyraine gave us orders, and I knew today wasn't the day to disobey her. From what I could tell, things outside were looking good. I hoped the same could be said for everything happening on the inside.

As I stood at the edge of the trees scanning the castle, I heard someone approaching me from behind. My gaze didn't waver, but I angled my body so I could see them out of the corner of my eye. It was a Hunter with gold, curly hair twisted into a braid, armed with her bows and arrows, and dressed in fighting attire.

"What are you waiting for?" she asked sharply, as though wondering why a swordsman watched the battle idly. She too searched the tree line for areas that might need extra assistance.

"My cue," I responded.

Suddenly, her face scrunched in confusion. I was about to ask what was wrong, but she didn't have to tell me; I felt it.

A tremor rumbled through the ground, making my legs wobble. It felt like an earthquake. I saw her mouth drop open, and her eyes grew wide. I followed her gaze to where she had her eyes pinned and what I saw made me straighten up. Danzinar roared tumultuously, and his warning echoed across the forest.

Out of the bowels of the castle rose a huge mass. It was dark as night, and its head was armed with heavy plates and spikes. Its eyes glowed orange like the pit of a volcano. Wings unfurled from its sides as it rose higher and higher into the sky. It let out a high-pitched screeching sound that made us cringe.

"And there's my cue," I said sideways to the Hunter, and jumped into action. I raced over to Danzinar and swung myself onto his back. He grunted impatiently. I could see it written in his eyes. He had the heart of a lion, and he itched with impatience to take on this threat. Azlaya's dragon, now airborne, began to shoot jets of fire from its mouth, causing Nymphs to rush to put the flames out. Streams of water started to flow upwards from the moat surrounding the castle, to quench the fires. Screams flew from the mouths of unlucky Hunters as they tried to escape the fire.

I kicked my heels into Danzinar, and we shot into the sky. I remembered Caden telling us long ago that Azlaya's dragon was named Kaida. I gazed upon her, taking in her sheer size, which was larger than my own dragon's. I tightened my grip on Danzinar's scales as he rose to meet his challenger. Kaida's eyes flashed in an ominous way that I recognized from being around Danzinar.

"MOVE! Danzinar, move!" He swerved to the left as a stream of fire just nicked my shin. I could smell the burnt flesh, but we kept moving. Danzinar roared in anger and flew like a bullet at Kaida.

Her entire body was covered in black scales and around her head were hints of red. As Danzinar sped towards her, she circled around. She was larger than he was, but I could tell that he was quicker and nimbler. Lowering her head, she waited eagerly as we approached. I braced myself for the impact, trying not to think about the long fall down. I knew that Danzinar probably wouldn't be able to grab me. I felt a shudder, and I was thrown backwards, but I clawed at his scales and spikes to stay on him. Boisterous roars and growls escaped the two dragons as they dug their claws into each other. They whipped their tails at each other and tried to catch the other's neck in their jaws. Pain-filled bellows emanated from Danzinar, and I saw his red blood sliding down his scales and over my hands.

"Hold on!" I yelled to him, barely audible over the shrieks of the dragons.

Kaida twisted around and seized a portion of Danzinar's neck. I heard the cracking sounds of teeth breaking scales. Only dragons had the strength and weapons to pierce the hide of another. I could feel Danzinar's agony, as he tried desperately to free himself. His roars turned from furious, to frantic, to weak, and Kaida still wouldn't release him. His pain-filled cries made me cringe. It was like listening to someone being burned as they screamed for help.

"Danzinar! Hold on!" I hoped he wouldn't give up. Both Kaida and Danzinar's wings beat rapidly to keep from making a quick and fatal descent to the ground, but his were slowing. If they stopped and Kaida dropped him, we would be dead.

I started to crawl up his sharp neck, which was on the verge of breaking with each passing second between Kaida's clenched jaws. I balanced myself, unsheathed my sword, and jumped from Danzinar to Kaida. I brought the sword down on her skull. My sword didn't break through her armor, but it made her recoil and release her grip on Danzinar. He kicked and flew at a very sluggish speed away from us.

I didn't have time to see where he was going because Kaida snapped her head around and almost caught me between her bone-crushing teeth. I jumped back and nearly tumbled off her thin back. My foot slipped down her slick scales, and I clung from the spikes that ran down her spine. I swung a leg up and hauled myself back up.

Kaida whipped her head around again, teeth bared. I knocked her away using my sword. She growled and thrust her head at me again. I held up my sword again, but the force knocked me backwards, and the sword fell from my hands. I cursed as I watched it tumble to the ground.

I tried to regain my balance when Kaida whipped her tail around, and I fell from her back. I hurtled towards the ground, still looking up as I fell. A furious Kaida dove after me, jaws wide open. As I tumbled towards the fast-approaching ground, I felt a jerk and my neck nearly snapped from the sudden change in direction. Then, I realized that my descent to the ground had stopped completely. Suddenly, I felt sharp talons close around my mid section. Kaida's menacing eyes studied me, as if trying to decide whether to crush me between her teeth, then eat me; or to just eat me alive. Then, she decided to just let me fall to my death, as she uncurled her claws.

On the doorway of death, I absentmindedly thought about how the Hunters would explain how I fell to my death fighting a dragon. I closed my eyes and resigned myself to my inevitable end.

I landed in a rather rough part of the afterlife. It wasn't a very soft landing either, and it felt cool and hard. A harsh wind attacked my face. It was an uncomfortable feeling, one I wouldn't expect to feel when I was dead. I was expecting a gentle breeze, with white clouds, maybe even a meadow—but not this. It bothered me so much that I forced myself to come to terms with the strange utopia. I peeled my eyes open, only to be very confused. I was flying. No, I was being carried ... maybe by an angel. I looked up excitedly, but to my disappointment more than to my relief, I saw Danzinar. He had a look in his eye that said, *do you really think I would let you fall?*

"You asshole, I thought you were going to let me die," I said lightly. I thought about my missed opportunity of being escorted into the afterlife by an angel, but we still had Kaida to take care of. Danzinar helped lift me onto his back again.

I checked his neck, which was healing quickly. Dragons were creatures that were nearly immune to injury. Cuts and gashes would heal very quickly and almost immediately for the younger ones. I leaned over and saw the cut across Danzinar's stomach closing up. I patted my dragon, and he torpedoed towards Kaida. From the low rumble in the pit of Danzinar's stomach, I knew he wanted her blood, and he wasn't letting anything stop him. Kaida looked up and saw us flying towards her, and again, she waited.

"Make it quick," I coached from behind.

Kaida spread her wings wide and started to arch her neck into a coiled position. It was the beginnings of a giant breath of fire. I felt an unsettling in Danzinar's own stomach. It was about to get hot. As if synchronized and on cue, the two dragons shot forth blazes of flames. I ducked my head and covered my face. I heard and felt the tremor of the impact. Their combined power knocked both of them back a couple feet. Through the smoke and sparks, I tried to locate Kaida, but she was hidden. My eyes became slits as I searched. The drum-like beat of Danzinar's wings became our clock as the seconds felt like hours.

I turned my head and saw her. Her massive black body moved like a sea serpent through the waves. I nudged Danzinar who spun just in time to grab hold of her in his jaws. The crunch of bone sounded no better the second time. Danzinar caught her chest in his mouth and snapped down. Then, he unclenched and brought his strong tail around like a whip. It hit Kaida square in the breastbone. I didn't need to direct or instruct Danzinar at all. It was any animal's instinct to know how to kill, especially when it's their own kind and survival is at stake.

Danzinar went in for the final blow. He tore one of her wings, as she tried to throw me from Danzinar's back. She missed and slammed her head against his shoulder blade, hard. She screamed in fury. Kaida desperately tried to fly away, but it was no use. With a severely damaged wing, it wouldn't keep her airborne. She managed to drift over to the castle and crash to the ground, still roaring in pain and hungry for revenge. She slithered back into the pit from which she rose. Danzinar moved to finish her off, but I called him to attention. It would be too dangerous to follow her into that tight space and not expect to get torched right away. With her injuries, it'd take days for her to even think about resurfacing, but when that happened, Danzinar and I would be ready. Danzinar let out a victorious and deafening growl.

I patted him. Both of us were short of breath. "Masterfully done."

We landed, relieved and ecstatic from our triumph, but the fight was far from over, and fires still brewed that needed extinguishing. Our little victory would amount to nothing if the flames weren't put out. I gave Danzinar one last pat of approval and rushed forward to help.

Chapter 34: Casey

ONCE VERONICA REALIZED it was me standing before her, her eyes were a mix of fear, guilt, and hate. She hooked her foot around mine and kicked it out from under me, and I stumbled to keep my balance. She scrambled to her feet and sprinted down a vacant hallway. I didn't allow myself to register the pain and raced after her.

I chased her down the hallway and away from the battle. We spilled into another room that was empty. No doors or windows lined the walls for her to escape through. She turned on me, knowing she was trapped. I stopped and stared at my betrayer. A large enough distance separated us so that we couldn't come into contact with one another. However, being alone with her made me feel like the walls were slowly caving in, forcing us to speak. Neither of us knew what to say as we watched each other's chests rise and fall, until we breathed inaudibly again. I had stared at her long enough, and I wanted to speak the words I had rehearsed in my head for this moment.

"How can you even look me in the eye after what you did?" I whispered sharply. "I trusted you!"

Her eyes looked anguished when they rose to meet mine. Her hard expression from before melted into one of regret. "It was a job. I needed to send money to my younger brother and sister, and Azlaya paid me well to get her what she wanted," she explained with guilt weighing on her words. I instantly remembered the day in the village when she rushed into the pub with a thick pouch of money. She must have been meeting with someone who would deliver the pouch to her siblings. "I won't try to hide the things I did. I was the one who notified the Sagen when you arrived in the clearing, and I sent them after you and Brennon in the woods. I took Irene and came to work for Azlaya to help my family, but Casey," her eyes locked onto mine, "you have to know I never did it with the intention of hurting you, even though that's what happened anyway. At first you were nothing but a stranger, but once I got to know you I regretted everything … but wouldn't you do the same if it were your family?"

My expression softened but remnants of my glare remained. I believed her story, but I couldn't trust her anymore. If she wanted to regain what she had lost in me, then she would have to convince me that she no longer belonged to Azlaya, and that she could fix what she had ruined. "If you want me to trust you again, then change what you did. Right here, right now. Help us bring Azlaya down. You may have siblings back at home, but you also have *sisters* out there," I pointed to where we came from, "who are dying for a cause that even you believed in. And somewhere inside you, I *know* you still do."

Veronica sighed and shook her head. "I can only warn you now. I helped with your sister's training, Casey, and I truly mean this when I say it … she may be your sister, but Azlaya has rooted something in her that is making her want your blood. You would be wise to fear what she can do. She is not the same person you've shared your life with and she will never be that person again," Veronica warned me. The intensity in her words and eyes spoke volumes.

I shook my head. I didn't want to think about Kate. I wanted to get Veronica back to the Hunters—to her sisters—and have her beg for their forgiveness. Despite everything she did, I wasn't ready to leave her at Azlaya's mercy. "Come with me," I begged her.

"I can't. I've already said too much and surely she knows by now. You have to tell the Hunters that I'm sorry for what I did and make sure that my brother and sister aren't forgotten," she whispered.

"No, Veronica. *You're* going to tell them. Come on," I beckoned her to follow me, but she just smiled hopelessly in response.

"Goodbye, Cas—"

But those were the last words I heard from Veronica. Her dark eyes grew distant as she fell to her knees and onto her side. I jumped back, and my hand flew to my mouth. My stomach churned and bile climbed up my throat. I thought I was going to be sick as I looked at the sword protruding from her mid-section. I started to take shaky steps away from Veronica's body, when I noticed to whom the sword belonged.

Her hair was an amalgam of waves and curls, pulled away into a messy bun from her round, pale face. She had immaculate red lips and high cheekbones. Her long eyelashes stretched out over almond-shaped eyes and brushed her cheeks when she blinked. Her features would have been coveted by women everywhere. It sickened me to think her beautiful, because I was, of course, describing the demon herself: Azlaya.

I recognized her from the day I saw her studying me from her balcony. She didn't even pay attention to the girl dying at her feet as blood pooled around her. She gazed right through me with those piercing eyes. I wanted to say something, but my mouth wouldn't form words. My shock, fear, hatred, and denial must have been written in bold ink all over my face. Azlaya saw it and it brought her to chuckle lightly. *Think; do something.* I could have done something. I should have stopped her. In my deep thinking, Azlaya spoke.

"We finally meet, Cassia Coles." Her icy words were like bitter medicine I had to choke down. I recoiled at the sound of my full name, especially hearing it from her. Suddenly, I wanted to be in the close quarters of my friends. I wanted to have nothing to do with that moment, but at the same time, I wanted to be right where I was. I wanted to make Azlaya regret what she had done—to me, my sister, my parents, and everyone else who had had to live under her tyrannical rule, and I saw this moment as my opportunity.

"I know what you want to do," she chimed. I knew too. I wanted to strike a hole in her heart as big as the hole of fear she had stricken in others. "But you must know, Cassia—"

"It's Casey," I snapped.

"Oh, you can speak," she exclaimed mockingly. I raised my hand, glowing with the energy of a spell, waiting to be released. A thin smile grew on Azlaya's lips. "This isn't my fight. It is your sister's."

"Where is she?" I asked through clenched teeth, my raised hand still glowing.

Behind Azlaya, a doorway shimmered into view, reminding me of the doorway I had entered to get to Alagia. It swung open, and Azlaya walked backwards through it. The door didn't shut or disappear. It taunted me to follow her. My initial fear from before started to melt away, and I could feel hatred boiling inside me again. I couldn't bear to steal a glance at Veronica's body as I ran past her and through the door. She was gone, her eyes still fixed somewhere on the ceiling above.

As soon as I crossed the threshold, a crisp wind hit my face. I shuffled forward into the pitch-black tunnel. I reached out and felt cold, damp, stone walls. *"Lux,"* I whispered. A ball of light sprung from my hand, and I held it out in front me as I advanced. I worried about what I would find at the end of this tunnel, but I kept my steady approach forward. It didn't take long before I saw a white light at the end of the tunnel. I extinguished the light I held, and, keeping my hand on the wall, I began to half-walk-half-run towards the end of the passage.

I burst through the tunnel's end and threw a hand up to shade my eyes from the beleaguering lights. It took a couple seconds for them to adjust. Once they did, I saw warriors darting chaotically around, but not Kate, who I thought I was going to run into. I was back where I was before I followed Veronica, but Myra had vanished.

The Hunters had pushed the Sagen deeper and deeper into the castle. At that point, the battle was no longer restricted to one certain part of the castle. Hunters and Sagen were everywhere. Gwen spotted me from across the room and rushed over.

"Where did Azlaya go?" I asked frantically.

Gwen was breathing in short, breathless gasps, "I don't know. No one has seen her."

I turned to look at the door I had emerged from, but it was gone. There was a fading ripple and glimmer in the spot that had been the portal. She gave my shoulder a quick squeeze as a final 'be careful' warning. I nodded, and she drew her bow and shot three arrows in the other direction. Each hit its target perfectly, and she sprinted away, shooting more arrows as she went.

I turned around and saw a Sagen warrior headed my way. He had his sword raised over his head, and his robes flowing behind him as he ran. I pulled water particles from the air and created a thin layer of ice under his feet. He barreled forward, and the sword skidded away from him. I picked up his sword.

As I was turning back to him, he tackled me to the ground. I had one arm pinned under me and the other was being held by the Sagen. He could have easily killed me, but the Sagens' orders were to deliver me to Kate, not kill me themselves. The side of my face pressed against the hard, chilled floor. I had bitten my lip when I hit the ground, and I could taste the blood pooling in my mouth. The warrior held me down, and I tried to wriggle from under him, but he was strong. I kicked my foot, trying to dig it right into his back, but I missed time and time again. I was spitting and choking on my own blood. It finally hit me that I couldn't get up. I couldn't throw him from me. Soon, Kate would come, ready to kill me with her dagger, just as I had seen in my dream.

Suddenly, I could breathe freely again. I remained still, coughing up blood that slid down my throat. I heard a grunt and a crash on the rock floor near me, and I rolled over. I saw a man and the Sagen warrior wrestling, throwing punches, and kneeing each other in the gut. Finally, after several minutes of struggle, the man grabbed a bundle of black cloak where the Sagen's neck should be and gave it a sharp twist. A shudder ran through my body when I heard the snapping sound. He spit on the Sagen's face. He lifted himself painfully and slowly to his feet. On the side of his face, he rubbed a fast-forming bruise. I gathered myself and stood to face him, but I didn't recognize him.

His chin and around his mouth were covered in stubble, and he had unruly, dark brown hair that hung in his eyes. His eyes were so dark they looked black, and his face was pallid, as though he rarely saw the sun. He found me staring at him, and he returned the gaze. His lifeless eyes started to brighten. They darted everywhere, studying and never leaving me. It was uncomfortable, as the stranger's gaze never wavered. When he looked at me, it was with love, a look I would have only received from my grandmother.

He took a step forward, but I stayed frozen. "Is that … you?" I wanted to turn around and make sure he wasn't talking to someone else, but I knew he spoke to me and to me only. "Casey?"

Then it struck me. His eyes—they were from the sketches in my mother's journals. I searched the features of his face. The high cheek bones, the warm face, the straight, pointed nose. They all matched up. The missing piece in my life, the never-present warmth I'd always wanted to feel, and the empty feeling that ate at me through the years, was standing before me.

I threw myself into his strong arms. My eyes released tears that I had held in for years, and I sobbed uncontrollably. A sense of guilt swept over me when I pulled away and saw how wet I had made his shirt, but when I saw his face again, more tears came. I don't know how long we stood in each other's embrace, but it didn't matter. All thoughts of the ongoing battle abandoned me, because where I was, I knew I was safe. He held me and led me forward, saying, "Yes, I'm your father. I have you now."

When I tried to separate myself from him again, I was in a different place. He managed to lead us behind a pillar that would shield us from the clashing swords and threatening arrows. I was blind to everything except the fact that I was in the arms of my father. He stroked my hair, kissed my forehead, gazed at me as if I were about to leave for prom. Except, I wore a sweaty cloak and tunic, dirty boots, with nothing but blood and dirt acting as my makeup. Yet, he still looked at me like I was the most beautiful thing he'd ever seen.

"Dad I—" I gasped, but those were the only words I could choke out. Suddenly Myra appeared. My father looked to her. Her mouth hung open, and her eyes didn't know whether to be guilty or happy.

"We thought you were dead," she said breathlessly, with disbelief plastered on her face. My father smiled, and then they had their arms wrapped around each other, too. It was a reunion that made us all forget our plight. "How did you escape?"

"Thankfully, some Hunters stumbled upon my room, and heard me banging on the door to let me out. They had to unlock it with sorcery." He placed a hand on Myra's shoulder. "They've been trained well if they can dismantle one of Azlaya's spells," he squeezed her warmly.

Myra mouthed her thanks from the compliment. "Are you all right?" she asked, spotting the now-purple bruise.

"I'm fine," my father said, waving aside her concern. "Where's Kyraine?"

"She's around here somewhere," Myra explained.

He nodded his understanding, and then turned back to me. His eyes searched my face. "I can't believe I found you," he said. I let out a short, breathless laugh in agreement.

"If I had known you were here, I would have come to get you," I told him fiercely.

"No." His answer confused me. "I'm glad you didn't know. Azlaya has been waiting for you, and you would have walked right into her trap." My mouth twisted, but I decided against telling him that I had willingly walked into one of her traps already. He was going to say something more, but he searched for the right words to say. Without even uttering a word, I recognized the look he gave me and immediately knew what he was trying to say.

"I don't know where she is," I spoke softly.

He nodded. Since we were infants, he knew what the prophecy foretold. What he didn't know, and probably would never get to know, was Kate, his other daughter who had been absent his whole life, and possibly forever.

I couldn't admit it out loud, but Kate had changed. I could feel the denial in the pit of my stomach, but the proof was everywhere. Just knowing I would have to face the Kate I didn't fully know or understand sent chills down my spine. Just after my brief encounter with Azlaya, I knew her influence would have made my sister unrecognizable to me.

"I have to find her," I said under my breath, surveying the battle beyond the pillar we took shelter behind.

I was still shaken by what had happened earlier with Veronica, but I was even more terrified that I might lose the father I just regained. It was even more difficult to rush into the battle, knowing I had one more person that could be ripped from me at any moment. That was the thing about war that I had never understood until that moment. I had to do all I could to win the fight and just pray that the people I cared about were alright.

My father told us he had waited too long for this day, and couldn't sit by idly and watch. We stepped out from behind the wide pillar, and a few nearby Hunters turned their heads when they laid eyes on my father. Those who had known him before he was captured stared in awe. My father raised his sword over his head, ordered the Hunters to keep fighting, and ran into the tangled crowd of slashing and thrusting swords. Sagen descended on Myra and me. Myra rushed towards one, but I stayed back.

As the warrior floated towards me, I flicked my hand, causing the marbled floor under his feet to shift. Rather than falling, he spun and launched a chunk of the floor at me. I had mere seconds to avoid the collision. I threw my hands in front of me and then swiped them down to my sides. The rock split and fell to either side of me.

I narrowed my eyes as he drew a lone sword from the ground and hurled it at me. The Sagen fed the sword's speed with some added wind. I thought of a shield and yanked stone from the floor with my mind just as the sword impaled it. The tip had come through from the other side, inches from my face. A short breath of relief fell off my lips. I pushed the massive stone with the sword lodged in it back at the Sagen. I watched as the gentle movement of his hand sent the rock and weapon crashing to the ground beside him.

He shot a stream of fire at me, and I reached my hand out to meet it. At first it felt hot, then cool, and before I knew it, it had melted into my hand as though it never existed. I smiled inwardly. I could feel the energy I had just absorbed racing through my body. A sharp snarl ripped from his lips. He started thrusting a variety of dark spells in my direction, and I fought hard to fend them off. When he saw that I wasn't going to yield, he tried a new approach. Suddenly, my world went dark. He used a blinding spell on me. My breathing accelerated; not knowing where he was made my insides tighten. I cleared my thoughts, trying to break his spell when I sensed his presence and swung an arm out. My fingers brushed his cloak. Before I could do it again, my knees buckled, and my back hit the marble. My breath came out in short, ragged gasps. I felt cloth around me, and I grabbed at it to feel where the Sagen was. A skeletal, cold hand snatched my wrist and something else held down my other hand. My vision started to return to me, and I saw the hooded figure leaning over me, a long, jagged knife in hand. I felt its cold, serrated blade pressed against my neck and his stale breath on my face.

"Your death will be a relief," he hissed slowly. He pressed the knife harder against my skin, and I felt the hot blood trickle down my neck. Even as he loomed over me, I still couldn't see his face. The only thing under the hood was a black space.

"You can't kill me." My choice of words was strange, but given the circumstances, anything to get the Sagen distracted bought me time.

"We will not hesitate if your sister does," he whispered.

My eyes flew everywhere, searching for an escape. I ripped my arm from his grasp and produced a ball of light, and as he went to restrain me, his bony hand grabbed the light I held. I smirked. Suddenly, a roar came from the Sagen as he pulled his burning hand away. He clutched the smoldering hand in pain. I punched him in the gut. He slid away from me, as I scrambled to my feet. I had stood back from the infuriated Sagen, when my toes began to tingle. The feeling gradually climbed up to my ankles and into my legs. Then, as if controlled by a remote control device, my legs began to rigidly carry me back to the waiting Sagen. I didn't know how to stop myself, and I was completely under his control. I cursed under my breath as my heart beat faster with every inch forward.

The Sagen rose from his crouching position and snatched the collar of my cloak when I was within reach. He forced me up against a wall, his forearm shoved into my throat. My eyes bulged as I clawed at his arm. I raised a hand to hit him with a spell, but he was quick, and pinned my arm against the wall too. I thought I heard his raspy laugh, when he suddenly yanked his arm away and spun around. I slumped to the floor and sputtered. I was level with his foot, and my chances of being kicked in the gut were high.

However, to my shock and relief, Adalia stood growling at the man she'd just bitten. The Sagen clutched his leg and robe and crumpled to the ground. Adalia kept snarling until all that was left of the Sagen was a pile of ashes. I painfully pulled myself to my feet and almost crashed to the floor again. I was lightheaded and needed a minute to recuperate. On the wall behind me, I saw a handle and used it to haul myself to my feet again. I was thrown off balance and fell through an empty space in the wall. As Adalia dashed towards me, the door I didn't realize I had opened slammed shut, leaving her in the other room. I grabbed the door handle and gave it several violent shakes, but to no avail. I gave up and leaned against the door, exhausted and drained. I pounded my fist on the door in frustration.

I languidly turned and scrutinized my surroundings. I could hear the noise of the battle all around me, but this room looked deserted. A haunting throne room spread out before me. The black marble floor sparkled, and candles lined the wall, with a giant chandelier hanging above. Huge pillars lined an aisle up to the dais where the throne sat in the center of the room. The chair was black with a red cushion and flecks of gold. I could easily picture Azlaya sitting on that throne. Behind the throne were wide arches and each arch had deep purple drapes, preventing me from seeing what was on the other side. Gargantuan stained glass windows lined the walls, casting an array of dark colors to dance all over the room from the light of the candles, and a huge dome-shaped ceiling spread above me. On the ceiling was another tiled picture of Azlaya's black dragon. The reflection of Azlaya's character through the décor of her throne room was suffocating.

I snapped to attention when I heard footsteps. Behind one of the curtains, in an archway, a figure emerged. She wore a deep red tunic with loose sleeves and dark boots that stopped below her knee. A black cloak was draped on her shoulders, and around her waist she had fastened a black belt, and her blonde hair was tied away from her face.

I wanted to say something. I wanted to tell her that maybe none of what we were there to do would have to happen. I wanted to do anything to stop that moment, but it was a standoff, and she was my enemy. She was Alagia's enemy … my sister.

Chapter 35: Kate

I WATCHED HER as a lioness watches her prey. She had more muscle and looked stronger than I remembered. Her eyes were sunken and tired. She hadn't slept that night. Her whole body looked as though it ached with exhaustion, which, I imagined, had to do with me. Her hair was braided down her back, and lighter from all the time she'd spent outdoors. Wild strands hung around her face and in her eyes. She wore a green, long-sleeved tunic that stopped above her knees, and shoes resembling moccasins on her feet. She carried no weapons. She had blood and ashes on her hands, face, and clothes, and I could see a fresh wound on her neck.

When Casey saw the light spill onto my face, I couldn't read her expression. It was a mix of so many emotions. Time seemed to stop as we held each other's gaze. Neither of us could comprehend anything outside this moment. Everything I remembered about her and our old life had vanished. The smile we always greeted each other with was absent. Nothing was the same anymore, and though I had known that from the beginning, seeing the concrete evidence gave me a peace of mind.

"Kate," she whispered as if trying to persuade herself that I, and everything that was happening, was real.

At the sound of my name, rage seized me. I hated her. I couldn't stand the sight of her. How could she join the very people who murdered our mother? After sixteen years of having no one, why would she want that for us?

"What happened to you?" she whispered. Casey gazed at me for a few moments, and then blinked away her stare. "You killed Jackson?" She sounded horrified and sympathetic all at once.

"He deserved what he got," I snapped. She recoiled as if I'd struck her across the face.

"Kate ..." she started, but couldn't find the right words to say. "I'm sorry." It sounded like a question.

"Don't be. He's in the past but this—" she gestured around her, "this is my future." Casey's face looked like anything she would say would be pointless. In her silence, I added, "So, you've been training to kill me this whole time?"

"I haven't been training to kill you. I trained to protect myself *from* you. You're the one who's been trained to kill!" Casey shouted at me.

"At least I'm doing it for our mother." Casey's head tilted. "They," I pointed towards the distant sounds of battle, "killed our mother for power and control." Casey was frozen, her mouth parted. "And Azlaya, can save her. Azlaya can bring her back, and rule alongside our mother as it should have been before she was murdered," I explained passionately. In that moment, I believed in Azlaya's promise so much, it made my heart impatient for the anticipated reunion with my mother.

"Do you hear yourself?" Casey scoffed. "Listen to what you're saying. It's insane. Azlaya has fed you lies, and you've believed every last one of them. She can't give you what she's promised. It's impossible!"

My eyes narrowed. "How would you know?" I spat at her with venom in my voice.

She looked at me hopelessly. "No spell can resurrect the dead, Kate," Casey said softly. "If one existed, then ask Azlaya why she hasn't used it for her own mother."

I didn't understand what she meant, and it showed on my face. I shook off whatever she meant. "I can do it. I'm almost strong enough to do it. And once I help Azlaya defeat the Hunters and Huntsmen, and take over the four kingdoms, my powers will grow, and I'm going to bring our mother back ... and you're standing in my way," I spat.

Casey's voice shook as she stressed each word. "Kate, she's gone."

I huffed impatiently and began to hurl spells at her. She deflected them but didn't attack. "Stop, stop, stop," Casey begged.

I threw darker spells, but she skillfully evaded them, catching the last one in her hand and throwing it aside. She breathed hard and looked at me in disbelief.

"Is this it then?" Casey screamed to me. "This is how it ends—how we end?"

I sent another spell in her direction. She sent it tumbling back at me so quickly that I didn't have enough time to react. I was hit square in the chest and knocked back a couple of feet. While I tried to catch my breath, I felt uncomfortably hot. I looked up and saw walls of fire circling me.

Chapter 36: Casey

I WAS STILL in shock about the things that Kate had accused me of, and then instead of trying to talk about it, she started throwing curses at me. I guess I shouldn't have expected anything less. We weren't anything like we used to be.

I created a ring of fire around us, leaving her nowhere to run. I was going to force a resolution to our confrontation, because I needed to hear all the lies she'd been told. Kate gathered herself and looked at me with dagger eyes. We stared at each other, both waiting for the other to make her move.

I could hear it before I even saw the beginnings of it. Myra hadn't allowed me to practice it. It was the source of power and the epitome of the dragons' fear. It crackled and sizzled, charging, waiting to be thrust at its target: me. *You're a Fire Bearer too*, I thought.

"Don't!" I tried to say, but Kate had already prepared herself for the discharge.

Thinking fast, I collapsed the wall of fire, making it wash right over Kate, who stopped feeding the lightning and threw her hands up to protect herself. Something inside me couldn't let her burn in fiery pain. I lowered my hands, and the fire extinguished. Through all the smoke I searched for Kate with frantic eyes. I saw two figures rise up, as if out of the smoke. I knew who it would be before I could see them clearly. Azlaya stood in front of Kate. However, she didn't stand protectively, because I knew her only desire was to be a witness to our fight.

"You," I hissed at her. Her lips tightened and pulled up at one corner in a half smile.

"I believe we've met before," Azlaya chimed, making my bones rattle with hatred. I couldn't say anything. My voice was caught in my throat, while Azlaya's floated around the room in a mocking manner. "Come now, Casey. Don't look at me that way. My hands are clean," she taunted, raising her arms and wiggling her fingers. I wanted to charge her, but thinking irrationally would lead me to my death.

"You've corrupted her," I spat at Azlaya, who was unmoved by my words.

"No more corrupted than you. You believe those Hunters really care for you? Do you think Myra actually loves you? She has trained you so you can face your fate, knowing that there was always the chance that you could die, but as long as you killed your sister, who cared what happened to you?" Azlaya said deliberately, letting each word sink in.

"That's not true. You're lying," I said evenly.

"Am I? Look around, Casey. Here you are ready to save this land that you hardly know. Those Hunters orchestrated your stay just for this very moment, so that they could have a chance at freedom, while leaving you the chance to die. But please don't get me wrong, I don't want to delay your death any more than your sister does," Azlaya continued. I stole a glance at Kate, who still cut her eyes at me.

The seeds of doubt and denial began to grow in the back of my mind. *It's not true. Nothing she ever says is true. You've been through too much for the Hunters not to care about you.*

I forgot Azlaya could read minds and jumped when she added, "What do you know of truth, Casey, when your whole life has been a lie? You were lied to about your world, your parents, and your past … you were even lied to about your sister's powers." Her words were suffocating and made it impossible to think clearly. I saw Kate shifting uncomfortably behind Azlaya, waiting to be released for the kill.

"How can you speak of truth when every word that leaves your mouth is a lie?" a new voice intruded. I turned my head and was relieved to see Myra standing right behind me. I could feel her energy supporting me. All the faith I'd lost just moments before came rushing back. She helped break the evil thoughts that Azlaya was trying to worm into my consciousness.

Azlaya began a rapid exchange of enchantments, charms, and spells in her frustration. Force fields exploded, as Myra and Azlaya cast illusions, invisibility charms, and binding spells. The atmosphere was charged and electrified. You could smell the ionization of oxygen as magical energy coursed back and forth. Kate and I joined the fight alongside our teachers. I forced spells at Azlaya that were warded off by Kate. She returned some of the spells I threw, and I redirected them away from Myra. All of us fought our own battles within the larger one.

We were barely moving, but the intense focus and concentration caused us to breathe hard and sweat to form on our faces. Unexpectedly, Azlaya shot a spell in my direction as I was deterring a charm from hitting Myra. It flew right past Myra, who didn't have time to reroute it, and she watched helplessly as it hurtled towards me. I raised a hand, my eyes glued to the spell flying at me. When it made contact, I wasn't prepared to absorb it. A flash exploded, and I staggered back. I blocked some of it, but the brunt of it hit me in the chest. Everything went black.

I thought for sure I was dead. Then, ever so slowly, a tiny light began to appear in the distance. I pulled myself to my feet and started to walk towards it. I glanced around and searched for Myra, but I figured she was in the light and walked straight into it. "Myra," I whispered into the distance. At first it was blinding, but my sight was gradually returned. I was so confused. Where were the castle walls, stained glass windows, and the throne? What happened to Azlaya and Kate? The whole castle and everyone in it disappeared, and I was left in this strange place. Then, a scene began to fall into a place, and a broken gasp escaped my lips.

My mother stood on a cliff overlooking a wild sea. The wind lifted her hair as she stared out over the ocean. She averted her eyes and looked straight at me. My heart skipped a beat when I saw her face. Her beauty was even more amazing in person, and her resemblance to Kate was frightening.

"Hello, Casey."

I couldn't answer. I could only stare. My mouth opened as if to say something, but nothing came out. I turned around and found a thick forest behind me. I spun slowly back to her. The fact that I stood in her presence confirmed for me that I was dead.

"Am I dead?" I asked flatly.

"No, honey," she replied warmly.

"Then how are you here?"

"This is a place where those who have passed remain if they still have things to finish with the living," my mother answered. Before I could stop myself, I immediately thought of the ghosts and spirits, and I didn't want to picture my mother that way.

I looked away from her and rubbed my eyes. "So, this isn't real, is it?"

"It's real and it's not, but it's just up here." My mother gestured to her head. My face furrowed with questions. Her soft, beautiful face studied mine. It was as if she tried to find the right words in my eyes. She turned around to gaze at the crashing waves again. "I came to you because we need to talk."

I imagined myself sitting on my bed with my mother, about to receive a lecture about something I'd done wrong. "What about?" I asked her.

"You," she responded, catching me off guard. She turned away from the ocean, and her eyes bore into mine, and I knew what she searched for. I hung my head.

"I just feel so lost," I whispered. "Kate has completely forgotten everything about us. It's like she doesn't even know that we're sisters and I ... I still do. I keep telling myself I need to forget our past and remember what is happening to us, but I just can't bring myself to do it. She hates me, but I still can't let her go."

"That's what Azlaya wants. She wants you to be at constant war with yourself, while Kate isn't."

"But we're sisters—twin sisters—and yet whatever Azlaya told her made her completely ignore that. Why has she forgotten me so quickly and so easily?" I said, almost pleading.

"The prophecy," my mother answered simply.

"That's not a good enough answer," I responded sharper than I intended, and crossed my arms.

"Maybe ... but it is the answer." I watched her, prodding her to continue. "The prophecy said that one of you would join Azlaya, and, since the time of your birth, that was predetermined, even though we may not have known. That's why it's so easy for her to forget you. There has always been something inside her screaming that something was wrong, that there was something she needed to do," my mother explained.

"Then what about me? If it was predetermined that I was going to side with the Hunters, shouldn't I feel the same way Kate feels about me?"

"No." I opened my mouth to protest, but my mother continued. "Think about it, Casey. Why is Azlaya doing all of this?"

I thought for a moment. "To conquer Alagia."

My mother shook her head. "No. She's doing it for her own vanity. Alagia is just another trophy for her glory. She's doing it all for herself, for her own personal gain. Now, why are the Hunters trying to stop her?"

"To protect the people of Alagia," I replied slowly. My mother lowered her chin, pushing me to think harder. "The Hunters are fighting for everyone in Alagia ... they aren't only concerned with themselves, but also with all the people they've sworn to protect."

"Yes. Kate has Azlaya's mentality, while you have the Hunters'. Kate is ignoring your relationship because she's only concerned with herself and getting what Azlaya has promised her, while you are worried about everyone, including your sister."

I gazed at my mother and nodded my understanding. A question sat on my tongue, and I debated asking it, but I finally couldn't resist the urge. "Why are you helping me so much?"

My mother's face scrunched together. "You're my daughter ..."

"So is Kate," I pointed out. "Have you been giving her the same advice?"

"No," my mother replied flatly and without emotion.

"What?" I asked, horrified. "You don't care about her?" I asked, trying not to sound accusatory.

"Of course I care. I care about both of you. When you two were born, I was heartbroken because I knew what the prophecy foretold. But I couldn't do anything to stop what was going to happen. For the first couple of weeks after you two were born, I cried in your father's arms every night. I questioned myself all the time, wondering if I was a good mother if I was allowing this to happen; if I could change your fate." My heart ached with a new and foreign type of pain at seeing my mother's guilt. "I know you don't want to hear this, but Kate will never be the same, and there is nothing you, nor I, could have done about it."

"You're saying she's evil, and would be all along?" I thought about what she did to Jackson, and realized I already knew the answer to my question.

"I don't want to believe that she is, but it's true," she replied in defeat. I wondered how Kate would cope with our mother's opinion of her.

"So, you're saying it's hopeless to try to save her from Azlaya?"

She shook her head. "Not hopeless. I tried, I sacrificed all that I was, but it was futile. It's too late, Casey. From the moment you two were born, it was too late." I exhaled and closed my eyes, defeated. Gentle hands grasped my shoulders. A finger slid under my chin and propped up my head so that I looked at my mother.

"Casey, look around. Everyone in Alagia has been waiting for you. You're the one who's going to free them from Azlaya. They need you."

"It was never up to me to decide. From the beginning, I would have to see this to the end," I concluded.

"Honey, I would never wish this upon you if the choice was mine, but I couldn't be more proud that you are fighting for a better future," my mother soothed me.

"How could I not fight after Azlaya killed you?" My mother's breath caught in her throat. Her eyes widened as she looked at me, and her rosy mouth parted, but she failed to form any words. "What?" I asked, afraid I had said something wrong.

"Casey, I … Azlaya didn't kill me." I opened my mouth to protest, but she kept explaining. "I know what Kyraine told you and what the Hunters believe, but … I didn't try to stop her," she said her last words so slowly that she paused between each word.

"Why would you—"

"Because I was scared, Casey. I was terrified." She spoke so gently, as if she were trying to lull a baby to sleep. "I knew if Azlaya captured me, I would have no way of protecting you and Kate. I was the only one who knew where you two had been sent, and I was only one who could bring you back. As long as you were in your world and I wasn't able to tell Azlaya your location, you would be safe."

"So you let her kill you to keep us hidden?" My voice cracked as I spoke. My mother nodded somberly, her guilt so evidently entwined into her face. "You left our dad—your husband—by himself, to be taken as Azlaya's prisoner," I said harshly.

Pain seized her eyes. A sullen shadow consumed her face at the mention of her husband. "I know," she sighed. "I thought it was my only choice at the time."

My mother's eyes stayed glued to me. "You were the greatest sorceress in Alagia. You could've beaten her!" I whispered in a strained voice, trying to keep my voice even.

"When I learned that Azlaya was coming for you two, I panicked. I sent you away to be with your grandmother, but I knew it wouldn't be enough to protect you. If anyone could get me to admit your location, it was Azlaya, so I let her kill me to give you and your sister more time." Her eyes were glossy with tears, and I sensed my own crawling to the surface. Suddenly, I lurched forward, and my mother caught me in her sturdy arms. The ground trembled, and the trees rustled violently in the distance. "You need to go," my mother ordered while steadying me. I didn't want to let her go, but she forced me to take a couple steps back from her. I didn't know what to say, but she said what I wanted to. "I love you, Casey. Everything I did was because I love you and Kate."

As I opened my mouth to respond, the world faded to black for the second time. I still felt shaky. My eyes fluttered open, only to find Myra leaning over me, rocking my body back and forth as she tried to wake me. I watched as spasms of relief, guilt, and happiness took turns flickering across her face. My head was cradled in her arms, and when I tried to lift it, she yanked me into a hug. "Oh, thank goodness! Are you okay?" She spoke so quickly that I had to think about each word she spoke and piece them together to make sense of it as I regained my bearings.

It was a couple seconds before I could answer. "Yes, I'm fine. What happened?" I asked as I rubbed my temples where a headache was quickly forming.

"I don't know. You blocked some of the spell Azlaya cast, but when it hit you, there was a huge flash of light. Azlaya and Kate fled, and when the light dimmed, you were lying on the ground," Myra replied. "It was strange. Before she left, Azlaya said your mother's name as though she stood right in front of her," Myra added absentmindedly. I wanted to tell her what I had encountered while unconscious, but decided to keep it to myself for now.

"Where did they go?" I sat up a little taller so I could look around the distorted room. Sections of the floor were cracked, pillars were missing chunks from being hit by spells, and the carpet that ran up to the throne was thrown askew.

"They vanished, Casey, I … I don't know where to."

I sat up straight, and Myra leaned back to give me room. As I did, pain flashed across my body and an exclamation of shock jumped from my lips. "I'm fine," I choked out. My head pounded with a headache. I winced as I stood with Myra at my side for support. Agonizingly slowly, we moved and approached the ten-foot tall wooden doors I had entered earlier. Myra flicked the doors open with the slightest movement of her eyes, and we walked through.

The Sagen seemed ubiquitous, but their numbers didn't appear to overwhelm the Hunters. Somehow in the mayhem, my father managed to locate us. He must have met Kyraine on the battlefield, because she was at his side as he rushed over to us. My father embraced me in his arms as soon as he reached me. My head fell against his chest, and a moan escaped my lips. The pounding in my head moved to my ears.

"Are you hurt?" he asked as Kyraine studied me.

"I'm fine." My eyes were clamped closed, and a fake smile spread on my face when I replied.

"Where are Azlaya and her sister?" Kyraine asked Myra.

"Gone. They escaped," Myra informed them.

Kyraine looked past us towards the doors. Her eyes seemed to lose life, and her shoulders sagged. Kyraine collected herself and nodded in disappointment. She turned to my father, who still had an arm wrapped protectively around my shoulder.

"We need to get her out of here," Kyraine spoke directly to him. I felt him tense, then ease again.

The two exchanged a brief, silent conversation, he nodded, and just like that, the decision about my future was made for me. My father stepped back from me and placed two firm hands on my shoulders. "Casey, it's time for you to go home," he said, trying to hide the pain of losing me again. I felt a lump in my throat.

"I can't go now," I said unevenly. "I have to stay and help."

"Azlaya and your sister are gone, and until we find them again, the risk is too great if you stay," Myra added. "And it's safer having you in the confines of your world."

Kyraine added, to convince me quicker, "Besides, you told me a long time ago that you had a life back home. I think it's time you returned to it. At least for a while, as we search for Azlaya," Kyraine offered.

"But ... but—" I stuttered, trying to think of a valid argument.

"Casey, look at me." I slowly brought my eyes up to my father's. "You have to go back. When we find them, we'll reach out to you. I promise." Looking into his eyes, so soon after staring into my mother's, made an even bigger lump close my throat.

"I just found you! I can't leave you now," I gasped, breathless. When I saw that my words weren't moving him to change his mind, I tried another tactic. "Come with me."

A smile curved his lips, but his eyes remained heavy. "I wish I could, honey." I sucked in a deep breath, feeling even more pain as my mother had recently called me the same thing. "I can't stay in your world for long, because I belong here. This is my home; it's time you went back to yours."

I swiped a hand across my face, refusing to cry. "It's my home just as much as it is yours. I was born *here*, remember," I said with more attitude than I intended.

"But until Azlaya's location is known, you are safer in your world. I won't jeopardize your safety anymore," he said shaking his head. He reached towards my face and tucked a strand of hair behind my ear. "Besides, your grandmother has missed you for long enough."

I hesitated before I said anything more. I could tell that he was determined and would have Myra figure out a way to send me back if I wouldn't go willingly. I realized I fought a losing battle, and gave in to his wishes.

"Promise me ... promise that I'll see you again." I looked at Kyraine and Myra too. "All of you, promise me."

I could tell that Kyraine and Myra choked back tears as they nodded. "Promise," my father whispered.

My father released me, and I jumped into Kyraine and Myra's arms. When we pulled away from each other, we all had tears streaming down our faces.

"Be safe," Myra said, more as a suggestion than a wish.

"You too."

Suddenly, I heard mad barking race towards us. Adalia darted through the battle, nimbly avoiding the weapons that cut through the air. She was so relieved to find me, after losing me earlier, that she nearly knocked me over when she reached me. I rubbed her ear, not sure how to tell her I was leaving for an indefinite period of time.

"Take her with you," Myra told me. I beamed down at Adalia, glad that I could at least take one thing back with me from Alagia.

"Find Brennon, and tell him I said 'Goodbye!'" I told Kyraine, and she nodded in agreement.

I turned back to my father. "All right, I'm ready," I said heavily, not wanting to leave at all. My whole life seemed to truly begin in Alagia. I'd found new strength and confidence in myself that I would have never discovered, had I not found my real home. And after so many weeks alongside Myra, Kyraine, Brennon, and the Hunters, it felt as though I was losing more members of my family, in addition to Kate.

"The necklace," Myra said as she pointed a finger at my chest. I numbly reached into my tunic and withdrew the necklace I had taken from the music box that had started this entire adventure. It had hung around my neck every day since my arrival, and seeing it between my fingers, it finally reminded me that I had left an entire life behind, and I was missed.

"Hold the ring that doesn't say 'Alagia,'" Myra instructed as I obeyed. "Now repeat after me." I nodded somberly. *"Domum redire ac iam non habeo propositum,"* she started. I no longer have purpose here and must return home.

"Domum redire ac iam non habeo propositum," I repeated.

"Dimittite me, ut tuto, quia unus dies revertar." Send me safely, knowing that I will return one day.

I hesitated and glanced around. I was leaving behind friends and family, who had supported me the whole way, to fight for me in my absence. It seemed so unfair. We had all worked so hard, only to come to the end of the chase and lose Azlaya and Kate. A part of me prayed that I would be able to return soon, but another part of me was eager to see what had become of my old life. Either way, I knew my mind would always be drifting back to wonder about the ones I loved, who lived amid this escalating war.

I placed a hand on Adalia's neck, bent my head, and muttered, *"Dimittite me, ut tuto, quia unus dies revertar."*

Chapter 37: Azlaya

I HAD TO transport Kate away from the battle. Once my spell hit Casey, I realized that the blinding light wasn't just a light. I saw Layna Coles, and out of fear that Kate would see her, too, and start asking questions, I made a quick escape from the castle, pulling Kate with me. She hadn't said anything about it, so I assumed I was the only one who caught sight of her mother. Kate huffed in frustration next to me as we walked down a dark hallway. She still hadn't noticed that we were no longer in my castle. I wasn't concerned with that fight anymore, because what I sought was where I teleported us to. I felt Kate's yearning to meet her sister again, but Casey had just proved to me that she was indeed strong. Even though my curse struck her, she was still able to block some of it, something a sorceress as young as her should not have been able to do. When Kate faced her sister again, I wanted to ensure that Kate would win. Suddenly, after seeing Casey, I wasn't so sure that would happen. That was why we left—for insurance. Of course, Kate couldn't know I doubted her powers.

"I could have taken her, she was right there," Kate exhaled irritably.

"You'll see her again." I waved aside her anger.

"But *that* was my chance," she exclaimed. I ignored her and focused on finding the room. "Funny you should be so indifferent about delaying her death when you've waited for that moment for years. Isn't that what *you* told me," Kate added slyly, playing with the very words I fed her.

I stopped walking and spun sharply on her. She drew back but stood her ground. "Yes, I have waited for that moment for a long time, which means I can wait a little longer. I underestimated your sister's strength, and you could use more training," I said viciously, to deflate her ego a little.

"You don't think I was ready?" Kate concluded, not hurt, just annoyed.

"No, I didn't expect your sister to be so prepared," I shot back at her. "Now you'll need more resources for when you confront her again."

I turned and opened a heavy, double door to my left. I pushed my way inside, closely followed by Kate. We walked down a dimly-lit hallway that spilled into a large, rectangular room. The ceiling stretched high above us with a black chandelier hanging over the desk. The tall windows around the room were decorated with dark purple curtains, drawn closed to keep out any light. A rosewood desk sat in the middle of the room, stacked high with papers and books that hid the face of the woman I was there to see. She sat in a matching wooden chair, cushioned with the same colors as the curtains. The whole room was dark and cold, much like her kingdom.

The Queen jerked her head up, surprised at my appearance. "Azlaya," she exclaimed. The candlelight by which she worked shed a small glow, outlining the sharp edges of her face. She straightened from her hunched position, but didn't stand. "I wasn't expecting you so soon."

"The plans have changed. Did you do what I asked?" she nodded nervously. She was always very uneasy around me. "Prepare a carriage for us," I ordered.

"You're going to the Shadowlands tonight?" she asked in disbelief.

"Yes, we can't waste any more time. Have you kept our document safe?" I stared at her.

"Of course. And you'll keep your promise. Aiden Redding will be mine?" she asked boldly.

"If Eileen stays out of the war and Casey Coles becomes mine," I reminded her, and she nodded curtly.

"What are you two talking about?" Kate interjected. She stared at the Queen curiously.

"It's none of your concern right now," I said to Kate, and motioned for her to walk back the way we entered. "I'll see you again, Gisele. Keep it safe; they'll come for it."

I saw a fire light in her eyes that was always present when we discussed the topic of our arrangement. She clenched her hand tightly around her writing utensil and muttered through her locked jaw, "He's the only person who knows where it would be." She chuckled softly, and then gradually her laughter grew louder with her nervous excitement.

"I imagine you'll have everything under control," I pressed her.

She still laughed, "Without a doubt. I've waited too long for him to return."

Chapter 38: Casey

I WATCHED AS several 'goodbyes' were mouthed to me as I vanished. For the second time that day, a flash of light blinded me, and I threw my hand up to shield my face. Wind whipped at my hair, sending it swirling in all directions and loosening my braid even more.

My knees hit a hard surface, and I thrust my hands out before I smacked my face on the floor. I peeled my eyes open and stared in wonderment. I was home. I bent over on my hands and knees in my mother's room, where books and papers were still disheveled and thrown about. My hand flew to my neck; the necklace still hung safely around it. It was strange being back. It didn't feel like I was home. Everything felt foreign, like I didn't belong in the world I grew up in anymore. In truth, only half of me really did. Adalia left my side to explore the strange room.

I stood and picked my way across the littered floor over to where the music box rested. The second necklace was gone, and I knew that it hung around Kate's neck. The words that had once been on the underside of the lid were gone, as though they never existed. By concealing the words from me until the time was right, I wouldn't be able to return to Alagia. The words' absence was like a lock on the gateway to Alagia. I sighed in defeat, knowing I had no way of returning until I was summoned.

Adalia growled ferociously, and I heard a creak behind me and whirled around, raising my hand and mentally focusing on a spell. I half expected to find Sagen ambushing me, but when my eyes fell on my grandmother, time rolled back. I mentally told Adalia to stand down. My grandmother wore the coral nightgown that I had bought for her for Christmas and a robe fastened around her frail body. I wanted to hug her, but I was afraid of crushing her. However, if my new strength didn't break her, I felt that my words surely would. Seconds elapsed as we held each other's gaze. Her eyes darted everywhere, examining the contorted room and her disheveled granddaughter in it.

"You found it." She didn't sound pleased or proud, but rather deflated. I stole a glance at the music box, and the emotions I felt when Kyraine first told me about my parents began to resurface.

"You … you knew all along and never told us that—that our parents—" I accused her.

Shame flooded to her face. I kept the indignant look on my face, but I allowed it to soften, realizing that I wasn't the only one hurt by Alagia's entrance into my life. Guilt took the place of anger. She did all those things only to keep Kate and me safe for as long as she could. I rushed over to her and collapsed into her arms.

"I'm so sorry," she whispered into my ear.

"You shouldn't have to be," I pulled back from her. "You only hid it from us to keep us safe."

Finally, something familiar engulfed me. Her lavender-smelling hair and sweet perfumes invaded my nose. I fit perfectly into her arms, like a missing puzzle piece. I loved and reveled in every second of it. Her shock from before must have worn off, because she instantly took notice of my bloody hands and clothes and recoiled, appalled.

"Casey! My God, what happened to you? Are you all right? Is that a wolf?" she shrieked.

I examined myself and half laughed at the atrocious sight I must have been. I returned my gaze to her face. She stared at me and Adalia in horror. My smile dropped. "No, Grandma, it's okay. I'm okay," I reassured her. "She's friendly," I added, referring to Adalia who stood at my side.

"Is that blood? And your neck!" she gasped.

I placed my fingers where the Sagen had sliced my skin with his dagger. "It'll take me a while to explain," I answered sheepishly.

"What about Kate, is she all right too?"

My mouth hung open as I searched for the right words. She stared at me intently and waited eagerly. "She's alive … but I don't know where she is."

My grandmother stared at me, trying to remember how to speak. "Well, you can tell me after you get cleaned up." She led me to my room, with Adalia in tow, and ordered me to shower. I left Adalia in my room and retreated to the bathroom.

It felt amazing to feel hot water rushing over my body, instead of bathing in the cold stream by the Hunters' camp. I turned the temperature on so high that it burned my skin, and the steam made it difficult to breathe. It took me half an hour to scrub dirt from every inch of my body. I must have poured half the bottle of shampoo and conditioner on my head, while massaging my fingers into my scalp. My body tingled with cleanliness by the time I stepped out of the shower.

I slipped into my room. I got down on my knees and started to grope for my chest of clothes under the bed, while Adalia peered at me curiously. It wasn't until I saw my dresser across the room that I remembered that I wasn't in my tent in Alagia anymore. I stood and went to my dresser to put on pajama pants and a shirt. Using socks, I covered the rough calluses that had formed in the past weeks. I buried my nose into my clothes, forgetting how much I missed the smell of laundry detergent. After sliding a comb through my clean hair, I left it spilling over my shoulders to dry, and went downstairs.

Adalia and I entered the family room and found my grandmother sitting on the couch that Kate and Jackson had sat on when she accused him of cheating. Suddenly, I remembered what Kate had done to Jackson. I paused, thinking about how to tell my grandmother, but with everything that I was about to tell her, I decided to gloss over Jackson's untimely death.

Two steaming cups of hot chocolate rested on the coffee table and logs crackled in the fireplace. I sat down next to her, pulled my legs under me, and turned my body so I was facing her. Adalia sat at the foot of the couch and rested her broad head on my thigh. I picked up the hot chocolate and let the warmth of it soothe me. She took a deep breath, telling me she was about to speak.

"When your mother first found the doorway to that world, she went to a college close enough to home that she just lived here. One day, she and a friend went to an antique store, and she fell in love with the music box. It was a whole year before she opened it and uncovered the secret it held. She had found a place she could call her own, away from your grandfather and me, and we couldn't understand what was making her so happy. We were really concerned when she'd come out of her room happier than ever. We assumed the worst, as parents do, but we never found anything that suggested she was involved in anything bad. It wasn't until much later that I found out it was because she was seeing your father. When I noticed she started wearing an engagement ring, I just laughed it off, thinking it was a joke. Then, she invited your father to have dinner with us, and they told us about their engagement and wedding plans, and I could tell by the way they looked at each other that it wasn't a joke at all. He was dressed in … peculiar clothes, and he had a strange accent that I couldn't quite recognize. It almost sounded British, but not quite. We had dinner, and when it came time for him to leave, your mother started leading him back upstairs, but your grandfather wouldn't allow it. It took your mother a good three hours to explain to us that he was from another world and that was where she went all the time. Anyway, to make a long story short, after seeing the two of them vanish into thin air and then seeing your mother magically reappear a few minutes later, we came to believe in Alagia. She loved going there so much, and even if we didn't want her to, we had no way of stopping her. Besides, she couldn't stand not seeing your father for long, and we couldn't bring ourselves to keep her from him, no matter how impossible the whole thing seemed."

"Your grandfather died before the wedding, and your mother was heartbroken. To soften the pain, your father moved the wedding up, and within days, they were married in Alagia. I had never seen her so happy. It was the first time I thought that something good had come out of that music box. She didn't tell me about the magic and her powers until she was pregnant with you two." I stared down into the cup of cocoa, letting the steam rush over my face. "And you were right. I knew about the prophecy. Your mother told me when she was pregnant. Then, you and Kate were born, and she sent you two to stay with me. She told me that if she didn't come to retrieve you girls after three days, it probably meant she was dead.

Of course, three days went by, and I knew I'd lost my daughter, with no way of contacting her children's father," my grandmother continued with a heavy heart.

Just hearing her talk about this made me shudder. Listening to her, realizing that she had known all this for years, I felt a sense of betrayal, but I couldn't let it consume me. She looked at me, and I held her gaze.

"As much as I don't want any part of that world anymore, it's a part of you and your sister. And that can never be taken from you. I should have told you girls years ago, but I couldn't bring myself to doing it. After I'd lost my own daughter, I couldn't bear to lose her children as well … but I know now that losing one of you was inevitable, and your mother knew it too." She let out a shaky breath and sounded close to tears.

I reached out my hand and rested it on hers, which trembled. I gave her hands a little squeeze telling her that I understood her motives and intentions. She only did what she thought she had failed to do with her own daughter: protect her. Her small lips formed a tight smile, and her eyes looked as though they brightened with my forgiveness. She sniffled, set her mug down, and turned to me.

"What should we tell people happened to your sister?"

My thoughts raced. I hadn't even thought about that. People would definitely start asking questions, if they hadn't already, seeing as Kate and I had missed several days of school.

"Grandma, don't worry about that. I'll take care of it," I said reassuringly, but still not knowing exactly how. I figured I'd sleep on it, in hopes I'd come up with something by morning.

My grandmother nodded absentmindedly. "Is it really as wonderful as your mother always said it was?" she asked quietly.

I looked at her in surprise. She was trying to let go of what happened and understand it all. Instead of shutting out the world that had claimed her daughter, she was going to try to accept the inevitability that it could not be ignored anymore. I smiled inwardly. "It's incredible," I replied, breathless, picturing myself still among the trees, the Hunters' tents spreading endlessly.

She smiled at my passion for the hidden world. I could tell she saw exactly what she had seen in my mother when she first told her about Alagia. "I believe it's your turn now," she said, opening the floor up to me.

I sighed, "I don't even know where to start."

My grandmother lifted herself from the couch and shuffled over to the fireplace. She tossed a few more logs onto the fire pit, making the flames blaze and radiate heat. I curled my toes with pleasure. She returned to the couch and positioned the pillows behind her back in a comfortable fashion and leaned against them, expectantly waiting.

"The beginning sounds like a good place," she offered.

So, I began my story. We talked through the night about my seemingly impossible adventure. As I spoke about my encounters, I could still hear Danzinar's deafening roars, the sound of arrows slicing the air. I still smelled Myra's scented oils and morning dew on the trees. She gasped when I told her about Danzinar, and looked horrified when I talked about Azlaya and the Sagen. Any time I said Kate's name, her eyes darkened, so I rushed through them, skipping details she didn't need to know. I was reluctant to tell her that my father was still alive, but decided he was imperative to my story. I couldn't bring myself to tell her about the conversation I'd had with my mother though. I couldn't tell anyone yet. The emotions I'd felt during it were tough to explain, and trying to remember them would be like reopening a healing wound.

Time once again meant nothing, because, suddenly, I felt as though I had all the time in the world. As I recounted my adventures to my grandmother, my yearning for Alagia lessened, and the ache I felt for it faded. In that moment, everything was good. I felt like my life was somewhat normal, and at least for a while, it would stay that way.

I drove the car along a winding road. Guardrails curved alongside to keep vehicles from plummeting over the edge and into the ravine below. I slowed to a stop at a sharp curve around a hill, glancing at the clock on the dashboard. It was three in the morning, and no one was on the road except me.

I parked the car and stepped outside to examine the spot I picked. I decided it would be convincing enough for the scene of an accident. I went around to the trunk and gathered my props. I placed one of Jackson's football sweatshirts that he let Kate have on the driver's seat, along with one of his baseball caps and some sweatpants. On the passenger's side, I lay Kate's fur-coated boots, leggings, and a sweater. I put her phone in a cup holder and set the GPS to a destination seventy miles down the road, a hotel right on Lake Michigan.

I had put some duffel bags filled with clothes in the trunk, and then littered the floor with open food wrappers. I shut the doors and checked over my work. When I first told my grandmother about my plan, she gawked at it. But it only took her a few hours for me to convince her that it would work. She told me that when Kate and I disappeared, she had called our school and told them we had a family emergency and not to expect us in school for a while. I told her that our family emergency was that Kate and Jackson had run off together. My grandmother and I had searched for her, but without any success. But, if I pulled off my stunt, the police would "find" her soon, and learn that she had run off with Jackson. With the swipe of my hand, I sent the car through the railing and over into the dark ravine. It was about a hundred-yard drop to the rocky, jagged bottom. When the sound of crashing metal met my ears, I ignited the wreck with a flick of my hand. Flames burst from the car uncontrollably. I watched it burn, letting what I'd done and what this symbolized sink in. I waited until the fire had died down a little and I was convinced that if Kate and Jackson had really been in the car, their bodies would have been burned so much that they would have been unrecognizable. Only their clothes and belongings that had scattered from the crash would be found to identify them. I felt silent tears beginning to roll down my cheeks and wiped them away.

I closed my eyes and whispered, *"Domum"* Home. I slowly began to feel myself fade away from the smell of burning fuel. A few moments later I materialized in my living room.

I saw my grandmother sleeping soundly on the couch. I took the blanket that had fallen onto the ground and laid it back over her. I curled up in an armchair in the corner and watched the clock as the hours ticked slowly by.

I felt numb. I knew Kate wasn't really dead, but Jackson was. I figured it was better for his parents to think he died in a car accident, rather than being disintegrated by his girlfriend. And even though the "new" Kate was still out there and waiting for me, I was grateful to have a moment to mourn the death of the "old" Kate. Because to me, the sister I grew up with now no longer existed.

It took the police several days to trace the car crash back to Kate and Jackson. My grandmother waited by the door anxiously as she saw a police car pull up in front of the house. Adalia, who I had disguised as a normal-sized Siberian husky with my powers, barked at the intruders, but soon lost interest after not sensing any real threats. When the officer broke the news to my grandmother, she cried out miserably. I think she had been holding in her sadness from losing the "old" Kate up until then, too. A female officer approached me where I sat, huddled in the chair. She knelt to be at eye level with me and gently told me how my sister had died.

When I didn't blink or make any sort of distressed sound, she asked, "Dear, are you all right?"

"Paris," I replied blankly, thinking about the day at lunch when Kate, our friends, and I were planning our birthday party. It felt like it had happened centuries ago in a whole different world. The officer's face scrunched in confusion. "She'd want a Paris-themed funeral."

Epilogue

IT WAS OUR seventh birthday. Ten years ago it was our seventh birthday, and our grandmother decided to take us to her friend's lake house for the weekend. Her friend, Charlotte, was out of town so we had the whole place to ourselves. Every summer we would visit Charlotte while she had her family reunion, so normally we were sharing the space with twenty other people. We liked spending time with her family. Uncle Eric was always making us laugh, and Aunt Emily's kids loved playing in the water with us. We loved visiting the lake house and thought of it as our second home.

However, the peace and quiet would be nice too. But that was the year when Kate began to prefer staying home and not making the four-hour trek to the lake. She was a smart seven-year-old and constantly tried to convince our grandmother that buying her a new doll was much cheaper than the amount of gas we'd need to go to the lake house, but our grandmother was adamant about spending our birthday there, and I was grateful.

I was in love with the lake that hugged Michigan. It was the most beautiful thing I'd ever seen. Kate and I could spend hours exploring the abundant trees that served as "our forest," or swimming in the lake that was "our ocean." But that year, Kate resolved to sit in the house on the couch with crossed arms and pouty lips. I decided to give her space and read two books while waiting for her attitude to improve. I stole furtive glances at her unruly curls that framed her delicate face and her caramel-colored, downcast eyes.

"Kate? Do you want to go play outside before it gets too dark?" She shifted away from me. "You can be the Forest Princess if you want!" I offered, knowing that my sister never got tired of the undeniable power people handed to her in attempts to console her.

"I want to go home," she replied sharply.

"But we love it here. We always have so much fun, and we never finished the Forest Princess game. Come on, it's our birthday, let's do something," I prodded. I watched as her expression softened, but her eyes insisted on remaining icy cold.

"I'm the Princess?" she asked, finally making eye contact with me.

I nodded eagerly. "You can even be the older one. I'll be the baby."

Whether or not Kate agreed to play with me out of guilt for the gloom she brought to our birthday, we did have an hour of fun out in the woods. When our grandmother called us in, she handed us both a wrapped package, and we squealed in delight.

"Kate, open yours first!" I told her. Kate didn't hesitate and ripped into the paper concealing her present. She uncovered a doll with blonde ringlets, a soft face with rosy cheeks, and sky-blue eyes. She wore a white lace dress and her red lips were slightly parted, showing her pearly teeth. Kate's face lit up at the sight of another doll to add to her collection.

"She's so pretty!" I exclaimed, scooting closer to Kate so that our shoulders touched, to get a better view of the doll.

"I want to name her Layna," Kate said proudly. She named the doll after our mother, but we never knew her, so the name didn't mean much to me then. Now I realize that it was another piece of evidence showing how desperately Kate wanted our mother back.

"Your turn, Casey," my grandmother encouraged me. Kate was too busy admiring her doll.

I carefully slipped my fingers under the tape to avoid ripping the beautiful wrapping paper and gently pulled the tape apart, one piece at a time. Kate took notice and grew impatient. "Any day now, Casey." She reached over and tore off a huge chunk to quicken the process. I was about to yell at her when the content of my present caught my attention. They were the last two books in the series I had been reading. Kate clearly disapproved of my present, but I was ecstatic. Kate darted off to get the other dolls she had brought, enlisting me to play with her as she ran away. I gave my Grandma a huge hug, still clutching tightly to my books.

When I turned seven, all I wanted for my birthday were a couple of books from my favorite series, but now that I was seventeen, all I wanted was the sister that I'd grown up with. It had only been two weeks since the police showed up at out front door proclaiming Kate would not be returning home, one week since the funeral, and a couple days of complete seclusion. Since Kate's funeral, I hadn't left my house or talked to any of my friends, and I wasn't planning on doing so any time soon.

A shrill beeping cut into my thoughts, and I slid down from the tall chair to get the cake out of the oven. I tried to tell my grandmother that I didn't want to make my birthday into a whole weekend celebration, as it would have normally been for Kate and I, but she insisted on at least baking a cake.

I placed it on the counter as my grandmother came out of the other room. I left the cake to her attention and escaped to the couch. My hand instinctively reached out for my phone, but then I remembered that I didn't want to face the things I would find on it. I would undoubtedly be inundated with birthday wishes, combined with people's condolences about having to celebrate my birthday without my "dead" twin sister. I turned on the TV and stared blankly at the screen, but my mind began to wander again.

I imagined I danced with Connor on a dark dance floor, surrounded by strobe lights. Our bodies rubbed against each other as we were pushed closer and closer together from the mass of people crowding onto the floor. We laughed and smiled, refreshed ourselves, and then returned to the party. I saw Kate and Jackson in a tight embrace in the corner, and saw my other friends feeding suggestions to the DJ. Everyone was running around doing something, whether it was dancing, talking, or taking pictures, and no one was doing nothing ... at least that was what I would have been doing tonight.

Instead, I was spending my seventeenth birthday alone. Shortly after Kate's funeral, I called off the party. All the planning my friends and I had done leading up to the event was for nothing, because my life had changed forever. I thought back to that day in the cafeteria when we were trying to decide on a theme, debating between the Enchanted Forest and Paris.

That led to me thinking about Kate's funeral. Since she couldn't have her Paris birthday party, the least I could do was give it to her in the form of a funeral. The spiraling black designs and splashes of pink created a sort of elegance that the "old" Kate would have been proud of. I had passed through that day numbly and didn't really remember much beyond the décor. I was told "I'm sorry for your loss" so many times that I began to tune everyone out. Even when my friends came up to me with tear-streaked faces and shaking hands, I was in too distant a place to register how hurt and torn up they must have been on the inside. Connor, Jackson's best friend, was the only person I clearly remember, because he didn't say anything. He just held me in a tight hug, and for the first time that day, I felt that someone finally understood what it meant to have just lost the most important person in your life. It was also the first time that day that I started crying.

"Do you want to help me ice the cake?" my grandmother called from the kitchen, interrupting my thoughts that were beginning to spin out of control. I found I couldn't sit idly anymore, or else I'd have episodes of deep depression, which undoubtedly would lead to tears, and I was done with crying.

"Sure," I replied and lifted myself from the couch. I joined her at the counter and spooned a glob of chocolate icing on the yellow cake. I had to admit that the scent of chocolate and freshly baked cake did brighten my mood. Adalia sat at my grandmother's side, waiting eagerly for anything to fall from the counter.

"So, Casey, I was thinking after you finish your school work for this year … I was thinking we could go on a trip," my grandmother said softly.

My grandmother had spoken with my school counselor. I was allowed, even encouraged, to finish the school year at home and give myself time to cope with my recent trauma. I gladly took the offer, because I didn't want to be reminded of how different my life was without Kate, from the looks people would surely give me as I passed by. Getting away during the summer would be a blessing too, so I wouldn't have to decline my friends' offers to hang out or go to some distant relative's vacation house for a party.

I scooped more frosting onto the cake. "Where would we go?"

"Well, you've never been to Europe, and I took your mother there when she was about your age." I met her gaze and stared dumbfounded. "I know you want to get away, at least for a little while. And this will give you the perfect excuse to get some distance between you and your friends while you all sort through things."

I fell silent for a while and became lost in thought. We finished icing and she placed seventeen candles on the cake. She lit them and, with a wide smile, pushed the cake towards me.

"Happy birthday, sweetheart." Adalia barked in agreement and playfully nudged my leg. I rested a hand on her broad head, and returned my grandmother's smile. It was the first one that reached my eyes in weeks.

Whether she knew it or not, that was the best present I could have received under the circumstances. She basically just handed me a means of escaping the life I desperately needed a break from. I didn't *want* to leave—I *needed* to. I had to relieve myself of this life plagued with memories of Kate and start to reconstruct one without her. I had to find a way to redefine myself without a sister, and if that meant running away for a while, so be it.

"When do we leave?"

About the Author

Taylor is a student with a passion for reading and writing who is in the process of matriculating to college. She started writing her book in 6th grade and has been writing ever since. Her first book in *The Sorcerers' Prophecy* series is called *The Unknown*, and is a young adult fantasy about twin sisters.

She enjoys sharing her gift with others and has created a program to encourage and inspire elementary/middle school students in reading and writing. She has been profiled by WLWT Channel 5 for her mentoring program, has won numerous awards for her writing, and was recognized by the Ohio State Legislature for her work. Her goal is to transform young children into avid readers and writers.

Taylor's other interests include cooking, volleyball, and soccer. She played Junior Olympics National Club Volleyball for four years and has been All-Academic GMC. Taylor has maintained a 4.0 GPA since her freshman year. She has been a volunteer at Operation Give Back and has also donated time to Cincinnati Children's Hospital's Neonatal Intensive Care Unit (NICU) and the Pediatric Research Organization.

Taylor lives in Ohio with her mom, dad, two sisters and brother.

Please visit Taylor's Facebook page at:

http://www.facebook.com/thesorcerersprophecy

www.ingramcontent.com/pod-product-compliance
Lightning Source LLC
Chambersburg PA
CBHW031718170626
46808CB00005B/1803